"I'm anxious *Mamm...*"

Martha made her way back to intensive care and took the seat by Paul's bedside. She stroked his good arm and spoke softly to the comatose man. Then, miracles upon miracles, his eyes became agitated under his lids and then he slowly opened them and stared at the ceiling.

She was so excited, she called out his name. Without moving his body, his eyes turned toward her as she moved her head to be in his line of vision. The hint of a smile came across his face.

"Oh, dearest, you hear me, don't you?" Martha said joyfully as tears of happiness flowed down her cheeks. "Paul, it's me. Martha! I'm right here with you."

His mouth broadened even more and it looked like he was trying to speak, but no sound came from his lips.

"It's okay, Paul. Don't strain. We'll have plenty of time to talk."

His eyes remained open and she reminded him to blink, fearing they'd dry out. He listened and followed her instruction—and smiled at her.

Dear Gott in heaven. Danki! *Paul can smile!*

June Bryan Belfie has written over twenty-five novels. Her Amish books have been bestsellers and have sold around the world. She lives in Pennsylvania and is familiar with the ways of her Amish neighbors. Mother of five and grandmother of eight, Ms. Belfie enjoys writing clean and wholesome stories for people of all ages.

HEALING HANDS

June Bryan Belfie

ISBN-13: 978-1-335-49976-9

Recycling programs for this product may not exist in your area.

Healing Hands

First published in 2018 by June Bryan Belfie.
This edition published in 2020.

This edition published by arrangement with Harlequin Books S.A.

For questions and comments about the quality of this book, please contact us at CustomerService@Harlequin.com.

Harlequin Enterprises ULC
22 Adelaide St. West, 40th Floor
Toronto, Ontario M5H 4E3, Canada
www.Harlequin.com

Printed in U.S.A.

HEALING HANDS

To the memory of the
Reverend Billy Graham—
one of the century's giants.

I found Jesus Christ through one of his
crusades in the 1950s.
It has changed my life forever.

Rest in peace, oh, good and faithful servant.

Chapter One

Martha and Paul were excited to tell her parents about their decision to marry and live nearby, but first they wanted to savor this special moment for themselves—the moment when they realized how much they longed to form this union. Indecisions were behind them now. They could enjoy their visit so much more, now that things were settled between them.

Sitting together on the sofa, they discussed all the ramifications of their new plans. Paul didn't seem upset to be moving to Lancaster, even though it meant breaking his contract with his partner, Jeremiah, and starting all over in the carpentry business. If truth be told, he'd be relieved not to be close to Hazel, who had almost destroyed his future with Martha with her forward behavior.

Between breaks in the conversation, Paul kissed Martha gently on her lips and reminded her about his love for her. She responded in kind. Their happiness and excitement were impossible to restrain.

While Martha and Paul enjoyed this time in private, her mother, Sarah, worked on the quilt with Martha's *Aenti* Liz and *Mammi* Nancy in the *dawdi haus* next door. The project had been started months before. Now it would be important to have it finished, since *Mammi* intended to give it to Martha as a wedding present.

After a few minutes, Martha went into the kitchen to check the roast venison browning in the oven. Her mother had placed potatoes around the roast and they were getting crisp, which was the way her father preferred them. Paul joined her in the kitchen while she cut up carrots for their meal.

Around noon, her father came in and washed up for dinner. He nodded over at Paul with a grin. "Have enough time to yourselves yet?"

"I'd never have enough time to be with Martha," Paul said, smiling back.

"*Jah.* Nice to see my *dochder* smile again. She's been a gloomy gus too long."

"Oh, *Daed,* I've tried to be cheerful."

"You ain't succeeded too *gut*," he said, chuckling. "So, when do we eat?"

"In about half an hour, *Daed.* Just have to wait for the carrots to cook," she added as she placed the saucepan on the back burner.

"I'll go tell the ladies and your *dawdi* then. I guess they're all next door?"

"*Jah*, and we have some news for everyone."

His brows rose. "Hope it's *gut* news."

"You have to wait and see," she said with a wink.

After he left, Paul grabbed her hand and pulled her onto his lap to give her a swift kiss before the family arrived.

"We have to be careful, Paul. My *mammi* would have a fit if she knew we've already kissed."

"I'll watch myself, but it will be hard to stay away from you."

"Help me set up the table. That will keep your hands—and your mind—busy."

As Paul poured water into the glasses and the roast rested on a platter for a few minutes covered in foil, Martha made rich brown gravy from the drippings.

Paul looked over. "I see you're doing a lot of cooking. Do you like it better now?"

"I always did like to cook, but it's taken a while to get the hang of it. I think you'll notice an improvement. Almost as *gut* as…" She stopped, not wanting to mention Hazel's name. Everything was going so smoothly, why bring up a sore spot?

Paul pretended not to hear her stop mid-sentence, knowing what she was thinking, and began whistling a tune as he straightened out the silverware.

The back door opened, and the family came in for their meal. Paul felt his heart beat faster, as he realized Martha's family would become his, as well. He was more confident than ever about his decision to move to Paradise. He was excited for Martha to tell them, but she waited till they had eaten their meal and were preparing for dessert.

After clearing the table, she set her mother's two fresh peach pies on the table and waited for the coffee to finish brewing. When it was ready, she placed the pot on a ceramic tile while her mother brought over mugs. Once everyone had been served, Martha spoke softly.

"I want everyone to know, we have made plans to marry this fall."

Her mother and Liz exchanged glances and then turned towards Martha.

"And?" Liz asked, hesitantly.

"*Jah*, and we're going to look for some land nearby and live near you all!"

Sarah's hand went to her mouth and Lizzy let out a "*Jah*! Praise Jesus!" as she reached over and patted Martha on her hand.

Her father grinned, as he nodded. "Now that's real *gut* news. It sure enough is."

Sarah wiped her eyes with her napkin and smiled widely. Then her smile turned down as she looked over at Paul. "I hope you didn't make that decision because of me. I am not going to stand in the way of Martha's plans for her future."

"I made the decision without even talking it over with Martha," he began. "I believe it was selfish of me to want my own way and have Martha leave her family and everything she knows. I'm real happy with this plan."

"What about your business? And your house?" her father asked.

"They aren't that important. What is important, is to make my future wife happy. Martha is more important than anything else. We want our *kinner* to be close to you as well."

"We welcome you to our little family," Martha's father, Melvin, said as he pulled on his beard. His voice faltered slightly. "We're small, but have big hearts."

"*Jah*, I know that already," Paul said, nodding his head emphatically.

"Wait till I tell your *Onkel* Leroy," Lizzy said. "He'll be so happy. I've been a bit gloomy myself."

Later in the day, Martha and Paul went over to the bishop's house to talk things over with him. The date was set for the wedding to be held on the first Thursday in November. The bishop seemed pleased for them and agreed to prepare them each for their baptism. This meant meeting frequently before the church service once Paul moved to Lancaster.

On the way back from the bishop's farm, Martha showed Paul a lot that was for sale. It was only two acres, but it would be large enough for a house and a future building if he wanted to open his own business in time—and it was walking distance to her parents.

The lot had been cleared for farming, except for along the property lines, which had large evergreens on one side and several small fruit trees bordering the other. The owner, who lived on connecting property, was still farming it. He was getting ready to retire and wanted to sell off his land, a parcel at a time.

"It's nice," Paul stated as he pulled the buggy over to the side. "We can always plant a few trees around the house for shade."

"I'd keep some open for our garden and a play area for the *kinner.*"

"You're right. And of course, I'd need a parking lot once I put up my building."

"Paul," Martha said, questioning with her eyes. "Are you sure about all this?"

"Absolutely. I'm actually excited. I'll talk to Jeremiah about leaving soon. He knows it's a probability."

"He may be glad to have you move. You know… because of…"

"*Jah.* And I think Ben would buy me out. I meant to talk to your *aenti* about a room at her place. Do you think she'd be okay with that idea?"

"I don't see why not. They have a lot of empty bedrooms now that their family has grown and moved into their own homes."

"See, sweet Martha? Everything will fall into place. That's because I've turned things over to *Gott*—where it belongs. Instead of trying to do everything on my own, I pray every day for His guidance."

"That's wise, Paul. I'm glad I'm marrying a man strong in *Gott*. It's so important."

The next day, before he left for his home, he asked his driver to take them to the shop where he'd be working, so Martha could meet everyone. They were very pleasant and she felt accepted right away. Then they drove over to the realtor's office, and spoke with the agent who was selling the vacant lot. They discussed the price and other details. Without making a decision on the land, Paul took the necessary information and said he'd get back to him shortly.

Last on the list was his housing arrangement. The driver took them to her aunt and uncle's home and waited while Paul discussed renting a room from them.

Lizzy and her husband seemed delighted with the idea of having Paul room with them and Leroy asked if Paul would be able to help a little at harvest time. Paul was more than agreeable to help out, and they agreed on a rent, which was reasonable and included any meals he wished to have with them. Everything was falling into place. After letting Martha off at her home, Paul left for the two-hour trip to Lewistown. It was easier to part this time, knowing they'd soon be together and had the wedding to look forward to.

Now Martha needed to hear about Sarah's cancer. Always, in the back of her mind, Martha feared for her dear mother's life. Soon, they'd all know if the cancer was gone.

Chapter Two

All the way back to Lewistown, Paul could hardly restrain his excitement. His driver, Skip, encouraged him to talk and before the end of the journey, Paul had invited Skip to their wedding.

After he arrived home, he made his way over to the workshop and was greeted by his partner, Jeremiah. After giving him the good news, he wrapped a leather apron around his waist and picked up a sanding tool along with a pair of goggles.

"Wait," Jeremiah said, holding up his hand. "You haven't told me where you two plan to live. That's real important, don't you think?"

Paul set the goggles and sander on the work table and folded his arms. "I was going to tell you at lunch, but since you've asked…we're going to live in Lancaster County, Jeremiah. I know that's not a shock, since we discussed it, but I've given it a lot of thought. I can't take Martha away from her family—regardless of the outcome with her *mudder*. I hope you understand."

Jeremiah leaned against the table and nodded. "I was

afraid that's what you'd decide. I sure will miss you. The contract—"

"I know, I'm breaking it."

"It's okay. I almost did the same. I just wondered about the amount you've invested already."

"I'd like to talk to Ben about buying out my share, if that's agreeable. Where is he, by the way?"

"He had to take his *mudder* to the doctor's. He'll be in later. Actually, I think I'll pay off your share instead. I can always offer him a partnership later."

Paul nodded. "Whatever way you want to handle it."

"Will you open your own place in Lancaster or Paradise?"

"Eventually. I'm taking it a step at a time. I've made arrangements to stay with Martha's *aenti* and *onkel*."

"And when do you want to leave?"

"Well, that depends upon you. As soon as you think you can get along without me."

"Things have slowed down a bit, as you know; so anytime is okay with me."

"Like I could be done by Saturday?"

"If that's what you want."

"You're making it so simple, Jeremiah. I'll never forget this."

"I'll miss you. You know that."

Paul moved over and clamped his hands on his friend's shoulders. He nodded and then turned away. No sense getting all emotional over it.

Paul put his goggles on and prepared to sand the drawer he was working on. He heard Jeremiah walk back to the cabinet he was designing.

A sense of relief spread through him as he realized that part was over. He expected to feel disappointment about leaving, but instead there was relief. He would no longer have to fear Hazel's sudden appearance, although she was no longer the slightest temptation to him. His love and loyalty were for one woman—and one woman only—the lovely Martha Troyer.

As Rose Esh sat having coffee, she checked her mail before returning to her latest manuscript. Setting two bills aside, she reached for the letter from her daughter. What a thrill to realize her only child was in her life again—not as prominent as she would like, but they corresponded now. Occasionally, she received a phone call, though it was usually through the mail that they touched base.

As she read, her mouth turned to a smile. So, Martha and Paul had reconciled their differences and were planning to marry in November. This November. She finished reading and sat back, picturing her beautiful daughter as a bride. Of course, there'd be no satin and lace bridal gown or champagne toast, but she'd still be radiant in whatever color dress she'd wear in the typical Amish style. Her perfect complexion and enchanting smile would be decorative enough.

Oh, if only she could be there. Foolish to even think about that possibility. She was sure Martha had not even spoken to Sarah about meeting with her. The adoption agreement had specifically made clear they were not to correspond for at least the first eighteen years of Martha's life. Rose had kept her promise, though every day she'd thought of the child she'd had to give to others to raise. After all, a proper Amish girl does not get pregnant before marriage—especially not with a non-Amishman. In her case, a student from Italy.

She had fallen in love almost immediately with the handsome young Italian. Only recently had she learned of all the letters he'd sent—which her parents had hidden or destroyed as soon as they'd arrived.

What if she'd kept up a correspondence? If she'd told him about being pregnant? They were so young at the time. Would he have even cared? Would he have wanted to marry her?

All in the past. She wiped a tear from her eye and re-read the three-page letter. Martha's happiness flew off the pages. Even her handwriting was larger and bolder than normal. She never mentioned the possibility of Rose attending the celebration. Of course she understood, but it still hurt. There'd be no pictures. Even when the babies started arriving, she'd hear about them, but with the ban against photography, she'd never even be able to picture her own grandchildren.

Though she wanted to write immediately, she knew her sadness at not being part of the wedding plans might show through her words. No, she'd wait a day before responding. By then she'd be able to write with a lighter heart. She really was pleased at the news and was quite surprised they were planning to stay in the Lancaster area, since he had already become established in a carpentry business somewhere else. It showed how much he loved her daughter, to be able to set all that aside, so she'd be happy and near her family.

She poured herself a second cup of coffee and took it with her to the computer. It might help to get back to work. The research was complete now and the manuscript was about twenty per cent written, though the edits would begin soon. When she finished her first draft, she went through the whole manuscript and made it as clean as possible. Then it would go to the professional editors and be checked for errors. It was a long process, but she enjoyed her career and rarely had writer's block, the way some of her friends did. There were always two or three stories running through her mind for future books. She began the fifth chapter and within minutes, everything else had been put aside.

That's how she got through the lonely moments.

Chapter Three

Paul packed up his few belongings that still remained in his parents' home.

Before heading over to the house he and Martha had planned to live in, he sat in the living room with his parents. His mother became quite teary as he sat and talked with them about his move. His father remained silent, but Paul could tell by his eyes, he too, was saddened by the news of his imminent departure.

"It doesn't mean we won't see each other—often," Paul tried to reassure them.

"It ain't the same," his mother said, wiping her eyes with her apron.

"I know. It was a hard decision, *Mamm*, but I had to think of Martha."

"Of course. I understand. And with her *Mamm's* cancer and all…"

"*Jah*, that was part of it. Also, as I told you both, she and her *mudder* are real close. She's their only child."

"And adopted at that," her mother added, nodding. "I understand. At least we have your five *bruder* and *schwesters* nearby."

"And the *grosskinner*."

"*Jah*. That's *gut*, but we'll miss you," she said.

His father nodded and folded his hands on his lap. He began to rock in the old family rocker. Slowly. "Do the Troyers know you're coming today?" he asked his son.

"*Jah*, I called Martha yesterday."

"Thought she didn't have a phone," his father said, lifting an eyebrow.

"I gave her one, and her folks allow her to use it now."

"Mmm. Guess there's no harm then. I thought their bishop was pretty strict."

"He is, but bending a little. He's a *gut* man. I like him a lot."

"You ain't been baptized yet," his mother stated.

"I'm going to get more instruction with Martha. He said he'd instruct us together so we can both be baptized before November."

"Ain't much time left."

"I know. He made an exception for us."

"Well now, that's real nice," his mother said, smiling faintly for the first time.

"You know her *aenti* and *onkel* real *gut*?" his dad asked.

"More the *aenti*. They're *gut* people. I know you'll like them."

"'Spect so. After all, they're Plain folk like us. What's not to like?" he added.

"*Jah*, true," Paul said, amused at his father's comment. In truth Paul knew an Amishman by the name of Daniel Beiler, who was 'not to like' but he didn't bring up the subject. Daniel was no longer in the picture. Apparently, he'd jumped the fence and was living the English way.

"I'll pack up some brownies for you to take," his mother said, rising from the sofa.

"You don't have to, *Mamm*."

"I want to, *sohn*. You can remember me when you see the tin I'm sending along."

"Goodness, I'm not going to forget you, *Mamm*." He rose and went over and hugged her. She stayed in his embrace for several moments and then looked up. "I hope Martha appreciates what a fine man you've become."

"We love each other very much, *Mamm*."

She nodded and moved towards the kitchen. "I'll only be a minute."

Paul returned to his armchair and sat down a few feet from his father.

"Do you have enough money to pay your expenses?" his dad asked.

"*Jah*, I've saved quite a bit and Jeremiah's going to buy out my share. In fact, I'll be able to repay what you gave me."

"It was a gift, not a loan. It's part of your inheritance, so I don't want it back. Besides, you may need it someday if you plan to open your own place."

"*Danki*, *Daed*. I'll bank it until I need it then. Actually, I've looked at a nice two-acre lot near the Troyer's place. With that money, I'd have enough to purchase it."

"If it looks right for you, don't wait. *Gut* land don't last long."

"True. I'll take another look at it next week and maybe consider making an offer. The location is *gut* and we'd have enough land for both the business and a house someday."

"Take my advice and take it real serious. Pray about it."

"I pray about everything now. I'm reading the Bible more, too."

His father smiled. "*Jah*, so important. You'll be the head of your own family soon. Be prepared."

"It's a big responsibility."

"Can't argue 'bout that. Your *mudder* and me have done pretty *gut*, if you ask me. Six *gut kinner* and we have a nice little nest egg built up."

"*Daed*, I mentioned once, if you ever retire, you're more than welcome to live with us."

"Paul, you ain't even got a house of your own, much less room for us, but not to worry. Your *bruders* have room anytime we need it. Hopefully, I have a few years left to be on my own."

"I just wanted to remind you. *Jah*, you're young yet."

His father chuckled. "Midfifties. Not young, but not old either. *Gut* age to be."

His mother, Helen, walked back in with a large colorful cookie tin. "I filled it up and even added three whoopee-pies."

"*Danki*! I hope they make it to Lancaster," he said, grinning over.

"They'd better!" his mother said, smiling back. "Now get going before I blubber like a *boppli*."

After packing everything up in their buggy, his father took him over to the house Paul had been living in. They climbed out and stood a few feet apart, silent at first.

"What's gonna happen to the house?" his father finally asked as he stood back and placed his hands on his hips. He perused the front of the building.

"I don't know. Maybe Ben will rent it out."

"Nice place. Musta been tough to make that decision, *Sohn*."

"We'll have a nice place someday. No hurry about it."

"Unless Martha gets herself triplets like Eb's wife."

"I know. Martha wants a bunch of *kinner*, but one at a time."

"The *gut* Lord decides that."

"*Jah*, for sure."

"So, let me say bye now. It don't get any easier." His father held out his hand for a shake. Instead, Paul embraced him tightly. His father's arms surrounded him in return. "Be *gut* and place your trust in *Gott*, not man," he told his son, softly.

"*Jah*." Paul could feel his throat tighten. "*Danki* for everything," he said softly.

"We'll see you soon, *jah*?"

"For sure. Martha and I will pay you a visit next month."

"You write to your *mudder* now. Women need that."

"I know. I will."

Paul watched as his father climbed into his buggy, directed his horse to turn around and then made his way onto the road. He looked back once and waved. His expression was somber.

Paul then went into the home he had hoped one day to share with Martha and packed up his few pieces of clothing. The furniture, what little there was, could remain until they needed it.

His ride was expected within the hour. It was time to say goodbye to Jeremiah and Ben. He'd already been over to his friends, Ebenezer and Deborah and their little ones, to say his goodbyes. He assured them that he and Martha would definitely make it a point to visit them several times a year, but it was still difficult to part. Goodbyes were never easy, but as his *mammi* used to say, "If you don't say '*gut*-bye,' you can never say '*hallo*'!"

Didn't make much sense then, but he was beginning to see the wisdom in her words.

He piled his belongings on the side of the shop building and walked around to the employee entrance. He noticed a couple of buggies and a shiny BMW in the parking lot as he opened the door. Ben was sitting at their lunch table with Hazel as Jeremiah took care of customers in the front.

Hazel's mouth dropped open when she saw him. "I thought you'd left already."

"*Nee*. I'm about to. I came in to say goodbye, but I see Jeremiah is tied up."

"So, you can say goodbye to me," Ben said, grinning.

"And me," Hazel said, giving him a sweet smile.

"*Jah* well, I guess my ride should be here soon."

"I have to admit, I was surprised when Jeremiah told me about you moving to Lancaster," Hazel remarked. "I guess Martha wasn't ready to make the move."

"She was, actually, but I insisted on relocating. It's too much to ask her to leave her family—especially under the circumstances."

"Wow. Oh well, it's your decision, but I don't think it makes much sense," she continued.

"It makes sense to us, and I think that's the important thing."

Ben remained silent as they spoke.

Jeremiah came back to the workshop. "I have to be brief. The customers are looking through some of our designs, so I thought I'd come back to say farewell. When's Skip coming for you?"

"Any minute." He stood and Jeremiah put out his hand for a shake.

"I wish you the best, Paul. And if you ever change your mind, I'd take you back in a split second. You do great work."

"*Danki.* It probably won't happen, but I appreciate the offer."

He saw Hazel rise from her chair at the same time they heard the car come in the drive.

Ben stood up, too, and shook Paul's hand.

"Don't forget to send us an invitation to your wedding," Hazel said as she drew close enough for a hug and stretched out her arms.

Instead of obliging, Paul patted her arm. "*Jah*, and you guys, too. We'll sure want to be here for your big day."

A look of disappointment sprang into her eyes, but she took a step back and reached over for Jeremiah's hand, which he willingly gave to her.

Then Ben and Jeremiah helped load up the trunk and back seat of the car. Once everything was in, Paul climbed into the passenger seat and removed his straw hat, tossing it back on the bags of clothing and bedding.

Skip started up the engine and headed towards the street.

"Hot today," Paul mentioned as he waved to his three friends.

"You'll cool off quickly. I've had the air on the whole way," Skip said. "Looks like this is more than a visit," he added, nodding towards the back seat.

"*Jah*, I'm going to live in Paradise, and in November, I'll be marrying Martha."

"Hey, good for you! I knew you'd end up doing that. You two have been stuck on each other for ages."

"*Jah*, true. We just had to iron out a few things first."

"Well, congratulations. I guess I'll have to find a new rider."

"Martha and I will want to come back to see my family and friends often, Skip, so don't fill up every day."

"Don't worry, you just call and I'll be happy to give you a ride anytime. I have a part time job now at a mechanic's shop, but I can call my own hours—usually."

When they arrived at the Troyer homestead, Paul asked Skip to honk, since no one was in sight. Immediately, Martha came out the front door with her parents right behind her. Oh, he wanted so much to grab her, but he merely nodded and then shook hands with each of them, holding onto Martha's just a wee bit longer than necessary.

This was a turning point in his life, and he knew beyond a doubt, it was the right move. Things were definitely falling into place.

Chapter Four

Paul and Martha sat with the family for their main meal. Then, after harnessing a young and recently purchased horse to the Troyer's family buggy, the young couple made their way to the nearest buggy shop. Chessy trailed behind on a long lead. If they purchased something today, they'd need to have two horses.

They looked at each shiny new buggy for sale. Paul's old one would have cost too much to have it brought by truck from his hometown of Lewistown. Besides being old, it was too small for a family. He'd sold it to a neighbor for a decent price and would put the money towards a new one.

Martha's favorite buggy sat facing the road. After examining it from every angle, she slid the doors open to admire the interior. "So cool, Paul. And the storm front is clear. You almost don't see the glass!" They both admired the closed fiberglass buggy, which also had comfortable seating with room in the back for future toddlers.

"Too bad your bishop won't let us get rubber tires,"

Paul stated. "They're so much quieter than these metal wheels."

"It's fine. You get used to it." She patted the plush seat next to the driver's. "I even like the upholstery. It's such a pretty blue."

"Then shall we buy it?"

"It's up to you, Paul, but it sure is nice."

"Then we'll purchase it. It should last for years."

After signing the necessary papers and counting out the money required, Paul removed the harnessing he'd brought with him from the back of the Troyer buggy, and he and Martha attached Chessy to the new buggy for the journey back to Martha's home.

"I'm getting my driving horse brought over tomorrow," Paul mentioned as they patted Chessy, who seemed a bit uneasy about the whole procedure. "Ben's borrowing his friend's horse trailer."

"That's nice of him." Martha patted Chessy to reassure him.

"*Jah*. I've had Frenchy for three years now. We're buddies."

"Why did you name him Frenchy?"

"His first owner was from Paris, Ohio, before he moved to Lewistown."

"Speaking of Paris, do you ever think you'd like to travel abroad?"

"I don't think about it, but now that you mention it, it might be fun to go to Europe. I've seen pictures of the Alps, and they sure are beautiful."

"I'd want to go to Holland where so many Christians left for America."

"Maybe someday we'll go. Now though, we'd bet-

ter get back home. You want me to lead or follow?"
he asked.

"I think lead. I'll drive my parents' buggy. Don't
worry if we get separated. I know my way real *gut*, Paul."

"Did you bring your cell phone with you? You could
call if you wanted."

"I forgot. Now that you're with me, I don't need it."

Traffic separated them, but they arrived back home
only five minutes apart. When they pulled in, her father came right over to examine the new buggy. "Nice
and shiny," he remarked as he pulled on his suspenders and nodded over.

"It runs real smooth, too," Paul said proudly.

Martha got out of the family buggy and joined them.
Their dog Spunky trotted over to get some attention.
Soon her mother came over after she finished hanging
sheets on their clothesline, and exclaimed over the brand
new buggy. "Sure is pretty," she said as she ran her hand
over the shiny grey side. "And lots of room, I see," she
remarked as her husband opened the sliding door.

"Guess we should think about replacing ours, Sarah.
It runs pretty rough."

"It's fine, Melvin. Just fine."

"Wanna have a ride?" Paul asked his future father-
in-law.

"Sure do," Melvin piped up quickly.

"You guys go out. I'll help *mamm* with supper," Martha said.

"Sure about that?" Paul asked. "I thought you'd want
a ride, too."

"I do, but you can take me after supper. Right now
I want to finish the potato salad."

"Can't argue with that," he said, grinning over. "We'll just take it a couple miles."

Sarah nodded. "We'll have supper ready in about half an hour, so keep an eye on the time."

Martha and her mother watched as the men headed back to the road in the shiny new buggy, after unhitching the new horse and releasing him in the pasture. "I think you'll have enough room for a while, Martha. Could hold three or four little *kinner*."

Martha smiled and took her mother's hand as they headed back to the kitchen. "*Jah*, that's what we figured. It cost a little more, but we're looking ahead."

"You're getting excited, aren't you, honey?"

"For sure. I can't believe this is all happening and we'll be neighbors—if Paul gets that land."

"Is he going to make an offer soon?"

"I hope so. It won't be on the market long, I know that."

When they arrived in the kitchen, they took turns washing their hands at the sink and then Martha chopped up celery for the potato salad while her mother sliced up the cold meats. They sang an old hymn together as they worked. Once the food was ready, they set up the table and Martha poured the water. She looked up at the clock. "They should be back by now. It's been nearly forty-five minutes since they left."

"Oh, you know men," her mother said, her mouth turned up. "They lose track of time when they're checking out new equipment or buggies. Man toys."

As Martha went to add more water to the pitcher, they heard an ambulance siren as the vehicle raced past their house. Then another followed. She looked over at her mother, who had stopped slicing pickles for their supper. Their eyes met briefly, fear revealed in their expressions. Several minutes later, they heard a car pull up the drive and stop by the back porch.

Martha reached the door before the driver even left the car. It was patrolman Harvey Whiting. His face was grim.

Sarah stood next to her daughter as she held the door open for him and his partner, young Bobby Storrs. "What's wrong? What's happened?" Sarah asked, her voice shaking.

"Sorry to be the one to tell you this, but there has been an accident. Your husband and a young man with him were just taken to the hospital. Now, they'll probably be just fine, but you'd better get over there. They took them to Lancaster Hospital. We can drive you both over, if you'd like."

"Oh, dear *Gott*," Martha said as she steadied herself against the frame of the door.

Sarah began hyperventilating and looked about ready to collapse. Martha quickly grabbed her arm. "*Mamm*, breathe slow. Everything will be okay. I know it. We have to go now though."

"Do you want to lock up first?" Harvey asked, as he took hold of Sarah's arm.

"*Nee*. No one bothers us. Just take us, please."

Patrolman Storrs opened the back door of the patrol car and waited for them to get in before taking the front passenger seat. Within a minute, Harvey was headed back to the road. He turned his siren on and headed towards the hospital at a high speed.

Martha's heart was pounding. She felt she might pass out, but her concern for the moment was her mother, who was extremely pale. She reached for her hand.

"Apparently, some kid was driving a motorcycle too fast on one of those side roads about a mile from your place, and your horse startled and freaked out. He flew into a ditch the road workers had dug for a pipe line just yesterday. The buggy turned over completely. Lucky there were a couple farmers who saw it and one was English and called 911 and then they pulled your husband out and laid him on the grass. They couldn't get the younger man out right away, but by the time we got there, several other neighbors had helped free him. I'm afraid we had to shoot your horse, Mrs. Troyer. He was in pretty bad shape and it was obvious he'd broken at least one of his legs. I'm real sorry."

"Dear Chessy. *Jah*, I understand."

Martha couldn't hold back any longer. "Were the men conscious?"

"Mr. Troyer was, but not the other fellow. I didn't recognize him as a local."

"It's my fiancé," Martha was able to say. Tears were streaming down her face, but she wouldn't allow herself the luxury of sobbing aloud. "Please tell me he was breathing."

"Yes, Ma'am," Bobby Storrs said. "He was definitely alive, I can assure you of that. Just not talking."

Sarah surrounded her daughter with her arms. She whispered in Martha's ears, using their *Deitsch*, "We must be strong. *Gott* will give us the strength we need, no matter what the outcome." Then she prayed fervently for their loved ones as Martha agreed in silence. *Jah*, the God of all creation was in charge. He knew their hearts and desires, and He cared for them with more than a human love—an unconditional deep love, which He extended to her father and Paul as well. They were

His children. But sometimes He took people home before their loved ones would have it.

Martha held onto her mother and continued to pray.
That's all she could do.

Patrolman Harvey pulled up to the entrance of the
emergency room. Martha and her mother got out of
the car and quickly entered the building, along with
the two policemen. Paul and Melvin were nowhere in
sight. "They've already taken them in," Harvey said as
he took ahold of Sarah's elbow and steered her towards
a chair by a receptionist.

The middle-aged woman looked concerned as she
laid several pieces of paper in front of Sarah. Martha
walked over to a door leading to the back. "Sorry," the
receptionist said, "but you can't go through there yet.
Someone will come to talk to you soon, I'm sure."

"But my father and fiancé are in there. I have to be
with them."

Sarah looked up and nodded. "They need us to be
there. I can fill out papers later. Please!"

"Well, let me go check. Just wait here," the woman
said as she rose and went towards the back. Several
moments later, she returned. "Mrs. Troyer?" she asked,
reading from a new chart, "you can follow me. Your
husband wants you there. They're just cleaning up a few
wounds and waiting for someone from x-ray."

"What about me?" Martha asked, panic setting in.

"It will be just a few more minutes. I'm afraid your
fiancé needs more attention at the moment. You don't
want to be in the way. There are several physicians and
staff with him at this time. He's being well cared for.

I'm sorry. I'm sure it will be soon, dear," she said as she nodded for Sarah to follow her.

Martha sat down at the vacated seat her mother had been sitting on and tried desperately to calm herself. She continued her silent dialogue with God, begging for Him to spare Paul's life. She soon felt calmer and closed her eyes as she pictured Paul smiling at her. Things seemed so perfect—just an hour or so before. How could this be happening? Oh, that it was merely a bad dream. But it was a reality. A horrible, unbelievable truth. How would it all end?

Chapter Five

Finally, a nurse came out to the waiting room and signaled Martha to follow her. Thinking she'd be taken to Paul, Martha was surprised when she was shown into her father's room instead. She went right over and kissed the side of his head. The nurse remained in the examining room with them as she took his vital signs. She barely spoke, but seemed pleasant enough by her expression.

"*Daed*, I'm so thankful you'll be okay."

Sarah held his hand and patted his head gently. "You don't look too *gut* though."

"I don't feel so hot, either. How's Paul doing?" he asked, looking over at Martha.

Martha fought back tears. "They won't let me see him yet. They're treating him, I guess. How did it happen?"

"Some stupid kid came up behind us on the noisiest motorcycle you ever heard, and then he tried to pass us on a bend. What a *dummkopf*."

"Melvin, you know they had to put Chessy down," Sarah said.

"I thought they'd have to. Poor old Chessy."

A male nurse came over to the bedside as an orderly followed him in to wheel Melvin down to x-ray. "This shouldn't take long. They've scheduled some x-ray films, Mr. Troyer," he said, checking his chart.

"Can I go too?" Sarah asked.

"Sorry, Ma'am. You can wait here though."

"I'll be fine, Sarah," Melvin said softly. "Your *dochder* needs you more than I do right now."

Sarah turned and took Martha's hand. "You're awful pale, Martha. Why don't you sit?"

A new male nurse looked over as she spoke. "I'll get you some water," he said as he reached for a paper cup.

Martha took a seat and accepted the water. "Can you find out about Paul?" she asked the nurse. "Please?"

"I guess while your father is out of the room, I can check. I'll be right back." He disappeared behind the curtain and they could hear him speaking out in the hall with one of the doctors. When he returned, his eyes were cast downward. Then he looked over at Martha. "He's still not responding, I'm afraid. They're taking him for a CT scan. It appears he's broken some bones."

"I need to see him! Why won't they let me see him?" Martha raised her voice.

"They will when they can, Miss Troyer. It's more important to care for his needs right now. They have to check for internal bleeding and…"

Martha couldn't hear the rest of what he was saying. Her mind had stopped functioning when she heard 'internal bleeding.' What if he bled to death? What if his brain was dead? What if? *What if?*

She suddenly rose and headed towards the hall. She had to be with him.

"Wait! Where are you going?" She heard the nurse

call out to her as she made her way along the hallway. She'd find him. She looked into each partitioned area. All strangers. Then she felt someone behind her tap her shoulder. She turned. It was a young resident. "Miss, who are you looking for? You can't just go wherever you want to. This is an emergency ward."

She turned and glared at the young man. "I know where I am. I know this is an emergency ward, but I need to be with my fiancé, Paul Yoder. He'll be okay if I'm with him. I know that. Help me find him, please."

"I know who he is. He's getting the best of care. I promise you. Right now he's not in the room. They've taken him for a scan, but I'll take you over to his room. I may get in trouble, but I know what you're going through. I've been there myself. Come with me. It's just down the hall."

"Oh, *danki*! Thank you so much. At last someone who understands. I won't be in the way. I promise, I'll stay in the corner if I have to. I just need to be near him and let him know I'm there for him."

"What's your name?" he asked as they entered a small examining room, empty at the moment.

"Martha. Martha Troyer. My father was in the same accident, but thankfully, he's talking and he looks pretty *gut*. A few mean looking cuts, but he's tough. I know he'll be fine."

"Yes, I heard the older gentleman would probably be okay. Now you can sit on that chair by the back wall. And please don't do anything to cause a stir. They'll have my head."

"I so appreciate you doing this." She sat down and the resident, whose badge said he was Dr. Patel, began writing on a chart, and then he checked some of the equipment. After several minutes, he went out and left her alone.

After nearly an hour had passed, she heard them wheel the gurney into the room. Paul was motionless. His head was bandaged and there were cuts and bruises on his face and neck. A sheet covered the rest of him. Her heart nearly ceased to beat as she looked at this stranger before her. *Oh, dear Paul. Don't leave me.*

A red-headed physician came into the room while the resident, who had returned at the same time, re-attached the cuff to the sphygmomanometer and checked an IV, which had been inserted in the ambulance by an EMT. After checking his chart and writing a few notes, the physician introduced himself to Martha as Dr. O'Reilly. He never smiled.

"Will he be okay?" she asked, trying to prepare for his answer.

"It's too soon to say. You're family?"

"I will be. We're engaged to marry."

"I see. Any of his blood relatives here?"

"*Nee.* They live a couple hours away. They don't even know yet."

"You should try to get word to them."

"It's that serious?" she asked, aware of tears flowing once again.

"We'll know more after we get the results of the scan. We know there was trauma to the head, which accounts for his being unconscious. We plan to do an MRI of the brain as soon as we can. That should tell us more."

"What about his bones?"

"I'm sure his right arm is broken in more than one location. He will most likely be operated on within the hour. A room is being prepared and an orthopedic surgeon is conferring with the radiologist now. I'm an internist. I'll handle things until he takes over."

"May I stay with him now?"

For the first time, the doctor allowed a slight smile. "Yes, that will be fine. It may help for him to hear your voice. We don't really know much about the comatose state and how it affects one's hearing. We most likely will keep him in a drug induced coma until the swelling decreases in the brain. Hopefully, we'll know more soon."

"It sounds so awful." She could hold back no longer. She covered her eyes with her hands and her body shook visibly as she wept. She could feel someone's hands around her and opened her eyes to see her mother as she embraced her.

"Hush now, Martha. He'll be fine. I know it."

"*Nee, Mamm.* No one knows yet."

"We must trust." They were now speaking in their *Deitsch.*

"How is *Daed*?"

"He's doing real *gut*. They are waiting for the reports to come back from the x-rays. He wanted me to come find you." Sarah looked over at the unconscious young man, who had only a short time before been so animated and cheerful. So much had happened.

Martha filled her mother in on what she'd learned. Dr. O'Reilly had left and there was a new nurse, a woman about Sarah's age, beside Paul's bed. She was checking his monitors and recording things on his chart.

Martha went to his side where she'd be out of the way and gently stroked his cheek. "I'm here, darling," she continued in her dialect. "You'll be just fine. They are taking *gut* care of you, my sweetheart. You must be okay. Please fight, Paul, my love." Her voice was trembling and Sarah touched her shoulder and whispered for her to be brave for Paul's sake.

After a deep breath, Martha continued to speak lovingly to him and her voice sounded somewhat stronger, though inside she was still frightened, no matter how hard she tried. She knew she needed to rely on God more during this terrible struggle and she went from prayer to words of love to Paul—back and forth, until it seemed like one conversation. Once, she thought she saw Paul's lips try to form a word, but it was most likely her imagination.

They came for him then and took him down for the MRI. Then the original nurse returned and asked them to leave the area so they could clean it for the next emergency. Paul would be taken to surgery after his MRI and then given a room in intensive care. Martha and her mother went back to check on Melvin, who was dozing. He woke up as soon as Sarah touched his hand.

After they filled him in on Paul's condition—as they knew it—he closed his eyes in prayer. They followed suit, but their prayers were silent. Intended for God alone.

Patrolman Harvey came into Melvin's partitioned room and talked to them about the buggy. "It's been pretty badly damaged, but it may be salvageable. We found the paperwork in the glove compartment and called the shop to come pick it up. Sure was new. When your young man is better, he can decide what he wants to do about it. They'll just hold it for him. They were real shocked, and upset. Nice people."

"*Jah*, for sure," Martha said. "What about our Chessy?"

"The vet was called in. He'll remove the body for you. It's gotta be hard for you with all these details to think about."

Martha nodded. "Nothing makes any sense."

"Oh, I also found this cellphone in the back of the buggy," he said as he removed Paul's phone from his jacket. "It must have fallen out of your fiancé's pocket. Thought you might need it. You'll want to get in touch with his family."

"*Jah*. I dread telling them such terrible news."

"I understand," he said, quietly. "If they don't have a phone, we can call the police near them and they can go to the home to notify them."

"Oh, *jah*, that would be *gut*. I'll write down their address in Lewistown for you. Oh, thank you so much."

"No problem."

The patrolman took the information, added it to his report and then went to Melvin's side and asked him how he was doing.

"Better than my future son-in-law. Can't believe this happened. I hope that young rider who spooked the horse repents of his careless actions."

"We have a pretty good idea of who he was. One of the men, who saw it happen, gave us a full description. If it's who I think it was, he's a troublemaker from the get-go. We'll be looking into it."

"Well, I hope he doesn't go to jail," Melvin said. "Youth makes people do stupid things."

"He will probably be fined at the very least. He needs to learn a lesson. Of course, if the young man in the buggy…"

Martha's heart skipped a beat as she filled in the rest of his thought in her mind. Nee, Gott, *please. Not that.* Oh, how she wished she could go back in time. If only she'd told them to wait and have supper first. How different the outcome might have been.

Chapter Six

Paul's mother, Helen, was changing her granddaughter's diaper when her daughter, Susan, came into the nursery. Her mouth was drawn and her usually bright blue eyes were dark.

"Mama, you'd better put the *boppli* in the crib and come downstairs with me."

"What's going on? You look so serious-like."

"Please, it's time for Mary's nap anyway."

"*Jah.* Okay." She placed the soiled diaper in the enamel container and laid the infant in her crib before following her daughter down the flight of stairs into the parlor where a policeman was standing awkwardly twisting his patrolman's hat in his hands.

"Ma'am, Patrolman Lewis here. I need to talk to you about your son."

"Which one? What did he do?" she asked, looking from him over to her daughter, who shrugged.

He glanced down at a paper he had in his hand. "Paul Yoder. You are his mother, right?"

"There are a bunch of Paul Yoders, you can be sure of that; but *jah*, I have a son by that name. He just moved away. He's in Lancaster County now. Is he in trouble or something?"

"I'm sorry to tell you, but he was in an accident. Now, he's alive, but it doesn't look real good right now."

"Oh, merciful *Gott*." Helen backed up and dropped down onto their sofa. Her daughter quickly took a seat next to her and placed her arm around her mother's shoulder.

The policeman proceeded to give them as much information as he could and then asked if they needed a driver.

"You mean it's so serious, we have to go to him right away?" Susan asked.

"I guess you could say that. Apparently, he's in a coma."

"Oh, dear *Gott*. My poor *bruder*," Susan said, her voice cracking. "We have to tell the others, *Mamm*. We should all go."

"*Nee*, that would be too many of us all at once. *Daed* and I will go first and then we'll get word to you through the Hopkins' family next door. We can call them from the hospital. You need to stay here with your little ones."

"Do you live nearby?" the patrolman asked Helen.

"Next door. I can walk over."

"I can drive you to help save time, and then we can check to make sure you have a driver. You can use my phone, if you'd like."

"You're so kind. *Jah*, that would be helpful. Oh Lord, help my *sohn*," she added as she embraced her daughter and then headed for the door with the policeman. It would be up to Susan to inform the rest of the family of the accident.

Helen had so many unanswered questions. Was anyone else hurt? Was Martha with him? Was it his fault? But most of all, would her son be all right? *Jesus, let it be the Father's will that Paul would make it through.*

Time dragged by as Martha kept her vigil with the unconscious man she loved so dearly. Her father had been discharged earlier, though he and Sarah remained at the hospital to be near Paul and Martha. They had not discovered any broken bones, and his blood work had come back without signs of internal bleeding, so he'd been fortunate.

Word moves quickly in the Amish community and it wasn't long before her Aunt Liz and Uncle Leroy arrived. The family stayed together for a while to support Martha. They suggested Martha have some supper in the cafeteria, but she had no interest in food.

Towards early evening, her uncle called his driver and the four of them returned home. Only Martha remained behind. She was told she could spend the night in the waiting room, and the staff would provide her with a pillow and blanket. Everyone was kind and solicitous to her needs.

Most of the time, Paul wasn't even in his assigned room. His surgery took over four hours as the splintered bones and damaged muscles were surgically repaired as best as possible. No one discussed the results of the MRI with her. Even when she asked, the staff was evasive. Of course, they weren't yet husband and wife, so she understood their hesitancy and privacy concerns.

Around nine-thirty, she was joined by Paul's parents. She wasn't surprised when they arrived. Where else would they want to be? Paul's family was close. She detected a slight chill emanating from Paul's mother when she embraced her. A hesitancy perhaps. Surely, she didn't blame Martha for the accident.

The neurosurgeon, who had ordered the brain MRI, came into the room and motioned for Paul's parents to join him in the hall. Martha was not included.

Martha moved her chair closer to Paul's bed, and she touched his motionless cheek ever so gently. She feared she'd injure him further if she wasn't careful. "Paul, my darling," she whispered close to his bandaged head, "Your parents have come to see you. We are all so concerned for you. You have to fight, my love. Fight to make it through this. Someday, you'll be all better, that's for sure and certain." Martha felt her eyes fill once again. She'd cried enough tears to fill a water trough. Oh, where did all that moisture come from?

"If you hear me, sweetheart, try to open your eyes... or raise your brows...or something."

She watched carefully, but there was no response. None. The nurse had warned her there most likely wouldn't be, since the physicians preferred he remain in a comatose state while healing took place naturally, and he was under strong sedation.

After several minutes, his parents returned to the room alone. They took seats on the other side of the bed and seemed to avoid Martha's questioning eyes. Unable to stand the wait any longer, she asked, "Well? What did he say?"

"Not too much," his mother answered finally. "They are just waiting it out."

"But, he'll be okay, right?"

Helen turned her eyes towards Martha and stared directly into her dark irises. "They can't say. I wish he'd never left home."

Martha felt a stab in her heart. *Jah*, if he'd remained where he was…this wouldn't have happened. It was her fault. She could have chosen to move to Lewistown. She touched the side of Paul's good arm gently. "We never expected…"

"Of course not," his father said. "That was not a nice thing to say, Helen. You owe Martha an apology. The boy is in *Gott's* hands. There's no blame to be had."

Helen nodded, without looking up. "*Jah*, you're right. It was unkind. *Es dutt mir leed*."

"It's okay. I know you're sorry. We're all emotional right now. It's so horrible to see him like this. Only a few short hours ago…"

Then his father spoke so quietly, Martha could barely make out his words. "We can't look backwards. It is what it is. But we can pray." He reached across the bed and took ahold of Martha's hand and then she extended her other arm towards Paul's mother, who placed her hand into Martha's. The three of them formed a circle of love and his father prayed in the *Deitsch* for his son and also for Martha's father. He also thanked God for His grace and His love. Peace surrounded the small group and Martha felt there were angels present. For the first time since the accident, she believed all would be well in the end.

At one point, Martha and her future in-laws went downstairs to have coffee and bagels. They had waited until the physicians were examining Paul before leaving his side. Confident of the good care he was getting, they took their time to discuss their plans for the next few days.

"Of course, we want you to stay with us," Martha said as she broke her bagel in half and spread jelly on it.

"We don't want to be a problem. We can stay at a motel," his mother said, setting her cup of coffee aside. George nodded.

"*Mamm* wouldn't hear of it," Martha continued. "Besides, we're practically family."

"Mmm. But not quite," Helen reminded her.

Martha's eyes filled. "I still hope we can marry in the fall."

"First, we have to pray he survives," Helen stated grimly.

"He will! He has to," Martha said, vehemently shaking her head.

"Now, now," George broke in. "Of course he will. He's young and strong and has everything to live for."

"We have to face facts though," Helen said, her voice cracking. "He's in a coma, and we don't know *Gott's* will, do we?"

There was silence. Martha shoved the uneaten bagel away from her and rested her head in her hands, struggling to regain her calm.

"Now, you should eat, Martha. You have to keep up your strength," Helen said, more gently. "And we must all continue to pray. *Gott* hears our prayers."

Martha removed her hands and nodded in agreement, though she left her food untouched. "We'd better go back up. The doctors should be done examining Paul. He needs to know we're there."

George popped the rest of his bagel in his mouth and loaded the tray with the dishes and mugs. Then they all stood and walked over to the trash area before heading towards the elevator.

When they got back to the room, only one nurse was in attendance. She had just adjusted his pillow to be flatter. "Any change?" Martha asked.

"No, dear. Don't expect any for a while. Don't forget, he's been heavily sedated."

The family took seats out of the way and sat silently, each to his own thoughts. Paul's father nodded off once and began to snore lightly, but he quickly stopped and adjusted his position. Still no one spoke.

Around midnight the nurse suggested they take turns watching Paul so they could get some rest. There were two faux leather couches in the waiting room. Martha fell asleep fitfully around two, but awoke only an hour later. Then Helen and George tried to sleep, while Martha took over her watch. The nurse was busy changing bottles and IV bags and checking on the machines, which occasionally beeped or lit up to warn of changes in his vital signs. Paul didn't look like himself. Without his smile and twinkling eyes, he looked like a Roman bust Martha had seen once in a museum on a class trip to Philadelphia. Sightless and…dead. She forced herself to think positively, though it was difficult at best.

The next day was a repeat of the evening before. Paul was now in critical, though stable, condition. He continued to remain unconscious and Martha stayed by his side constantly. Her mother appeared around ten along with her aunt and uncle. Sarah talked with Paul's parents about staying at their home and convinced them it was the best solution. "We don't know how long your *sohn* will be in the hospital, and we have plenty of room."

Helen nodded. The strain of the past hours was showing. "*Jah*, we'll take you up on your offer. It would be better to be with other people. This is not easy."

Sarah placed her arm around Helen's shoulder. "Such a shame. We all care so much for Paul."

"I know. Martha barely leaves his side."

Martha looked over at the women who had congregated in the corner of the room to be out of the way. Liz came over and stood next to Martha. "He's strong, dear, and he will fight to get better."

"I know. All that's true, but I'm still scared."

"*Jah*." Liz embraced her niece. "Of course you are. I'll stay the night with you, if that would help."

"*Nee*, I can't let you do that."

"It won't be a problem. This way you'll have company. It has to be difficult to sit hour after hour with no response from Paul."

"It's horrible, *Aenti*. You can't believe it."

"Then that's final. I actually brought a change of clothing with me. Your *Mamm* has a change for you as well. We figured you'd want to stay."

"*Danki*. Thank *Gott* for my family."

There was a slight knock on the door and there stood Paul's ex-partner, Jeremiah, along with Hazel Miller, his fiancé. They stood at the entrance appearing uncertain about entering. The attending nurse turned towards them. "I'm sorry, we already have too many people in the room. You can wait in the waiting room until some of the others leave."

Martha went right over and shook Jeremiah's hand. Hazel reached over and hugged her as she whispered how sorry she was about the accident. Martha didn't even think about her old feelings towards this young woman who had nearly caused a break-up in her relationship with Paul. She was merely an Amish friend now, and her embrace spoke of her caring. "I'll go out with you until we have permission to return."

As they talked about the accident, Lizzy and Leroy appeared. "You young people can go in now. We're going to the cafeteria for coffee. Take your time. It was sure nice of you to come," Lizzy added.

"We came as soon as we heard," Jeremiah said. "What do the doctors say?"

"Not much," Martha answered. "We just have to wait and see. They already operated on his arm, but now they mentioned casting his leg as well. It's not a major break, but they want to be sure he has full use of it when he's better."

"Then he will get better?" Hazel said, questioning with her eyes.

"He has to," Martha replied, firmly.

"*Jah*, for sure." Hazel and Jeremiah nodded at the same time.

As they headed to his room, Paul's parents came out and joined the others as they walked over to the elevator.

"Paul's *schwester*, Susan, came by to tell us. *Gut* thing because Ben was planning to bring Paul's horse over," Hazel said to Martha as the three of them walked back to Paul's room. "She had her three little ones in the buggy with her. She's so upset. Paul and she are very close."

"*Jah*, he talks about her a lot. He gave up so much to move here, and look what's happened," Martha said, choking on her words.

"Now, Martha," Jeremiah said, "It was what he wanted. Don't go blaming yourself for what's happened."

"I just can't help it. Things would be so different if…"

Hazel shook her head. "Jeremiah is right, Martha. It was Paul's decision. No one can see the future. No one."

"I guess you're right. It's hard, is all."

"Of course."

They stood at the foot of the bed and stared as the nurse changed his IV bag. "It doesn't even look like him," Hazel said.

"Shhh. He may hear. We have to be careful," Martha whispered over.

"Oh my. Should we talk to him?"

"You can."

Hazel moved closer and touched his free arm. "Paul, it's Hazel. Jeremiah is here, too. We heard about what happened and we're so sorry, but we pray about you a lot and we know everything is going to be just fine. You have to get better to come to our wedding. We're getting married pretty soon, you know."

"*Jah*," Martha said, coming up beside her. "And we're supposed to get married in November. *Nee*, we *are* getting married in November." A tear fell from her eye to her hand. Oh, that he could hear. It might make such a difference. *Lord, bring him out of this terrible coma, please.*

Chapter Seven

Rose Esh turned the thermostat on her air conditioner down three degrees. This heat wave was draining. It was August. One had to expect heat, but it was the humidity that got to her. It was a good thing the writer's conference was to be held indoors. She was flattered to be asked to teach a course in historical fiction at such a well-known and esteemed event.

At first she was hesitant, since it would mean staying in New York City for several days and that could be pricey, but she was being paid rather significantly and it would certainly look good on her résumé. It had been years since she'd spent any time in the City. Maybe she'd take in a Broadway play. She was so out of touch with the theatre world, she wasn't even sure what was playing.

One other thought, which had occurred to her when she was debating whether to accept the offer, was the possibility of seeing Alexandro.

How in love they'd been back in that other lifetime. She'd been swept off her feet by the handsome Italian exchange student who was spending a year living with the Plain people in her town in Ohio. It had quickly turned to love and the result was Martha. Dear, sweet Martha. Thankfully, she'd been raised in a loving Amish home, since it was impossible for Rose to raise her in her own strict Amish family. Her parents had been so shamed by their teenage daughter's pregnancy. By the time she realized she was in a family way, Alexandro had flown home to Italy. Later, she discovered his letters had been destroyed, so there had been no correspondence. Perhaps, if he'd known…

Rose walked over to her mahogany desk and sat down to begin revisions on her latest manuscript. While her computer booted up, she opened the bottom drawer and removed the New York Times article she'd saved about a man by the same name, Alexandro Gionnardo, who owned and operated an art gallery in metropolitan New York. The man in the photograph could have been him. It was not a close-up and it had been twenty plus years, so it was impossible to know if it was the same Alexandro she'd known and loved. Foolish to think about renewing something after all these years. Surely, he had married in the meantime. He probably had several children as well. He'd mentioned wanting a large family someday. Besides, even though he was a tender, caring young man, who knew what his character would be like after all this time?

She probably wouldn't have the nerve to speak to him, but it might be fun to at least check the man out and see if it was indeed her love of long ago. She tucked the article in her attaché case, which would be traveling with her in less than a week. It would be nice to get away. She had been cooped up in the house due to the unbearable heat, and she missed being with people. At least she'd had her weekly bridge game and church to look forward to.

Before getting back to her writing, she decided to drop a line to Martha. She hadn't responded to the letter she received a couple weeks before. Things certainly seemed to be coming together for her daughter. She'd be busy making plans for her upcoming wedding. Rose had decided on sending her a check for a gift, since she had no idea what the couple would need and money was always acceptable. Though it was early, she wanted to include it with her letter. That way, Martha could use it toward any wedding expenses. From her past, Rose knew weddings amongst the Amish were often very large and even though everyone tried to help with providing food enough, there would be expenses.

After their visit to the hospital, Jeremiah and Hazel made their way back to Lewistown. They sat in the back of the driver's car and held hands. Hazel was unusually quiet. Finally Jeremiah asked how she felt seeing her ex-boyfriend in such bad condition.

"It didn't even look like Paul. I was shocked. Weren't you?" she asked, turning her head towards him.

"*Jah*. I was. He looks terrible. I'd be surprised if he made it."

Hazel gasped. "He *has* to."

"For your sake or Martha's?"

"Jeremiah, it's all over between Paul and me and has been for a while now. You know that. Don't act that way."

"I'm sorry. You're right. The green devil still plays around with my brain sometimes. You looked so devastated when you saw him, I guess I feared you might still love him."

"Only as a friend. I don't even know why it took me so long to realize it was you I truly loved. I think I just didn't want to admit I'd failed where Martha had won. Not a real *gut* thing for an Amish woman, *jah*?"

He squeezed her hand. "Give me a quick kiss," he whispered. "And then we'll pray for Paul. He needs all the prayer he can get."

She closed her eyes and received a sweet kiss on her lips and then they prayed and ended with the Lord's Prayer.

Three more days passed, the hours jumbled together. Sometimes, Martha couldn't even tell what day it was, or if it was morning or afternoon. She continued her vigil and there was only minimal change in Paul's condition. The last image of his brain showed less swelling than he had originally, so the doctor reduced the amount of sedation, allowing him to begin his return to consciousness. His brain waves were improving, and one nurse encouraged the family by saying he had moved his good leg several times while she was caring for him.

Paul's parents spent the mornings with Sarah and Melvin. George and Melvin had struck up a comfortable relationship, and spent much of their time in the barn or the fields until it was time to have their rider pick them up for the daily trip to the hospital.

Before leaving for the day, Helen asked Sarah about her cancer. "You seem real *gut*, if you ask me," she said over her second cup of coffee.

"I feel pretty *gut*, but the proof is in the pudding, as they say. I go for a CT scan tomorrow, so I'll go to the hospital when you do, if you don't mind me sharing your driver."

"Of course it's okay. Anytime. *Danki* for all you do for us, Sarah."

"Oh, mercy. It ain't anything much. I'm glad things seem a little better with Paul. Are you feeling better about your *sohn*?"

"*Jah*, we're real encouraged. Now we need to make plans for when he's discharged. We'll have to take him home with us, Sarah. Martha realizes that, right?"

"We haven't talked about it at all. Of course, I don't even see her. She practically lives at the hospital. She agreed to come back with you folks tonight though— according to Liz, who was there yesterday. The *maed* needs to rest and take a shower, for heaven's sake."

"*Jah*, she's been so faithful to our *sohn*. It speaks well of her."

"She's a *gut* girl. She's been my pride and joy."

"*Jah*, I'm sure. She's very devoted to you. Paul has explained it to us."

"But I didn't stand in her way, Helen. I hope you know that. I want only for them to be happy. It was Paul's decision to move here."

"That's what he told us. I just hope it was *Gott's* will. You have to wonder—with the accident happening so quick and all."

"I don't think *Gott* works that way."

"Oh, you know that?" her tone turned sharp.

"I don't try to figure out *Gott's* mind, Helen. No one can. Not you, either."

"*Jah*, that's true. I spoke out of turn. Forgive me. We must take things as they come and hope to please *Gott*. Jesus loves each of us and wants what's best for us."

"That's for sure."

"And for certain," Helen said, smiling faintly over at Sarah. "I'd better get ready for the ride. I can take anything you want for Martha. She finally ate some of your crumb cake yesterday. She's getting so skinny, her dresses hang on her. Poor thing."

"Once Paul is back, she'll be just fine. I'll pack up a few pieces of the cake I have left. I know George likes it, too."

"Oh, *jah*—Mister Sweet Tooth. I think he married me for my snickerdoodles!"

Sarah laughed for the first time in a week. She thought she'd forgotten how.

Chapter Eight

It was difficult to leave Paul's bedside, but Martha was so exhausted, she felt physically ill. She finally listened to everyone's advice and went back home around supper time when his parents had scheduled their driver. To Martha, nothing seemed to have changed with Paul's condition, though the nurse was encouraging and said she had worked many cases like his, and his vital signs had improved significantly. His nurse, Shelley, was about thirty-five and very efficient. Martha felt better able to leave, knowing Shelley would be Paul's nurse for several more hours.

When Martha arrived home, Sarah embraced her for several moments and kissed her cheek. "You must be so tired, child. Once you've eaten something, you should take a nice long bath and then go right to bed."

"That sounds like a really *gut* idea, *Mamm*. I'll help clean up first though."

"No you won't. I wouldn't hear of it. Are you going to take a break and stay home tomorrow?"

"Mercy, no. I feel guilty taking the evening and night off."

"Did you see any change in him?"

"Not really, but the nurse was pleased. She thinks he's doing well."

Helen had taken a seat at the table and looked over at the mother and daughter. "I think he opened his eyes once, but my head was turned slightly, and before I could get a *gut* look, they were closed."

"Oh, maybe I should have stayed after all," Martha said, pouting.

"Nonsense. You'll fall apart if you don't think of yourself once in a while," Helen said, drawing her brows together. "It will be easier on you when we take him back to Lewistown later."

"Lewistown? He'll stay here—with us, when they discharge him."

"Now, Martha, that's real sweet of you, but he'll need his mother," Helen said firmly. "There are things you won't be able to do for him. It wouldn't be proper."

"But maybe we could hire a nurse or something. Or maybe I could come stay with you, if he goes to your place."

"That would be fine," Helen responded, though a frown had formed at Martha's words.

"*Jah*, that way I can help you take care of him, and then when he needs you, I'd take a break or something."

"Don't you think people would talk?" Sarah asked. "After all, you ain't married yet."

"Let them talk. We'd know we weren't doing anything improper."

"Well, I'm afraid we're a long way from having to make that decision anyway," Helen said. "The *bu* can't even talk yet. It's going to take time, I'm afraid."

"*Jah*, you're right." Martha sighed as she rose to set

the table. After she was done, she went next door to ask her grandparents to join them for supper. Her *dawdi* and *mammi* were delighted to see her, and they asked a million questions before they headed over. Martha barely made it through the meal—she yawned several times and added little to the conversation, which was sparse at best.

Instead of a long tub bath, she showered and then collapsed on her bed. It had never felt so luxurious, and before she finished her night prayers, she fell sound asleep and didn't wake up until nine the next morning. When she went downstairs, the men were already outside and her mother and Helen were talking away as they peeled potatoes for the noon dinner.

"There she is," Sarah said when she spotted Martha. "You've never slept so long in your life, honey. Just shows how exhausted you were."

"I know. I can't believe it! I'll grab some Cheerios and then help you with dinner."

Helen smiled over. "We've got it under control, Martha. Why not take a walk and get some fresh air. It's finally cooled off a little."

"I love the idea. I have to admit, the walls were beginning to close down on me in that hospital. I bet Spunky will be glad to see me."

"He's been acting kinda strange," Sarah said. "Dogs sense when things aren't quite right. Give him an extra pat."

After washing her bowl and spoon, Martha walked outside and immediately the dog barked and sprinted over, nearly knocking her down with his enthusiasm. She laughed and rubbed his head. "You missed me, didn't you?"

Spunky whimpered in response.

"Come on, we'll go for a nice walk," she said as she breathed the refreshing cool air and headed for the path around the pasture. There was a lightness to her step. The past few days had been pure agony, but now that Paul was progressing, she felt her hope restored.

She sat on a large rock and her dog laid down next to her. There she prayed. When she thought about her mother and the possibility she was not yet healed, her hopes began to fail. *No, Lord, I refuse to think the worst. I'm going to enjoy this perfect August day.*

After an hour or so, she and Spunky walked back towards the house. Her father and George came out of the barn and greeted her. Then her father asked when she planned to return to the hospital. "You know, your *mamm* has to get her CT scan at three today."

"Oh my goodness! I'd forgotten all about it with everything that's going on. This is so important!"

"*Jah*." Melvin turned toward George. "We'll learn from this if Sarah's cancer is gone or not."

"Oh, that's a biggy for sure. Our family has been praying for her."

"I'll head over to radiation to wait with you, *Daed*. Will they tell us anything today?" Martha asked.

"I don't know. I hope so." He pulled on his beard. "If it ain't so *gut*, she'll have to have more chemo, I reckon."

"Oh, she's been through so much. I do hope it won't be necessary. Should I use a different driver? It may be crowded."

"We can manage," George said. "He drives a van, anyway. We can leave a little later, Melvin, so Sarah and you won't have to hang around so long."

"That's okay. We want to spend some time with Paul while we're there, anyway."

"I wish I hadn't slept in so long," Martha said. "I may as well go in with you, rather than try to get another driver then. It's nice having someone across the road to call on."

"Sure has helped lately. Without phones, it can be a problem if you don't have a close neighbor to help," her father said. "You must have needed the rest, Martha, or you wouldn't have slept all those hours."

George nodded in agreement. "You need to take care of yourself, Martha. It's not like Paul even knows you're there."

"We don't know what he knows. The nurse even told me that. She warned me to be careful what I say in his presence. Strange things happen, and we need to assume he does hear us."

"Well, I'll be. I didn't know that." George clucked his tongue. "I'll tell Helen to watch what she says."

They heard the farm bell ring for them to come in to eat, and the three returned to the house. Martha's grandparents were already there and they all sat and had meatloaf together. Martha looked over at her mother and noted her expression. She looked anxious. No wonder. So much hung on the results of the scan. The three of them had been through so much together. The least she could do was be there for support.

On the ride over to the hospital in the van, Martha was squeezed between Helen and her mother. She took hold of her mother's hand. The men, who were seated in the third seat, spoke quietly on their way to Lancaster.

Oh, Lord, please let my Mamm *be free of the cancer. I don't know how I could stand watching her suffer any more…and now with Paul… Lord, I need your strength.*

I'm just not strong enough for all these burdens. I need to be under your yoke, just like you tell us to be, in Matthew 11. You make all things easier.

By the time they got to the hospital, the doctors had already made their rounds. Paul had a new nurse named Betty, who gave out little information. She was efficient, but not particularly friendly. When it got closer to three, Martha and her parents headed over to the radiation area, where her mother was to be prepared for the CT scan. Her hands shook slightly when she was called back for the procedure. "So, here I go." Her smile was strained and Melvin, who was usually unemotional around others, rose and gave his wife a tender hug. "We'll be here, Sarah. Be strong."

"*Jah*, I try, Melvin." She nodded and then Martha embraced her, before she disappeared into the back.

Melvin folded his arms and sat back down in the chair.

"Want a magazine?" Martha asked as she reached for a copy of *Field and Stream*, which was over a year old.

He shook his head and stared straight ahead.

"It will be okay, *Daed*. Even if it's not totally gone, she's strong. She's prepared for more treatment, if necessary."

"She broke down last night, Martha. She doesn't want to go through any more chemo. She said she'd probably refuse it and just accept whatever happens."

"Oh, dear *Gott*, we need her, *Daed*. Surely, she knows that."

"I told her that and she knows, but she said we could manage okay and *Gott* would give us the strength."

Martha tried to hold back tears for her father's sake.

He looked too close to weeping himself. "I think she'd change her mind if it got to that."

"I don't know. She said she'd been giving it a lot of thought."

"I can't imagine…"

"*Nee.* I can't either. She's my sweetheart. Always has been. I can't think about it now."

A few minutes later, Sarah came back out, adjusting her prayer *kapp* and tucking a few stray hairs underneath it. Her hair had thinned so much, there wasn't much to worry about. Her face was drawn.

"Well? Did they tell you anything?" Melvin asked, rising from his chair.

"Nothing. It was the technician. He said we'd probably hear tomorrow. They're backed up, apparently."

"Well, this ain't just any old scan!" His voice had risen, and people in the waiting room looked over, surprised to hear anger expressed—especially from one of their Amish neighbors.

"Hush, Melvin. We'll talk later. Let's go back and see how Paul is doing."

Martha walked behind her parents as they headed slowly to the elevator.

"I could use a cup of tea," her mother said. "What about you, Martha?"

"Actually, I'm anxious to get back to Paul, *Mamm.* You two go down. I'll give his parents a break. They've been by his bedside all afternoon."

Martha made her way back to intensive care and Paul's parents were just coming out of his room as she arrived. They decided to join Sarah and Melvin in the cafeteria, so Martha went in alone and took the seat by his bedside. She stroked his good arm and spoke softly to the comatose man. Then miracles upon miracles, his eyes became agitated under his lids and then he slowly opened them and stared at the ceiling.

She was so excited, she called out his name. Without moving his body, his eyes turned towards her as she moved her head to be in his line of vision. The hint of a smile came across his face.

"Oh dearest, you hear me, don't you?" she said joyfully, as tears of happiness flowed down her cheeks. "Paul, it's me. Martha! I'm right here with you."

His mouth broadened even more and it looked like he was trying to speak, but no sound came from his lips.

"It's okay, Paul. Don't strain. We'll have plenty of time to talk."

Betty, the nurse, stopped what she was doing to come over to his side. "Now that's a real good sign. Keep talking to him. He needs to remain responsive for a little while longer."

Martha talked about the wedding, about all the people who had been by the hospital to see him or check on his condition; she even talked about her dog giving her such a hearty welcome, and how she slept all those hours. His eyes remained open and she reminded him to blink, fearing they'd dry out. He listened and followed her instruction—and smiled at her. *Dear* Gott *in heaven.* Danki! *Paul can smile!*

Soon he closed his eyes and his smile disappeared as he went back into a coma-like state, but the nurse assured her, he would not be as deep into his coma. She smiled broadly, and Martha decided she really was a nice person, after all.

When the family returned, they were all elated at the news. His mother looked disappointed not to have seen it for herself, but she patted Martha on the shoulder. "He needed to see you by his side first, Martha. It will give him the courage to go on."

Whatever strain had been present earlier between the two women seemed to have vanished as they each put Paul ahead of their own issues. It was a good sign for the future.

Temporarily, though Martha had been able to appreciate the joy of having Paul returning to life, in the back of her mind, her father's words prevented her from being free of the fear of losing her beloved mother.

Chapter Nine

Martha's parents made an office appointment with the oncologist for the next day, hoping to get the results of the scan, and then spent an hour with Paul and Martha before returning to the farm.

Paul was in and out of consciousness most of the day. His parents were elated to be present once when he formed their names with his lips and offered them a frail smile. He had not yet uttered a sound, but the doctor came by while Martha and his parents were in the room and told them he was more than pleased with Paul's progress. Then he motioned for them to follow him out to the hall so they could talk in private. He now included Martha.

"We're moving him into a different section tomorrow. He'll still get round the clock care, but we're upgrading his condition from critical to serious."

"Thank *Gott*," his father said.

"Then you can truly say he'll live?" his mother asked.

"I'm fairly confident he'll make it if he continues to progress. Whether there is any permanent damage to his brain, is impossible to determine at this stage. He may have difficulty working with his right arm. It was severely broken and there was damage to his muscles and nerves."

"He's a carpenter," Martha said. "How will that affect his work?"

He shook his head. "Time will tell. We'll make sure he gets physical and occupational therapy as soon as he's able. It will be a while."

His mother shook her head. "It would kill him if he couldn't work with wood. He has such a talent."

Martha and his father nodded in agreement.

"He's young and strong and I'm sure he'll work hard to restore the use of his arm. I wouldn't concern myself with that just now. What's important is to bring him back to normalcy in every other way. We've cut back further on his medication. We want him conscious more of the time now. It would be helpful to continue your vigil—for his sake. I know it's not easy…"

"I'm going to spend my nights here again soon. I missed one and I have to go back home today, but after that…" Martha said.

"Well, that's not necessary, miss. I was thinking of the day visits."

Helen agreed. "We'll be able to take him back home with us. We have a large family, so he'll get *gut* care."

"It's way too soon to discuss his next step, Mrs. Yoder, but it's good to be thinking about the future. He'll go from the hospital to rehab first. He's an adult, and caring for him at this stage would be far too difficult in a regular home. He still requires strong medication."

"*Jah*, I guess," she conceded.

"Let's just listen to the doctor, Helen," her husband said. "He knows what's best."

"*Jah*, I know that, George."

The doctor told them he'd check in again later in the day, and then he left the room.

"We'd like to leave around five, Martha," Helen said as they stood in the hallway. "Will that be okay with you?"

"*Jah*, I need to spend time with *mudder*. She's nervous about tomorrow—I can tell."

"No wonder. Poor thing." Helen clucked her tongue as she shook her head. "We may go back home in the next day or so. George doesn't want to be away from the farm too long and now that we know our *sohn* is improving, it will be easier to leave for a while."

"I understand."

"It also helps to know he has you, Martha," Helen said as she patted Martha's arm.

"I'll be here every day—that I can. And I have a cell phone. You can take Paul's. It would be so much easier to talk."

"*Jah*, we'll take it. Our bishop is understanding. Not as strict as some."

"Just remind me when we get back to the house. I forget things all the time now," Martha said.

"You have too much on your mind," George said.

"*Jah*, that's for sure."

When his parents took a break and Martha was alone with Paul, she whispered how much she loved him and talked to him about their wedding plans. At one point, she realized his lips were moving and he formed the words, "I love you," in the *Deitsch*. She kissed him several times until she noticed the nurse was standing next to the bed. It was Betty, who smiled at her as she went on with her job of checking the IV tubes.

"So I understand they're moving your fiancé tomorrow. That's a good sign of the progress he's made."

Martha smiled over. "*Jah*, we're thrilled." Then they heard a low, weak voice coming from the bed and they turned toward Paul, who was attempting to be heard. Martha put her head close to his, once again. "What did you want to say, Paul?"

"We…we…marry…soon."

"*Jah*, we will!"

"Well, isn't that nice," the nurse said directly to Paul. "Good for you. Your fiancée has been here night and day waiting to hear those words. Right, Martha?"

"Oh *jah*!" Martha was ecstatic. At that moment she knew in her heart, someday things would be right once again.

The next morning Paul's parents went to see their son while Martha remained home so she'd be able to go with her parents when they got the report about the scan. Lizzy insisted on going, too. They rode in their buggy, arriving at the oncologist's office a half hour before their scheduled visit. They sat together in the waiting room, but Melvin couldn't remain seated. He got up and paced the floor, until Sarah finally snapped at him. "You're making me a wreck, Melvin. For Pete's sake, sit down."

He huffed, sat across from her and began fidgeting with his straw hat. Then he whipped through an old magazine.

Lizzy and Martha sat on either side of Sarah and remained silent. Finally, they were all led down the familiar hallway to the doctor's office. Dr. Harriman, her oncologist, was seated at his desk and rose when they entered. He pointed to two chairs, which Lizzy and Sarah took. Martha stood behind them next to her father, who was now pulling on his suspenders, occasionally snapping them against his chest.

"The good news, is the cancer cells have decreased significantly. More than we'd even expected."

Melvin let out an audible sigh of relief, but the doctor looked over with a somber expression, which caused everyone to freeze.

"The 'not so good' news, is that you are not totally free of your cancer, and we'll need to put you through another regimen of chemo—"

"No!" Sarah interrupted. "I'm sorry, but I can't go through that again. I was so sick, and I want to just let things alone."

"But, the chemo is working, Mrs. Troyer. We just need to give you a few more treatments. Surely, you want to survive."

"I do, but I think if it's *Gott's* will that I will survive, then it will happen—regardless of what you folks do for me."

"*Mamm*, you can't just give up!" Martha couldn't hold back her tears. "What about *Daed*, and Lizzy, and me? Aren't we worth living for?"

"Dearest, you'd all be fine in time."

"*Nee*, not true!"

"You need to try for us," Melvin said emphatically.

Lizzy wiped her eyes and nodded. "Think of our *Mamm* and *Daed*, *schwester*. You can't just give up."

Sarah looked down at her hands and smoothed her apron across her lap. "I'll pray about it." Then she looked up at the doctor. "I'll let you know what I decide."

He nodded. "I believe with the progress you've already made, you'd get good results with only three or four more treatments. I urge you to reconsider your decision."

"I can't promise, but I will think about it some more."

Dr. Harriman stood up and nodded to everyone as he went out the door to the hallway. No one moved. Lizzy let out a faint sob and then blew her nose. Finally, Melvin suggested they head for home and the group followed him out to the back where Melvin had tethered the horse and buggy.

It was even quieter on the trip home. Sarah held Lizzy's hand on one side and Martha's on the other. Her hands were moist. When they arrived at the house, Sarah excused herself and went upstairs to her room. Melvin and Lizzy sat at the kitchen table, and Martha put a pot of coffee on the stove before joining them.

"My folks will want to hear the news," Lizzy said, quietly.

"The '*gut*' or the 'not so *gut*'?" Melvin asked, his jaw taut from stress.

"I guess both."

Martha shook her head. "I don't want to be the one to tell them *Mamm's* not willing to go for more treatment. It would break their hearts."

"You're right," Lizzy said. "I'm going up to talk to Sarah. She has to be made to see how selfish she's being. Look at all the people it would affect! My goodness! I'm shocked at her sometimes."

"She thinks it will be easier on the family in the end," Melvin said softly.

"Well, she's wrong! Dead wrong!" Lizzy said, her brows creased.

"Don't go up now, Liz," Melvin said. "Let's give her a chance to think it through on her own without pressuring her. It has to be her decision. It ain't right for us to say what we'd do in her place."

"But *Daed*, she really thinks we'd all be okay, and it simply isn't true!"

"*Jah*, I know. I still want her to have some time to come to the right decision without our pressure."

"I'll give her two days," Lizzy said.

"Now, Liz, it might take three…or four. We have to respect her wishes."

"But what do we tell my folks in the meantime?"

"I don't know for sure yet. Maybe just the *gut* part. We don't have to mention that she'd need more treatment quite yet. One thing at a time."

"I know it would absolutely kill them to know what she wants to do."

"Then, we'll keep that part to ourselves for now," he said firmly to his sister-in-law.

Lizzy nodded. "I'd better go over and talk to them. Martha, you want to come with me?"

"I don't want to, but I will. Then I must go see Paul. I'm going to spend the night."

"At this point, your *mamm* may need you more," her aunt said.

"Oh goodness, I feel torn in half. I keep expecting something else horrible to happen."

Melvin's mouth dropped open. "You poor *maed. Jah*, you're going through too much right now. You go to your Paul. We shouldn't tell you what to do." He looked over at Lizzy and glared at her. "We have no right."

Lizzy pouted and then stood up. "I'm going next door. If you want to come, Martha, you know where I'll be." She slammed the door behind her.

"I never saw *Aenti* Liz act like that," she said to her father.

"Oh, she can be a spitfire, that woman," he said. "She's always wanted to boss your *mudder* around."

"She loves her, is all."

"*Ach.* I know her better than you do. She can be downright bossy."

"She has a *gut* heart though, you have to admit."

"I'll give in on that. I guess I need to be more patient."

"I'll go next door as well. How about you, *Daed*?"

"I have work to do. But first, I'm going up to see your *mamm*."

Martha went over and gave him a hug. "*Gut* luck."

"I ain't gonna say too much. I just want her to know I'm with her—whatever her decision will be."

Martha went next door and arrived as her *mammi* was pulling chocolate chip cookies out of the oven. Even they had no appeal today. Nothing did.

When Melvin quietly opened the bedroom door, he found Sarah sleeping. Rather than disturb her, he went outside and shared his thoughts with God. His heart remained heavy, but he would accept whatever decision Sarah made—no matter how it affected him. His prayers spoke his heart and there were no secrets between him and his Lord.

Chapter Ten

On the way to her car, Rose stopped at the mailbox, inserted a letter to Martha and raised the flag to alert the mailperson. She wheeled her suitcase to the car and placed it in the trunk. She hated driving in metropolitan New York, so she planned to drive to a parking area outside of the city and take public transportation to the hotel where the conference was being held. She'd arrive a day before the event began in order to be completely ready when the conference started. Her time slot was ten in the morning until noon. Then the rest of the day she would be free.

It would be fun to walk along Fifth Avenue again. It had been many years since she'd been in New York. She also planned to go to the Metropolitan Museum of Art one afternoon. Hopefully, she'd know some of the other attendees and would not have to do everything alone. She'd read one of the instructors was a woman she'd met a few years before at a conference in California. They had shared taxis and become quite friendly, so not everyone would be a stranger.

When she finally got to her hotel room, she showered and then rested on the enormous king-sized bed. Before she realized it, she fell asleep and dreamt about being a child again. She pictured the home she grew up in and dreamt about cows, of all things. She'd always hated milking cows, and even though it was only a dream, she felt the distaste, even these many years later.

When she awoke, she stretched her arms above her head and allowed her mind to return to her Amish roots. It had been painful to leave her home in many ways, though her parents had been strict to the point of alienating one of her older brothers. He had left the home when she was but a toddler, so she heard only whisperings of his existence from others. She didn't even know his name. How sad to have a brother somewhere and not even know his name.

She was close to two of her sisters, but after she left the area, she no longer felt welcomed by her family and wrote them off mentally to avoid any further anguish. It was often when she slept that she'd picture her Amish childhood. Her mother had been dominated by Rose's father, who rarely smiled and expected perfect obedience from her as well as his children.

His disapproval of Rose's behavior leading to the birth of a child was something she couldn't live with. It was total disdain, and though he claimed to be a Christian, there was no forgiveness in him. At first, after leaving her home, she prayed he'd repent of his hard heart and come to her begging for her to return. Eventually, she realized it would take a miracle and though she believed it was possible—since anything is possible with God—she gave up hoping and made a life for herself.

Her marriage with an older man she'd met was short-lived, since he died suddenly of a heart attack after only five years. Though she missed his company, she had never loved him the way she'd loved the young Italian student.

Rose heard her stomach growl and felt strong pangs of hunger. She suddenly realized she hadn't eaten since breakfast and it was now close to seven. She went down to the dining room in the hotel and was invited to sit with several other women who were there as guest speakers or instructors at the conference.

It was pleasant to be part of a group with whom she had so much in common. Whatever fears she had of finding herself alone, were quickly extinguished. When she mentioned wanting to explore the shopping the next day after her obligations were met at the conference, two others asked to join her. Her past was forgotten and she was in her writer's skin, and happy to be there!

Mammi Nancy and *Dawdi* Rubin were already having coffee when the others arrived. "I'll make a fresh pot," she said, looking over at her daughter, Lizzy, and her granddaughter, Martha.

"Don't bother, *Mamm*," Lizzy said. "I have to get home soon."

"You sure look serious. What is it? The cancer? She still has it?"

"It's better than it was," Lizzy started. "But it's not totally gone."

Mammi nodded. She bit down on her lip and stared at her daughter.

"Well, now Sarah doesn't want to go through any more chemo treatment," Lizzy continued, despite Melvin's warning.

"But, she'll…die," *Mammi* said, her voice cracking.

"Don't she care?" *Dawdi* asked, as he leaned forward and stared at Lizzy who had taken a seat across from him.

"I guess not," Lizzy answered with a touch of anger.

"It's not that," Martha said, as she took a seat next to her grandmother. "She just can't take any more. It's made her so weak."

"Well, I'll be." *Mammi* wiped her eyes with her apron. "Don't she know how it will affect the rest of the family?"

"Apparently not," Lizzy said, still fuming.

"Maybe she'll change her mind," *Dawdi* said, patting his wife's hand. "When she thinks it through, she'll come around."

"Oh, I do hope so," *Mammi* said. "Poor child. It's been hard on her. Even losing her hair…."

"Oh, for pity's sake," *Dawdi* said. "Hair? You ain't even able to tell with her *kapp* on."

"A man simply wouldn't understand."

Martha nodded. "I don't think that has much to do with it, *Mammi*. I think she fears she will never be cured and these treatments will go on and on. Maybe she thinks it would be harder on all of us to keep hoping and then to be disappointed."

"I'm going to talk to her about it," *Mammi* said. "Have you said anything to her, Martha?"

"*Daed* said we should give her more time to think about it. I'm respecting his feelings." She glanced at her aunt and frowned.

"Poor man," *Mammi* said. "They're so close. It would be real hard for him."

"For every one of us," *Dawdi* added. "I guess all we can do is pray for her to come around."

"*Jah*, we must continue," Martha said. "In the meantime, I want to talk to her about our feelings. I'll just give it a couple of days and then talk to *Daed* about it first. I don't want to upset him."

They all agreed that was the best way to approach it.

"Now, you get back to Paul," Lizzy said. "He may be watching for you."

"*Jah*. My driver is coming in a half hour." Martha got up and hugged each of her family.

"And give that young man our love," *Mammi* said as she smiled weakly at Martha as she headed for the door. She waved back as she stepped out onto the porch.

Rose enjoyed teaching and barely referred to her notes as she taught her classes. Her students were enthusiastic and the time went quickly. She also spent the afternoons with three of her newfound friends, and they purchased tickets for a Broadway play for one evening.

In the back of her mind, Rose kept thinking about a certain man—Alexandro Gionnardo. If she was going to stop by the art gallery mentioned in the article from two years before, this would be the time.

One afternoon, her friends decided to remain at the hotel to get preparations done for their respective classes.

Rose knew the address of the gallery. Lexington Avenue was a mere fifteen-minute walk from the hotel. The weather was perfect. Nothing was holding her back, except…her fear that it might indeed be him! The man, who had stolen her heart and given her a child. The man, who knew nothing of Martha's existence.

She spent an extra few minutes trimming her eye-brows to perfection, and then brushing and re-brushing her blonde hair till her scalp was sore. She used a sub-tle brown shadow on her eyelids and added a touch of mascara to her long lashes. Finally, she picked out her favorite casual white trousers and added a teal blue silk blouse which complimented her coloring. In spite of the fifteen minute walk, she wore high white heels. She checked the full-length mirror on the closet door before heading to the elevator. She noted several men glance her way as she walked over to the revolving door in the lobby.

The walk seemed to take longer than expected, and she wished she'd worn her sandals, but she was not about to turn around. She did say a short prayer, ask-ing God to help her through this.

When she arrived, there were three customers in the gallery. They stood together talking to a pretty young woman, who was obviously working for the gallery. There was no one else in the showroom. After making the effort to be there, she wasn't going to rush out. She might as well look over the artwork. Slowly, she made her way from painting to painting. They were all Italian artists, mostly contemporary. Some of them were too modernistic for her taste, but there was one that caught her eye. It was a landscape, an inlet viewed from a hill-side. The deep blue sky drew her attention with its dra-matic cloud formation over the water, which reflected in the still water. So peaceful.

"Do you like it?" a deep male voice asked from be-hind her.

"It's lovely," she said, turning to see the source of the voice. A tall, very handsome Italian man with a mass of curly black hair and sparkling eyes looked down at her, a smile hovering over his cleft chin. Alexandro had had a dimpled chin.

"Yes, I agree. The artist is from my home town in Italy."

"Positano."

He stepped back abruptly. "You know it?"

"I..."

"Please, have we met? Do I know you?"

"Perhaps."

He stared into her eyes and soon his face relaxed and he smiled as he shook his head. "You are Rosie? Rosie Esh?"

She nodded. "You haven't forgotten my name."

"I will never forget your name," he said in a whisper. He took hold of both her hands and kissed the side of each cheek and then stood back slightly to gaze at her. "You have grown so beautiful. You're no longer Amish."

"No, I left the Amish years ago."

"I can't believe you're here in front of me. I have dreamt I would one day see you again. How did you know I was here?"

"I saw an article a couple years ago in the New York Times, and I read your name."

"You kept it all this time. But we can't talk here. Let me take you to lunch or the park, or anywhere so we can talk." He moved quietly over to the group and apologized for interrupting. Then he spoke to the young woman and reached for a jacket before steering Rose towards the door. "I still can't believe this is happening."

Rose was thinking the exact thing. Oh my, if only her heart would slow down!

Chapter Eleven

Each day, Paul remained awake for longer intervals. His parents had returned to Ohio, but Martha continued to spend hours by his side. He had other visitors as well. Martha's bishop stopped by occasionally, and a few of his family members made the trip from Lewistown. Their visits were brief since it was difficult to leave their responsibilities in the hands of others for more than a few hours.

The doctors made arrangements for Paul to be sent to a rehab center right in Lancaster, after explaining there was little more they could do for him. At this point, no further surgery was scheduled and now that he was out of his coma, he could make progress with the therapists in rehab. It was located about four miles from the hospital.

It would still require a driver for the twenty-five minute trip from Paradise. Fortunately, Martha was a saver and she had been able to put money aside when she worked as a waitress. Anytime she received money as a gift, it went into her savings. Hank, who was one of their favorite drivers, charged very little for his services. Sometimes he stopped in to visit with Paul. The last time, Paul had been able to utter his name, which pleased everyone. His memory was improving and so was his ability to speak, though it was still an effort for him.

Two days after being told of his pending move to rehab, a bed opened up at the center and he was transferred by ambulance. Martha sat with the driver, but peeked back frequently to check on Paul. He was still in a lot of pain from the accident and riding, even in a new ambulance, proved to be difficult, though he never complained. Fortunately, it was a short drive.

The room he was given was bright and cheerful, and everyone they came in contact with was welcoming. It was a big step forward, and Martha could tell Paul was excited to be making progress. She no longer spent the night away from her home, but went in later in the day, so she could help her mother clean up from the noon meal.

Sarah continued to ponder her decision about further treatment, though she kept silent on the subject. More than once, Martha had started to talk to her about it, but Sarah had merely listened politely and then changed the subject.

Before leaving one afternoon in August, Sarah and her mother were drying the dishes and putting them away. Once the kitchen was in order, Martha sat a few moments with the women. Lizzy arrived and joined them at the kitchen table.

"Before you leave, Martha, I think we need to talk to your *mudder* about something."

"Now Lizzy, don't start that again. We've been over this so many times," Sarah said, letting out a long sigh.

"Well, you need to look your *mudder* and your *dochder* in their eyes, and tell them you aren't willing to keep trying. Go on."

Sarah shook her head. "You have no idea unless you've had to face this. No idea at all, Liz. I wish you'd make some effort to understand."

"I don't!" Liz threw up her hands. "Do you, Martha? *Mamm*?"

They shook their heads, but remained silent.

"How about your husband, Sarah. Does he understand? Or *Daed*? Don't you think your husband would do everything in his power to live if it were on his shoulders? For your sake, if not his own?"

"Please." Sarah sank back in her chair and put her hands over her eyes. "I'll think about it some more."

"Every day, you wait, you could be growing more of those dirty, nasty cells. Just remember that."

"Okay, enough. Martha wants to leave. I think I hear your ride," Sarah added. Though Martha hadn't heard anything, she stood and went to the window.

"Not yet, but I think *Mamm* needs to be left alone now, *Aenti* Liz. She knows it's breaking our hearts. If she feels this strongly about it…"

"I can't talk anymore." Sarah rose abruptly and made her way up to her room without turning back.

Martha's driver pulled up at that moment so she hurriedly kissed her aunt and grandmother and left the house. Her heart was heavy with sorrow. *Oh, help her change her mind, Lord. Please.* She rode to the rehab center in silence. Hank knew enough to allow her her privacy.

* * *

Around four, Melvin knocked softly on the bedroom door before turning the knob. Sarah was lying on the bed. A tissue box lay beside her and several wads of used tissues were tucked in a plastic bag for the trash. Her eyes, though reddened, were no longer forming tears. He sat on the bed next to her and laid his hand against her cheek. "Are you okay?"

"I guess so."

"Do you want to talk?"

"I don't have much to say."

"It might help to talk to me."

"I thought I was sure about my decision, but now…"

"And now, you're wondering if it might be better to live?"

She nodded and sniffed loudly. "Something like that."

"It's got to be your decision, sweetheart. We have no idea how difficult this has been on you."

"You'd be okay with whatever I decide?" Her eyes focused on his.

"Sarah, my heart would break to lose you. You know that. I want you to stay with me as long as I have breath in my body. If I had my way, I'd beg you to keep trying, but it ain't right for me to put pressure on you."

Sarah let out a soft laugh. "I think you just did. How can I not try when you talk like that?"

"*Jah*? You think you'll try, honey?"

She slowly nodded her head. "It would be selfish of me not to. And when I saw Martha's face and my *schwester's*, I realized it wouldn't be right not to keep fighting. And my dear *mudder*. But mostly for you, Melvin. You can't find anything around here without me."

A grin formed on his face. "You got that right."

"I'll get word to the doctor tomorrow somehow."

"I'll take you in the buggy myself." Melvin's smile was radiant, and he leaned over and kissed his wife. *"Danki."*

She wrapped her arms around his neck, pulled him down and held him closely. Through freshly shed tears, she spoke in their language. "You are the light of my life. I want to make it. I want to see you as an old man and care for you. I want to see my Martha marry and be with her when she brings our grandchildren into the world. No, I'm not ready to give up yet."

He laid next to her then and held her in his arms and they wept together and then prayed for her healing. They prayed fervently and felt confident that their prayers were indeed heard.

When Martha got home just in time for supper, her grandparents had already come over to join them.

After the grace was said silently and the food passed around the table, Sarah cleared her throat. "I have something to tell everyone."

They stopped what they were doing and looked over at her.

"I'm going to the doctor tomorrow to tell them to start my therapy again. I'm ready to fight."

"Amen!" her father said loudly. Everyone let out an elated cry and Martha got up from her place and went over and laid her head against her mother's chest, surrounding her with her arms.

"Danki."

"Jah, I was being selfish. It ain't that bad—the treatment and all. I'll get through it, and if it still isn't

enough to kill off those bad cells, I'll try again. Life is too precious to cast it away."

"You'll have to stop at *Aenti* Lizzy's tomorrow on the way to the doctor. She was so upset," Martha said.

"*Jah*, I might even run over tonight. You couldn't ask for a better *schwester* than Liz."

Mammi put her fork down and looked over at her daughter. "You've just given me a reason to live to be a hundred."

Martha hadn't told Paul her mother was ready to die rather than go through more treatment. He wouldn't have understood. He had been through so much himself and learned only hours ago that he might not ever get full use of his right arm. It came as a stunning blow, but he remarked how watching Sarah go through the cancer with so much courage and grace was giving him the encouragement he needed to accept his uncertain future.

People need the example of others, she thought, to get through some of their own difficult days, which lie ahead for everyone. It wasn't the trial, but the way one handled it, which built character.

Chapter Twelve

Rose stood outside with Alexandro as he hailed a cab. "Are you hungry?" he asked.

"I could eat something light, perhaps."

"I know a nice little café where you can get just about anything." After giving the address to the cabbie, he sat back and looked over at Rose. "I still can't believe this is happening. You have to tell me all about yourself. I'm sure you're married…"

"No, I'm widowed. Two years now."

"And I too, am alone now. Three years ago my wife was killed in a car accident."

"Oh, how horrible. I'm so sorry, Alex."

"It was a terrible shock. At least she was killed immediately and didn't suffer."

"I guess that's some comfort. Was she alone in the car?"

"My daughter was in the car with her, but miraculously, she was only slightly injured. You saw her. She was helping me in the gallery."

"Oh, she's lovely."

"And you, Rose, did you and your husband have any children?"

"No," she said in all honesty.

"I see. What do you do? Do you work?"

"From my home in Ohio. I'm a writer."

"How terrific! What do you write?" They discussed her books at length and the reason she was in New York. She also told him her pen name.

"Wait, I'll write it down. I need to buy all your books." He pulled out his phone and made some notations. A few minutes later, the cab pulled over to the curb.

"We're here already. That was fast." He drew out his wallet, paid the driver and then they got out of the car. She felt his hand under her elbow as he guided her into a small, cozy restaurant, half-filled with customers. It shocked her to feel a slight thrill at his casual touch.

Once they ordered some gourmet-style burgers, he leaned back in his chair. "You never wrote back, Rosie. I looked every day for months."

"I never got your letters, Alex. My sister told me only recently that my parents destroyed them. Every single one. I didn't have your address."

"So that's what happened. I couldn't understand it. We cared so much for each other. But why would they destroy them? What were they afraid of? After all, we had an ocean between us."

"I think they were afraid I'd leave the Amish."

"Still…it seems so severe. Would you have written if you'd had my address?"

"Yes, I believe so. You were very special."

"How long did you wait to marry?"

"Nearly three years. I guess I was still hoping…"

She looked over and his beautiful dark eyes showed his inner pain as they penetrated her own eyes.

"I was too hurt to wait that long. I married about a year later. My daughter just turned nineteen. When she was three, we came to the States to live. I wanted to open a gallery here to promote Italian art. My father encouraged me since he was an artist himself—a very successful one. He footed my expenses in the beginning, but business took off quickly and I was able to pay him back within five years."

"That's amazing. I remember you loved the art world even when you were young. I thought you'd end up being an artist yourself."

"I still like to fool around with oils, but I prefer the business end of it. I knew I could never excel as an artist."

"So, will you turn your business over to your daughter someday? Does she paint?"

"No, she has no interest in the business. She just helps me when she has the time and I need her. She's attending Columbia University."

"What is she studying?"

"She's in pre-med. Rosalind wants to be a pediatrician. She loves kids. She never quite forgave us for not having more children, I guess," he added with a crooked smile.

"Why didn't you?"

"We weren't happy together. It was not a good marriage."

"I understand. I married for companionship. I don't know if I ever really loved him, though he was kind to me. Just much older."

"We should have married, Rosie. You and I."

She shook her head. "I can't think that way."

"I try not to, but it's true. We were so close. I think you knew what I was thinking before I did."

"I remember."

"I'm sorry."

"What about?"

"You know. Taking something precious from you."

"Oh."

"Forgive me?"

"I never held it against you. It wasn't like you forced me."

"I should have had more strength of character. You'd been so protected and—"

"Alex, it was a long time ago."

"And we've both moved on."

"Yes."

"May I see you again?"

"I leave in two days."

"Then we can have the rest of today and all of tomorrow."

"Well, not all of tomorrow. We have a closing ceremony at noon and—"

"Then as soon as it's over. I can pick you up. I'll take you to a show."

"Oh, I'm supposed to go with some friends tomorrow night. I forgot all about it."

"Can you give the ticket to someone else?"

"Sure."

"I'll reimburse you."

"I wouldn't think of taking money from you, but of course, I'll just give it to someone. I'd rather be with you."

He reached across the table and laid his hand over

hers. "It really is you. I pictured you exactly as you look. Well, actually, you look younger. I have a photograph of you, you know. A friend took it when you weren't looking. I probably didn't tell you for fear you'd insist on ripping it up."

"I didn't know you had one. Martha has one of you," she said without thinking.

"Martha?"

"Oh, someone I know. I'm not sure where she got it."

"Didn't you ask her for it?"

"I'm not sure."

"It doesn't matter. All that matters is you're here with me right now. Do you still like to dance? Remember when I taught you the Rumba?"

Rose giggled. "How could I forget? It was so funny. Our dog kept barking at you. He thought you were hurting me."

"And then your father came over."

Her mouth narrowed and she cast her eyes down. "He wasn't happy. *Daed* passed away. I didn't even know it until a couple years later."

"Why did you leave the Amish?"

"For many reasons. I'd rather not talk about it."

"I'm sorry. I won't ask again, but it must have been a difficult decision."

"It was. Very. Someday, I'll tell you. I just don't want to spoil this day." She looked over and smiled tenderly. "You're just the same. A really sweet guy."

"Sweet. Is that good?" he asked with a chuckle.

"To me, it is. I lived too long with someone who never smiled or laughed."

He nodded. "Sounds like my wife. Sorry, I shouldn't speak of the dead that way."

"Why did you marry her, if you weren't in love?"

"I thought I was at the time. She was cute and smart and it helped to get my mind off of you. I didn't want to be alone."

"But you were in college," Rose said.

"Yes. But it can still be lonely when all your friends are partying and you're in your room studying by yourself. Sharon was a student, too. She liked to cook and she'd invite me over nearly every night to have supper with her and her family. They seemed to like me and encouraged us to get together."

"So the way to a man's heart is—"

"Through his stomach. Yup, I guess it helped. We weren't married six months when I realized I'd made a mistake. I couldn't divorce her. I wasn't a practicing Catholic anymore, but I didn't—and don't—believe in divorce. Besides, she discovered she was expecting. That's the best thing that came out of the marriage. Rosalind is a wonderful young woman."

"I'm sure she is. Rosalind? Any reason for that name?"

"I think you might be able to figure it out. Sharon didn't mind. She kind of liked the name and I never told her about you."

"It must have been difficult on your daughter when her mother died."

"She was in the car at the same time, but she was only slightly injured. Yes, she missed her mother terribly. It took a long time for her to get over it. Probably never will entirely."

"Was it your wife's fault—the accident?"

"She'd actually been at a friend's house for part of the afternoon. School was over so Rosalind went along with her. She liked playing with the woman's new baby. Sharon had a glass or two of wine, but I doubt she was intoxicated. She never drank much, but she went through a red light, and our car was hit by a pick-up truck. She was killed immediately."

"At least she didn't suffer, poor girl. And thankfully, Rosalind was all right."

The waiter came over, set down their burgers and refilled their water glasses. After he left, Alex took hold of her hand and bowed his head. Surprised, but pleased, she followed suit and he prayed over the food. Then they began to eat.

Rose smiled over after sipping water. "I'm glad you take the time to pray for your food."

"I learned that from being with you and your family. Now it has more meaning."

"It's a good reminder of who provides everything in our lives."

He nodded. "I'm learning."

Rose took a small bite of her burger. It was difficult to swallow. She was surprisingly nervous as she realized how much she cared about developing a relationship with him—once again.

Chapter Thirteen

Paul was able to speak more easily now, though sometimes his words sounded slurred. He had a speech therapist come in daily and also a physical therapist, who encouraged him to sit in a wheelchair for short periods of time. Though he still needed pain medicines, they were decreasing the potency and frequency of his doses.

Martha often read to him when he seemed too tired to talk and she read from the Bible and also from the *Book of Martyrs.* Martha's bishop came by and prayed with them. He offered to work with them on their baptismal requirements once Paul recuperated more, though it was too soon at this point. There was still extensive recovery to take place first.

Paul and Martha did not discuss his arm. They each knew it could be a problem in the future, if he was to continue his desire to return to carpentry. Everything Martha talked about was meant to be encouraging. They drew closer through their trial.

Rose and Alexandro enjoyed their time together. It was difficult to part at night, but they were still testing their relationship, and there was no intimacy shared physically. It amazed Rose that they were nearly able to pick up from when they had parted more than twenty years before. Perhaps it was an illusion and there'd be a moment when reality would set in and she'd see him as a stranger who invaded her life for a brief interlude— only to end in more pain.

After the closing ceremony finished up, some of the instructors and most of the attendees who were staying at the hotel made preparations to leave. Rose was glad she had another night before leaving for Ohio, and she went to her room and freshened up before going down to the lobby to meet Alex. When she got out of the elevator, she saw him standing near a water fountain, his arms folded as he waited. She felt a sudden elation. This was real. This man—the only man—she'd ever loved was right there in front of her. It was almost too much to believe. They'd have all day together and maybe even some of tomorrow, but then it would be separation once more. Would she ever see him again?

Her eyes caught his as she made her way over to him, and he gave her a wonderful familiar smile and put his hands out to grab hers once she was close enough. He held them for several moments before letting them go. "You're free now—I have you for the rest of the day."

"Yes. I'll let you decide how we spend our time."

"Are you hungry for lunch yet?"

"Not really. They had donuts and coffee for us and I managed to get two down."

"Still have a sweet tooth," he said as he guided her out of the hotel to the waiting sidewalk.

"Always."

"You certainly haven't put weight on."

"If I get carried away on desserts, I give myself a lecture and stay away from them for a week or so. I have more energy when I don't overdo."

"Do you still like to dance?"

"I like to, but I can't remember the last time I went dancing. It might have been with you."

"Tonight I'll take you to a lovely restaurant where they have a small dancefloor. You'll like the music. Not the wild stuff they play today, but good dance music. Even their food is special."

"Sounds wonderful!"

"Now, I'd like to stop by the gallery for just a moment. I want you to meet my daughter."

"I'd love to. She knows nothing about me, I'm sure."

"Actually, I told her once, not that long ago, about my time in the States as a young student."

"You have very little accent, Alex. I'm surprised."

"And disappointed?" he asked, his chin dimpling as he grinned.

"Perhaps, just a tad. Just don't forget your Italian."

"Won't happen. I go back once or twice a year to see family and freshen up my Italian."

When they arrived at the gallery, Rosalind was sitting at a small desk, working on her computer. When she saw her father and Rose, she smiled and went to greet them. There were no customers at this point.

Alex introduced Rose, and Rosalind's brows arched when she heard him speak her name. "Rose?" she turned towards her father. "Is that why I'm named Rosalind?"

"Perhaps," he said, clearing his throat. "This is the young woman I told you about whom I'd met years ago in America."

"Ah." She nodded at Rose and continued to smile. "The one you fell in love with. I thought you were Amish," she added.

"I was when your father was there, but I left the Amish soon after."

"Oh. I'm fascinated by the way they live. You must take me to visit your family one day."

"I… I don't see them very often, but perhaps it can happen."

After a few minutes discussing Rosalind's future plans for her schooling, Rose and Alex left the gallery. The sidewalks were crowded with shoppers. Now that the heat wave had terminated, people were anxious to visit the stores once again. At one point, Rose dropped back due to the crowd. Alex turned and stopped until she caught up with him. He took a firm grip of her hand. "I've lost you once, I won't allow you to disappear again." His hand felt good upon hers.

They decided to go to the Metropolitan Museum of Art. When they grew tired towards the end of the afternoon, they sat on a bench and talked more about their time together so many years before. She remembered things he'd forgotten and he was amused at some of the events she'd placed into her memory bank. One was when he had slipped into the brook and ended up soaked for a couple of hours. "You didn't like it when I suggested taking my clothes off and drying them in the sun," he said, grinning.

"Well, no! Goodness, how naughty of you to even mention such a thing."

"I really had no intention of following through," he said. "I just wanted to see your pretty face turn red."

"And blush, I did."

"You have such pretty skin. So fair and smooth. I still can't believe we're together again. I hope you'll let me come to Ohio to visit you."

"Of course, though there isn't much to do there, I'm afraid. Not compared to the City."

"Sometimes, I wish I lived in the country. I loved my time in the States. The Amish lifestyle really appealed to me then. I even thought once about returning, but my father had a stroke right after I got home, and my mother needed me to help out at home. I told you all about it in my letters, but of course, you never got to read them."

"I should have known you'd write, but my parents made sure my sister always brought the mail in. I was not allowed to get it. Now I know why. They wanted to destroy them before I'd see them. It was a terrible thing to do."

"Did they know we loved each other?"

"I told them, and they were furious with me. I've tried to forgive them."

"I guess they were afraid I'd come back and take you away with me. I should have."

Yes, life would have turned out so differently.

"I try not to look back. Maybe I should return to the hotel and change into something more exciting than slacks—especially, if we're going dancing."

"It's not terribly formal there, but I guess most of the gals do wear fancy dresses. I went with my daughter and her boyfriend once, just to see the place."

"No date?"

"I may have had a date with me. I've dated quite a few women, Rose, but nothing serious ever happened. My daughter tried fixing me up a couple times with single faculty women she'd met in college, but I detest blind dates. They're usually so boring, I would end up wishing I were home with a good book."

"Sounds like one of my friends. She's convinced I can never be happy unless I have a man in my life."

"And what do you think?"

"I... I have found something—maybe not happiness, but peace. I have friends at church and I'm quite active there. My peace is with God, so I never feel totally alone."

"I understand. I'm the same way. I haven't found a church here in the city though. I just read the Bible on my own and once in a while, I watch a preacher on the TV."

"Maybe if you visit me some weekend, I'll take you to my church. I think you'd like it."

"I'd love to attend with you. When can I come?"

Rose giggled. "Goodness! You are in a hurry."

"Rose," he said as he leaned over to be closer. They were actually alone, except for a guard who walked back and forth between rooms. "I believe my feelings for you have never gone away. I feel young again, just being with you."

She could feel his breath on her cheek. It looked like he had plans to kiss her, but she drew back. "We're in public. I—"

He tilted his head. "And if we weren't, would it make a difference?"

"Oh, Alex, you're still a tease, just like you were years ago."

"I feel like I'm a teenager again. Yes, I'll get you back to your room and maybe you should take a rest. I plan to keep you dancing until your coach turns back into a pumpkin."

When she was alone in her room, she filled the large tub with hot water and turned on the jets as she laid back with her head against a towel. What a luxurious feeling. Peace. And happiness. My, what a wonderful combination!

Chapter Fourteen

The evening was everything she dreamed it would be. At first they danced together stiltedly until she relaxed enough to follow his lead. They kept a slight distance apart. Rose feared being too close at this point in their budding relationship. She didn't want it disrupted or colored by her emotional desires. He seemed to understand, and never pushed her, though she sensed it was difficult for him to keep his distance as well.

When the small band finished its set, Rose and Alex ordered supper. It was still difficult to eat in front of him, but she ordered soup and a plate of assorted sushi, which she ended up sharing.

"Why don't you stay a few more days?" he asked looking over. "I'd be happy to pay for your hotel room, or you could sleep in my guestroom."

"Alex, you know I couldn't do that."

"I figured you'd say that." He grinned over. "But what about staying on at the hotel?"

"I could afford to. Yes, maybe I will. I don't have anything pressing at home. Can you take so much time away from your business though?"

"I made a call earlier to a guy who helps me out from time to time—when my daughter's unable to work. I asked him if he'd be available for the next couple days and he said he could help. All I need to do is text him. Please stay." He reached across the table and placed his warm hand on hers.

She looked into his gorgeous dark eyes. "All right. I'll stay two more nights, as long as they have room."

"I'll call them right now and you can check. I have the number." He took his phone out, pressed in the number of the hotel, and handed it over to Rose.

After being assured of her room being available, she hung up and handed it back. "I'm not usually so impulsive," she added, grinning.

"Thank you for changing your plans last minute, and please allow me to pay for the room. When I was young, I had so little money, I couldn't take you anywhere. Now I want to dazzle you," he said, as he touched the tip of her nose with his index finger.

"Let me think about it. You're kind to offer, but I feel funny about accepting your offer."

"There would be no strings attached. It would be a gift from an old friend. Nothing more—unless you wanted more."

"I'll pretend I didn't hear that last part," she said, winking over at him. "But that makes it easier to accept your offer. Now, how about if you dance with me again. You won't believe it, but they're playing a Rumba."

"You're right! I wasn't even listening. Come lovely Rosa, we'll show them how it's done," he said as he stood and reached for her hand.

Sarah began her treatment again. She knew what to expect and resigned herself to the side effects of the chemo. She was relieved she'd made the decision to continue, and reprimanded herself for considering only her own feelings. She had so many who loved her and wanted her to make it through this, surely she could do her part. Perhaps there would be a total cure or remission, after all.

Martha felt torn between being with her parents and spending her time with Paul. Dividing her time was draining, but she felt she'd come up with the best solution—mornings and evenings with her family, and afternoons with Paul.

One afternoon, when she arrived at the rehab center, she found Paul sitting in the group room watching television. He barely looked over at her, and continued to watch the gameshow. She tried not to be hurt by his actions, but as she sat down in a chair next to his wheelchair, she reached for his hand. "Better not hold that one," he said in a low voice. "It's pretty useless."

"Let me take you back to your room. We can't talk here, Paul. People are trying to watch the show." Without waiting for his response, she got up, unlocked the wheels and pushed the wheelchair towards his room. When they arrived, an aide had just changed his sheets and was getting ready to walk out.

"Wait. I need help getting in my bed."

"I'll get your nurse," the young girl said and left.

"Have you been sitting long?" Martha asked.

"No."

"Are you tired?"

"I guess."

"Paul, what's happened? Why are you angry?"

"I'm not angry at you."

"Well, it feels that way. Who are you angry with?"

"*Gott*, I guess."

At that moment, his male nurse arrived and Martha sat back as she watched him struggle to get Paul back in his bed. Paul seemed so weak. Once it was accomplished, the nurse left and Paul laid his head back and closed his eyes.

"Paul?"

"What?"

"Open your eyes. We need to talk."

He lifted his lids and stared at her. "It's not going to work. Our marriage. You should go home and try to forget me."

"What are you saying? Did you take 'crazy' pills today?" Her dark eyes flashed.

"I'm never going to get better. I'll never have a job again. I'll be useless till I die."

"Don't be absurd! You're getting better every day."

"Not my arm. My doctor told me today, I'll never have full use of it again. Do you realize what that means?"

"I have a pretty *gut* idea, if you take his word for it."

"He's a doctor! Who knows more?"

"Sometimes, doctors are wrong! Sometimes, we need to pray and get our strength from someone greater!"

"Martha, you think I haven't prayed about it? That's all I do when you're not here."

"Well, then give it time. But if you think you can chase me away just because you might not be a carpenter again, then you sure don't know me very well. I love you. *You!* It doesn't matter if you ever work again. We would manage somehow. Besides, you can do other things and your arm may heal completely someday. And you're angry with *Gott*? Seriously?"

"I couldn't be more serious. Why did this have to happen? Things were going so smoothly and I thought I'd made the decisions He wanted me to make. I wanted to do what was right for you, your family, everyone. And now look at me."

"I am looking. And I picture you the day of the accident. Paul, we didn't know if you'd make it or not. You couldn't move or talk. You were in a coma. Your brain was damaged. You needed surgery. You've come through so much in such a short time and look at you! You're doing so well now. You should be singing *Gott's* praises!"

He lowered his eyes and remained silent. She went over to the other side of the bed and lifted his good hand to her lips and kissed it. "We'll get through this, my *liebschen*. Together."

"Martha, Martha, what would I do without you. Please hold me." His voice cracked.

She surrounded him with her arms and kissed his cheek and then his lips. "*Gott* is with us, Paul. You may not see Him or hear Him, but He never leaves us or forsakes us. We just need to be patient. *Gott* has His own timing."

"I know. You're right. I guess I was having what the English call a pity-party. Forgive me, darling. I will work as hard as I can to get the full use of my arm back, but if I can't, I'll find another way to provide for you and our *kinner*."

"I know you will. I'm marrying you in the fall, Paul. Get used to the idea." She moved back and smiled at him broadly.

His eyes were filled, but he blinked back his tears and smiled back. "I love you, forever."

Jah, they'd get through this together—with the Lord Jesus by their side.

Jeremiah called Martha one morning to see how Paul was doing. He was pleased with his friend's progress, but concerned when he heard Paul might not get full use of his right hand and arm. "How's he taking it?"

"It's hard on him, Jeremiah, but he's trying to accept it. I think if he keeps up with his therapy, even when he leaves rehab, he'll be fine one day. We all need to pray for his healing."

"*Jah*, Hazel and I pray every night together for him—and for you. I know it's hard on you as well. How's your *mudder* doing?"

"She's shown improvement, but she still needs more chemotherapy. She tries to be brave, but I know it's not easy on her."

"I'm sure. Cancer is nasty. Do you think Paul would be up to company next Sunday? We want to come visit with you both."

"I think it would do him a world of *gut* to have friends stop in. He doesn't know many here. Just us."

"I stopped by to see his parents a couple evenings ago. They're making plans to bring him back, as you know."

"I know that's what they plan to do. I'll probably come visit frequently if that happens. I just wish there was some way to care for him in my home."

"That would be difficult. Is his leg healing?"

"*Jah*, I guess, but it's slow going. He still needs a wheelchair."

"Poor guy. I bet it's hard on him. Well, tell him we're

coming. Maybe that will cheer him up. His *mudder* gave us the address of the rehab center. Now we'll get a driver."

"*Danki*, Jeremiah. It will be *gut* to see you both again."

After she hung up, she thought about Hazel. Finally, it seemed the girl had given up on Paul and was really going to marry Jeremiah. Though her fears had nearly been extinguished, there was still a thread of concern. If Paul ended up back in Lewistown, would Hazel try to work her way back into his life? Surely not! After all, she was going to marry Jeremiah. For sure and for certain!

Chapter Fifteen

The following evening, Alex included his daughter in their plans. He picked Rosalind's favorite Italian restaurant, and he and Rose met her there around seven.

After ordering, Rosalind told him she had sold a major piece of art at the gallery, netting them over twenty thousand dollars, and how she had convinced the buyer and his wife to purchase it for an investment. "It was easy, Dad. It helped that they liked the subject matter, of course, so they can enjoy it on their wall."

"What was the subject matter?" asked Rose.

"Oh, a landscape."

"In oil?" Rose asked.

"Of course. What else?" Rosalind answered rather sharply.

Alex glared at her. "There are other mediums, Rosalind."

"But not selling at that price in *our* gallery."

"She wouldn't know that, now would she?"

His daughter shrugged and turned to Rose. "Tell me about being Amish. Is it true they beat their children?"

"Goodness, no. Of course, there are bad people in

every group, so maybe occasionally you hear about abuse, but the Amish love their children just like English do."

"English?"

"Non-Amish. That's what we called them."

"Why did you leave?"

"Rosalind, that's pretty direct questioning. Let's settle down." Alex's mouth was drawn.

"Sorry, I didn't know things like that were secret. Did you go on to school?"

"Actually, I did. I majored in English in college."

"She's a writer. I thought I mentioned it to you," Alex added, as he reached for a piece of bread.

"Maybe. I forgot, if you did."

They were silent for several minutes. The waiter brought their salads and filled their water glasses.

Alex put his head down to pray. Rosalind rolled her eyes and muttered, "How embarrassing, Dad. Why do you always insist on praying, even in public?"

"Doesn't God provide your food, even in restaurants?"

"It's so old-fashioned," she whispered loudly as she lowered her head to comply.

Rose was disturbed by her attitude and wondered if his daughter acted like this with everyone, or whether the girl had just taken a dislike to her. It was an uncomfortable hour, and she was relieved when Rosalind prepared to leave to meet up with friends before their coffee arrived.

"It was nice to see you again," Rose said, forcing a smile as his daughter reached for her purse.

"Same here. I probably won't see you again, so have a nice life," she added. She leaned over and pecked her father's cheek. "See you tomorrow."

"Not tomorrow. Todd will be working with you."

"Oh. I thought Rose was leaving."

"I'm staying on a couple days."

"Oh. Nice. Well, whenever you get back to work, Dad, I'll see you. Thanks for dinner."

She left quickly and Rose noted Alex looked none too happy. She sipped at her water and waited for him to speak. When he did start a conversation, it was about her latest book. They discussed the historical aspect and she was impressed with his expertise on American history.

"I love history, of any kind," he mentioned. "Listen, I'm sorry my daughter acted rudely towards you. It really isn't personal. She's just had her hopes set on another woman I was seeing, even though it's been over for a month now. It never was that serious. She read more into it than there was."

"Maybe she's just used to having you all to herself."

"Perhaps, either way, I'll have a talk with her."

"Don't feel that's necessary. Teens can be complicated."

"By not having children, you've avoided some of the difficulties parenting brings, though there are many pluses. I'd hoped for more children. Maybe it's not too late."

That didn't sound like he was getting serious about her. After all, not many women had babies at thirty-nine. "Perhaps," she said, hoping not to sound disappointed.

"Would you still want to try for a child—if you ever married again?" he asked as he laid his napkin by his plate.

So he was thinking of me. "I guess it would depend upon my age at the time."

"I guess that's a pretty personal question to ask."

Wouldn't now be a good time to tell him about Martha? Why was she so hesitant? She really didn't know, but the words never came. If they were to become interested in each other again, she didn't want it based on the child they'd produced together. He might pretend he cared about Rose, when it was really just their child he wanted to get to know.

The conversation ceased altogether as the waiter left a check on a small tray and thanked them profusely for allowing him to serve them. After he left their table, Alex shook his head. "That's the nicest our waiter's been all evening. I guess he figures it's tip time. Pull out all the stops."

"He was rather indifferent, wasn't he? Though he certainly kept his eyes on Rosalind."

"She gets a lot of attention. At this point, she's more concerned about getting into medical school than getting serious about someone. She's already researching her choices. I just hope she can get into one in New York. How about going back to my place. I'd like to show you the view from my apartment. It's quite amazing."

"I guess that would be fine. I'm a bit of a prude, I guess. I don't usually accept invitations to visit a man's home."

"We've been friends a long time, Rosie. I think you should feel safe with me."

She nodded. Safe was not the word that came to mind. She feared her own feelings for him, which she'd finally admitted were strong. If this was the end of their relationship, she could no longer pretend it wouldn't hurt. They had two more days to be together. Of course, he'd talked about driving out to see her. Maybe he really would.

Before leaving the restaurant, she excused herself and checked her hair and makeup in the restroom mirror. After refreshing her lipstick, she went with him to the curb, where they took a cab to a magnificent building on Madison Avenue.

A doorman greeted Alex by name and bowed slightly as he held the door open for them to enter. Marble floors, glistening walls and huge glass windows gave the large foyer an elegant and airy look. The high ceilings echoed their footsteps as they made their way over to the elevators. As it travelled swiftly, she could barely feel it move, but suddenly the doors opened and they'd arrived on the seventeenth floor.

Alex led her to his apartment entrance and unlocked the door. After touching a silent switch, lights went on throughout a large, immaculate great room, furnished in white contemporary furniture, with accents in black. It was very dramatic. She was almost unable to speak, shocked at his obvious success to be able to afford such a luxurious apartment. The art he'd selected was surprisingly traditional, and most of the paintings were landscapes of Italy.

"Wow."

"Do you like it?"

"It's amazing! You've certainly done well, Alex. I kind of always knew you would, but I'm really impressed."

"All this, and no one to share it with. Even Rosalind has left me and shares a place with a friend. It gets lonely. Maybe that's why I work so many hours. I go in seven days a week, even when we're closed. It gives me something to do."

"I'm surprised you're still single."

He shrugged. "I'm not going to make another mistake. Sometimes, it's better to expect less in life. Then you're not disappointed."

"I guess that's how I feel. I, too, don't wish to be hurt again."

"Did I hurt you, Rosie? By not coming back? I would have, you know, if you'd asked me to."

"I can't think about what might have been."

"No. It gets you nowhere. So I'll show you the rest of the apartment, if you'd like."

"Please."

He took her by the hand and walked her through. She loved the sterile white and stainless kitchen with all the latest equipment. "Do you cook much?" she asked him.

"No. I like to, but if I'm not cooking for someone, well…it's not as much fun."

"And too much clean-up. Would you like me to make dinner tomorrow night? I'm not a great cook, but I could make one of my Amish meals for you. You used to rave when my mother made chicken and dumplings. Do you remember?"

He grinned. "Do I? They were the best! I'd love to have you cook for me. We can shop in the morning for the ingredients. Do you have the recipe with you?"

"It's here," she said, pointing to her head. "I used to help mom make it every week. I could probably make it in my sleep."

"This will be fun, Rosie. I'm so glad you're here." He reached for her hands, and gently pulled her into his arms and before she could respond, his lips were upon hers. She trembled at his touch, remembering how it was to be embraced by him those many years before.

Her resolve to keep things from getting serious, was melting and she pulled back slightly.

"I'm afraid, Alex," she whispered.

"It's okay. I won't pursue anything more. I know what you're thinking. We'll go slowly, I promise."

Oh, she wanted so much to let her emotions take over, but it wasn't the way it should happen. She made a mistake once. She would not make the same one again. Even with the same man. Slightly shaky, she asked to see the rest of the apartment. After going through the five thousand square foot apartment, they came back and sat on opposite sofas to chat.

"Can I get you any wine or brandy?" he asked.

"Maybe just water," she said, fearing anything stronger might be dangerous. While he was getting her some, she looked around. There were two photographs of his daughter on a bookshelf—one taken when she was a toddler and the other at her high school graduation. She resembled her father—and even Martha, with her beautiful dark eyes and black silky hair.

After about an hour, Rose decided she should head for the hotel. As they waited for the taxi to arrive, they made plans for the next day. Then, holding the car door open for her, he smiled widely. "See you at ten. I'll come by for you, and we'll go to my favorite market. I can't wait for that dinner."

"I hope it's as good as you remember it," she said as she sat back in the seat. She waved as the car pulled away from the curb. She'd made it. She'd managed to keep things on an even keel, though the memory of his kiss replayed itself over and over. She hadn't realized how much she'd missed having a man in her life. One she loved.

Chapter Sixteen

Before picking Rose up the next morning, Alex stopped by the gallery. His daughter was already there, sitting at the desk with a textbook in front of her. She looked up and smiled when she saw her father. "Have fun last night?"

He frowned. "Once you left the restaurant."

Her brows rose. "Why? What did I do?"

"You know very well how rude you were to Rose. It was uncalled for, and it was very embarrassing. Why on earth would you act like that?"

"Maybe I shouldn't have said some of the things I did, but I was nice to her most of the time. She certainly doesn't seem like your type though."

"What's my type?"

"You know. Like glamorous. Worldly. Sophisticated. She's like a small-town girl out of her element."

"You don't even know her. And what makes you think I like the kind of person you just described?"

"That's what Beth was like."

"And we broke up. Remember?"

"It was a major mistake. I can't imagine why you did that."

"Because, my dear, I didn't ever love her."

"What were you looking for? Someone you could dominate? A little woman who would cook your meals and—"

"Hold on, Rosalind. You're getting beyond yourself. I really don't want to discuss it any further. You're a different generation. You have no business saying these things. I'm leaving now."

"Already? To see her again?"

"We plan to spend the whole day together."

"Well, I hope you're not getting serious. She's probably just interested in you for your money."

"That's a pretty nasty thing to say."

"I guess I can't say anything right. Hey, it's your life."

"Yes, as a matter of fact, it is." He quickly sorted through the unopened mail and then left without adding any further comment. Instead of using a cab, he walked briskly through the crowds and tried to calm himself down before reaching the hotel. By the time he arrived, he had his anger under control. Using his cellphone, he called to alert Rose of his arrival.

She had been ready for several minutes, and joined him in the lobby.

They took their time walking the narrow aisles in the grocery shop and purchased the necessary ingredients for their meal, adding hors d'oeuvres, chips and salad fixings for their lunch.

"I bought tickets for the show at Radio City Music

Hall," he mentioned as they waited at the check-out with a small cart filled with food.

"How exciting! Tonight?"

"Tomorrow night. The best seats available."

"Thank you, Alex. I've always wanted to see a show there. I confess, I've never been to a Broadway show either."

"Did you give your ticket away?"

"Yes."

"Was it hard to do?" he asked with a crooked smile.

"Not in the least. The person I gave it to was thrilled. She's from South Dakota and this is the first time she's been to New York. I'd rather be with you than a bunch of girls."

He laughed. "I'm glad to hear that."

They finally reached the cashier and Alex paid for their groceries. After they got back to the apartment and unloaded, they sat down at the small glass topped kitchen table to relax and plan their day.

"If you were staying longer, I'd take you over to see the Statue of Liberty, but I thought it was too hot today. You might get sunburned on the ferry ride."

"Oh, can we do that tomorrow? I'll put sunblock on."

He smiled at her enthusiasm. "Of course we can. We can do anything you'd like. Have you been to the Library on 5th Avenue?"

"No."

"You have to see that. And the 9/11 Memorial?"

"I really have to see that, too. I hope it's not too depressing."

"It's not easy to go to, but we need to. As Americans, we shouldn't ever forget that tragic day."

She nodded. "I wish I could stay longer."

"Why can't you?"

"I'm committed to two book signings back in Ohio. I really can't get out of them. I know they've advertised the events already."

"Well, we'll pack in as much as we can while you're here. Hopefully, I can talk you into coming back soon."

"You mentioned visiting me in Ohio. Is that still a possibility?"

"Absolutely. Yes, I want to see where you live and meet your friends."

"It's pretty humble, compared to your way of life."

"Does that bother you, because it doesn't affect me?"

"I don't know how to answer that. I guess, I'm a bit overwhelmed."

"And I'm overwhelmed to be sitting with you here in my own kitchen. The girl I loved so fiercely and then who evaporated from my life. It was almost as if it was a dream, but you're real."

"Do you think we're moving too quickly? I'm scared, Alex."

"Don't be. God's in control. We're together for a purpose."

"You truly believe that?" she asked, leaning towards him.

"Yes." He leaned forward and kissed her softly.

"I'm afraid of my strong feelings, Alex. I hope you can be strong for me."

"It's taking every effort I have not to grab you and… well, it's difficult. After all, we're both adults now."

"I know, but I want our relationship—however it ends—to be right in God's sight. We kind of forgot our values when we were young."

"I know. I agree, but my heart and my mind are in two different realms."

She nodded and leaned back in her chair, anxious to change the subject. "How about if I make a tossed salad for lunch."

"Sounds good," he said as he rose from the chair. "And after we eat, we'll do the tourist thing and walk till we collapse from exhaustion."

"Well, we need to save enough energy to cook dinner."

He laughed. "You'll have to leave right after we eat, so we won't be tempted. I'll even do the clean-up."

"Oh, you won't get an argument over that!"

She pulled out a head of Bibb lettuce for the salad and rinsed it while he set out salad plates and laid them on the counter beside her. They also decided to split a cheese sandwich on rye.

They left right after lunch and spent the day sightseeing.

After going through the library, they spent a couple of hours just walking down Fifth Avenue and through Central Park. Finally, exhausted, they returned to his place and Rose removed her shoes and laid back on the sofa. "My feet are killing me."

"You should have worn sneakers," Alex said as he sprawled on a large armchair across from her. "I don't know how you walk in those things."

"I didn't even bring sneakers, but I could have worn my sandals. Maybe I can pick up a pair of sneaks tomorrow."

"Good idea. Do you want me to make dinner for you? You can tell me what to do."

"I'll be fine in a few minutes, but you can help. Do you mind if I go barefoot?"

"Of course not. Anything you want, Rosie. I'd give you my slippers, but my feet are a bit larger."

She laughed, looking over at his size eleven feet. "Just a bit."

A while later, they worked together on the food preparation, and then sat down to a tasty Amish meal. "This is fantastic!" he remarked. "I can't remember enjoying a meal this much in years."

"Goodness, it's such a simple meal."

"Sometimes, simple is better. There are times I just grab a salad bar."

"Alex, do you think your daughter will get over her feelings towards me if we go on seeing each other?"

"She'll have to."

"It's not always that easy."

"I love my daughter with all my heart, but I have my own life to live. She's practically independent now. I don't see it as a problem. Please don't worry about it. I guess we're lucky you don't have kids to consider. Simplifies things somewhat."

Rose pushed some noodles across her plate as she stared down. *Now?*

"So do you want to watch a movie when we're done?" Alex asked.

"I'd like to stay, but actually, under the circumstances, I think I'll head back to the hotel when we're finished cleaning up."

"I have a woman who comes in to clean every morning, Rose. I'll just rinse the plates off and stick them in the dishwater. We can leave the pots for her."

"Okay. No wonder the place looks so perfect."

He smiled over. "Believe me, if I didn't have her, it would be a disaster."

She tried to laugh, but the secret she kept from him was beginning to torment her. She didn't even understand herself why she didn't disclose the fact that she'd borne his child.

Once she got back to the hotel, she took a long bath and then laid awake for over an hour pondering her decision. Maybe before she left for Ohio, she'd share the whole story of her pregnancy and be open with him. She owed him that.

Chapter Seventeen

Paul was asleep when Martha arrived in the afternoon. After tiptoeing over to his side, she seated herself next to the bed. His pale face was still somewhat distorted from the accident. How much she loved him. It pained her to see him so weakened by his injuries. Though he tried hard to be positive about the future, sometimes his expression showed defeat. The doctor had warned them that often depression went along with serious injuries like his, so she was somewhat prepared for his fluctuating moods.

At home, she experienced the same thing with her parents. Even her aunt and grandparents showed signs of melancholy when she was with them. Life was not easy. Trials came to everyone, but she believed with all her heart that they built character, just as the Bible taught. Going through them, though difficult, was part of the process. It just seemed sometimes there were too many crises going on at the same time. She was getting through them, but not without the strength of Jesus to gird her up. *Danki, Gott*.

After a few minutes, Paul stirred and opened his

eyes. He smiled when he saw Martha next to him. "I didn't hear you come in."

"I know. I wanted you to rest."

"I can rest when you leave. Always wake me up when you arrive."

"If you want me to."

"I do. I don't want to lose any time with you while you're here."

"Has anyone given you an idea as to when you can leave the center?" she asked.

"No. It shouldn't be too long though. I need to get around better by myself first. I still can't bear any weight on my leg. As you know, I can't add pressure by using crutches because of my damaged arm. It sure complicates things."

"I see. *Jah*."

"I feel *gut* enough otherwise, but it would be too hard on my folks to try to care for me at this point." His lips were drawn. "I don't want to be a burden to anyone. Ever."

"Paul, I'd never consider you a burden, no matter how things worked out."

"The bishop was by earlier. He worked with me for a little while on the baptismal preparations."

"He should have waited for me to get here."

"He said he's already talked to you about it."

"Oh."

"I don't think I'll be ready this fall for marriage, Martha. I want to be pretty normal first."

"I see. I understand. It's too soon to predict, don't you think?"

He nodded. "I guess so. This just isn't the way it should be."

"I know, but we can't be defeated by it, Paul."

He let out a long sigh. "I try to be positive. It's hard."

"I know." She leaned over and kissed his cheek. "For me as well, but I know it will all work out in the end."

"*Jah*." He didn't sound as positive as she was, but of course, he was the one trying to recuperate. The pressure was on him.

"If you don't feel ready in the fall, I'm sure they'd make an exception and let us marry in the spring. After all, you wouldn't be in the fields and all."

"*Nee*. I wouldn't be doing anything. This is so hard." He turned his face away from her.

She knew he was close to breaking. "Honey, someday you'll be able to do anything again. I know it."

"*Nee*. You don't."

"I have faith."

"Martha. Martha."

She turned his head with her hand and kissed his lips. "We can't accept failure. We'll make it through this together, and come out stronger."

"You're an amazing woman. I love you with all my heart."

"And I love you. Remember Paul, *Gott* is *gut*."

"*Jah*, all the time." They stayed close for several minutes, no words spoken between them. There was no need.

Sarah took her anti-nausea medicine and laid down. She was glad she'd made the decision to fight the remaining cancer cells still present in her body. Life was too precious not to fight, and her family still needed her. Martha had enough of a struggle dealing with Paul's condition right now, without worrying about her. She needed her mother to help her through it.

Melvin returned from the barn and called out for her. Then she heard his footsteps on the stairs and he strode into the bedroom. "What's wrong?"

"Just taking a short rest."

"Did you *kutz*?"

"*Nee*. Just felt like it, is all. I took my medicine. I'll be okay in a few minutes. Please don't worry so much about me."

He walked to the bed and she moved over to allow him to sit beside her. "I can't help it, Sarah. I try not to, but this is tough on everyone."

"That's why...but it was wrong to not fight. We'll get through this, Melvin."

"*Jah*, for sure. You're real pale. Can I get you some juice or something?"

"*Nee*. I'd better not eat anything now. I want the medicine to work first. Besides, I'm not hungry."

"You look like you've lost weight, Sarah."

"I probably have. My clothes are looser. It's okay, I was gaining too much."

"You look wonderful-*gut* no matter what you weigh. You're such a pretty woman. I'm sorry we didn't have *kinner* of our own."

"I kind of like having a beautiful dark-haired *dochder*, but *jah*, it would have been nice to have more little ones around. Maybe someday, we'll be able to enjoy *grosskinner*."

"Hope so. Do you think Martha will really be able to marry this fall—the way things are with Paul?"

"I don't know. I don't talk to her about it. She probably wonders the same thing. Poor *maed*."

"*Jah*, she's had a rough time lately, between Paul and you and your troubles."

"And she was mighty concerned about you when the accident happened."

"She's a *gut* girl. Always thinking of others. You did a *gut* job raising her."

"We both raised her, Melvin. You deserve some of the credit yourself."

"I'm glad Paul was willing to come here to live."

"He's a fine young man. We should visit him again."

"Do they know when he'll be able to leave the rehab?"

"It hasn't been decided yet. When he goes back to his parents' home in Lewistown, it's going to be harder on Martha. She may want to go stay with them."

"She still has responsibilities here with you, Sarah. She has to understand that."

"Well, we need to not put pressure on the girl. She's divided enough. Promise me, you'll let her make that decision herself."

"I'll try to keep my mouth shut, but you're my first concern."

"*Danki.* I'm feeling a little better. Maybe I'll go down now and work on dinner. Is Martha downstairs?"

"She was working in the vegetable garden. Cool this morning. She mentioned canning some tomatoes before leaving for Lancaster."

"Mercy, she's a hard worker."

"She's Amish—she'd better be," he said, grinning as Sarah prepared to rise. He stood and held out his hand, which she took as she moved over to the edge of the bed and then sat a moment before getting up.

"I sure don't have time for this cancer. Later today,

I'm helping *Mamm* sew up new curtains. Her other ones wore out *gut*."

They went downstairs together and walked hand-in-hand out to the garden to join Martha.

Liz pulled in to the drive and tied her buggy to the fence under a shade tree. Melvin went to check for eggs as the three women gathered tomatoes for the canning process. Then they went into the kitchen and laid them near the sink to be washed. A stew simmered in a large Dutch oven on the back of the stove.

Martha took a deep breath, enjoying the combination of food smells, enhanced by fresh chopped garlic and basil, waiting to be added to the stew. She had learned to appreciate cooking during these last few months. Her fear of being a good cook had evaporated and she felt better prepared to be Mrs. Yoder, an Amish housewife. Now it was up to God to determine when that event would take place. He was after all, the great healer.

Chapter Eighteen

Rose and Alex took the ferryboat to the Statue of Liberty and walked in the gardens. They took selfies with their phones and then made their way to Ellis Island. Fortunately, Alex had purchased tickets ahead. It was a busy time of year for tourists and they still had waiting lines for everything. Rose didn't want to take the time to check out her family's arrival, so they went into the museum and walked around reading about the early immigrants.

After returning to Manhattan, Alex took her to a pizza parlor for lunch and then they rode a cab to the 9/11 Memorial, where they reflected on the events that had shattered the world on that horrible day. Alex was still living in Italy at the time and mentioned how affected his family and friends were at the news of the catastrophe, and how they were glued to their news channels for every word.

Then Rose told how she was attending a class when the news came across the air. The class had been dismissed so the students could watch in the student lounge. "It was difficult to understand how people could hate complete strangers enough to want them dead," she said.

"It's detestable," Alex said. "A spiritual battle."

"Yes, I agree."

After taking a guided tour, they made their way to the exit.

"We never bought your sneakers, Rosie. Should we head over to the shopping area?"

"I'll skip it. My sandals are working out okay. I put band aids on my blisters this morning."

"Maybe we should go back to my place to rest up then. We have the show tonight."

"Okay. I hope you can brew some java," Rose said as he hailed a cab. Immediately, one pulled up to the curb and they got in and gave his address.

"I not only have coffee beans to grind, but great bottled spring water."

"Sounds perfect," Rose said as she leaned back on the seat. "We have leftovers from last night. Maybe we can stay in and eat before the show," she suggested.

"You sure? I have more restaurants to take you to."

"I think, if you don't mind, I'd rather eat light tonight. I bet I've put on five pounds this week."

"Eating home is fine with me. More relaxing."

"Do you want to invite Rosalind to join us for supper?"

"Actually, I'd rather be alone with you."

"Sounds good. I'll miss you, Alex."

"You have no idea how much I'll miss you. Can I come visit you in September?"

"Of course. I don't have any plans right now, other than a writing deadline, which I'm ahead on. Please realize that I live very simply, Alex. You'll have to lower your standards, I'm afraid."

"You think that matters to me?" He took hold of her hand and squeezed it. "Things aren't that important to me. I've been fortunate to be successful, but if I had to give it all up tomorrow, I could do so without regrets. If I've learned anything in life, it is that relationships are far more important than material things. Of course, that includes God. I have a personal relationship with Christ now, Rosie. Something else that began in my time with the Amish when I was there. I saw they had something special. They had so much more than the people I knew at home, who were more concerned with creating wealth than developing strong bonds. It was a good time for me that year. One I'll never forget. Of course, it didn't hurt that I fell in love for the first time."

"You really did love me, didn't you?"

"Do you have to ask?" He leaned over and pressed his lips against hers. "I think I still do."

"Oh dear," Rose said. "That's frightening. It's too soon, don't you think?"

The cab pulled over. "We're here," the driver said as he pushed aside the glass window, which was between the seats.

After Alex paid, they got out of the cab and walked through the door held open by the doorman. They were greeted by a couple exiting the building. The ride up the elevator was shared by three others. Once in his apartment, their thoughts centered on coffee, and they worked together in the kitchen to prepare a full pot of fresh brew. His statement about still loving her floated through her mind, but the conversation did not return to her last question.

"I have my daughter's room for you, if you want to lie down a while," Alex said, while they waited for the coffee to brew.

"I might just take you up on that. I don't want to conk out at the show."

"I have to make some phone calls while you rest. Todd texted and we've received an offer on a painting. It's lower than he's allowed to accept, so we need to discuss it."

"I've kept you away from your work too long," Rose said.

"It's been a wonderful break. I never take off."

"Then I'm glad I'm here. Everyone needs a break from work sometimes."

"I'm finding that out. So, let's relax first. The coffee's ready and I think I have some Oreos somewhere. My daughter loves them." He found half a box while Rose poured the coffee in two large pottery mugs. Oh my, it tasted good after so many hours running around in the crowd-packed city.

On the way home after the show, the cabdriver left them off at her hotel. In a way, she had hoped Alex wouldn't feel it necessary to see her into the building, but she knew his manners wouldn't allow him to do otherwise.

They took the elevator up together, holding hands. Though there was no one else in the elevator, they remained silent. After she unlocked the door to her room, he stood for a moment. "Do you mind if I say goodbye inside your apartment?" he asked, almost apologetically.

"I was hoping you would," she said as she stood to

the side and motioned for him to enter. "You could stay a few minutes, if you'd like," she offered.

"I'm afraid to, Rosie."

"I understand." She didn't ask him to sit. He drew her into his arms and gave her a long, lingering kiss, passionate, yet tender. Then he stood back slightly and looked into her eyes. "I see tears. Don't," he added, wiping them with his hand. "We'll see each other soon. I promise."

"Yes, it helps to know that," she said. "You know I'm emotionally a mess over this whole thing."

"It will work out, Rosie."

"But how? So much time has passed."

"You still care?"

She nodded. "Yes, I still care."

"Then we'll go as slowly as you want. Time will come when you'll know if you can ever love me again."

"I already know. I do love you. I don't believe I ever stopped."

He smiled and kissed her once more, then again, and again.

"Oh, stop, Alex. Please."

He drew back and put his hand on the door handle. "I'd better leave."

"Yes."

"I'll call you at your home tomorrow night."

"Okay."

He turned and left quickly. She closed the door without following him with her eyes. This was so difficult. It would have been easy to have him stay, but she knew this was the right way.

She walked to the bed and laid down without even taking her shoes off. Perhaps it was just a dream and she'd wake up. Hopefully, it was reality and just the start of something special.

She wiped tears from her eyes as she rose and went into the bathroom to prepare for her night. Tomorrow, she'd return to her world, but she knew her life would never be the same again.

Chapter Nineteen

Dan, Paul's occupational therapist, was pleased with his progress. "You'll be able to get around with a walker soon, as long as your arm continues to heal enough to take the extra pressure."

"How long should that take?" Paul asked as Dan lifted his leg and bent it gently at the knee several times.

"Oh, I'll guess another two or three weeks will do it. Your physician is the expert. It helps that you're young and strong. What do you do for a living? Farm?"

"I help with the farming for my family, when I'm needed, but in the past I was in carpentry. Don't know if that's in my future anymore."

"Your arm will probably heal eventually. I saw the x-rays. Not pretty. You had multiple breaks, but the pins they inserted should be able to do the job. Depends upon how much weight you have to lift."

"I thought I wouldn't be able to get the mobility back."

"If that's what they told you, don't listen to me. I work on getting people back to living their lives pro-

ductively again, but I can only go so far with that arm
of yours. It's going to be slow progress, I'm afraid."

"And what do I do in the meantime? I'm supposed
to get married soon. I don't want my wife to starve."

Dan chuckled. "You'll get there, man. You just have
to be patient. You may have to depend on others for
a time. It's not the end of the world. Amish have big
families, right?"

Paul nodded.

"Good thing."

Martha knocked and then came in, carrying a cake
box. She was introduced to Dan and asked him if he
wanted a piece of spice cake before he left.

"I can't take a break yet—too many cases; but I
wouldn't mind taking a piece for later," he said as he
finished up with Paul's last exercise.

"How's Paul doing?" she asked as she went over and
took Paul's hand.

"Pretty good, if you ask me. He had a nasty accident."

"*Jah*, for sure." She looked over at Paul, who was
frowning. "He's strong," she added.

"That's going to help," Dan said.

Martha walked back to the counter where she'd set
the cake and cut a large piece. She placed it on one of
the paper plates she'd brought along, and covered it with
a napkin. "Do you need a fork?" she asked.

"Yeah, thanks."

After he left, Martha returned to Paul's bedside and
kissed him gently. "How are you feeling today?" she
asked.

"Same."

"Dan seems nice."

"He's a *gut* man. Puts me through a lot though."

"Are you tired? I can let you rest for a bit."

"*Nee*. Stay near me."

She pulled a chair close to the bed and reached again for his hand. He hadn't smiled at all yet.

"He thinks I'll be able to go home in two or three weeks."

"You don't seem very excited," she said.

"It means we'll be apart again."

"I know, Paul. But it also means you're getting better. That's wonderful-*gut* news."

"I'll miss you. Can't you come and stay with us?"

"I'll be going back and forth. You know…my *mamm* needs me now too."

"*Jah*, you're right. I'm being selfish. I'm sorry, Martha. Forget what I said."

"Paul, look me in the eyes. You keep avoiding me." He turned his head and looked directly in her eyes, still somber. "I want more than anything, to be with you. You know that. I'm torn in half now trying to spend time with you and yet helping my family. I'm drained."

"Martha, I'm sorry. Of course, you are. I forget how hard all this is on you. You've been so wonderful coming every day…staying with me night and day in the beginning. I couldn't ask for anyone more devoted than you have been. I'm being plain stupid."

She laughed gently. "Plain, maybe—but never stupid. Now, I'm going to cut you a piece of spice cake. I made it myself last night and I used creamed cheese for the frosting, just the way you like it."

She saw his first smile of the day as he licked his lips in an exaggerated gesture, which made her giggle as she prepared their snack.

His spirits improved as the afternoon progressed. She took him around the hallways in his wheelchair. He knew everyone on staff and most of the other patients. If one had to recover away from home, she couldn't think of a better place. According to Paul, even the food was good.

Eventually, it was time to leave him yet again. Each parting was a struggle. Oh, how they wished to be wed and living together. It didn't matter where. Their home would be their sanctuary, no matter where, or how humble.

When she arrived back home, Sarah was busy slicing meat for their supper. She looked up as Martha came in through the back door and greeted her with a frown. "There's a letter for you on the kitchen table," she said, nodding over.

"Oh, *danki*," she said, walking over to pick it up. It was addressed from Ohio. She recognized Rose's handwriting. In the past, Martha caught the mail first and sneaked any mail from Rose into her room before her mother saw it.

"Who's it from?" Sarah asked.

"A friend."

"You have a friend in Ohio?"

"*Jah.*"

"Martha, look at me. Something is funny here. Tell me about this friend."

"I guess I may as well tell you. It's from Rose Esh."

Sarah let out a gasp and covered her mouth. "Well, for heaven's sake. When did you start communicating with Rose?"

Martha explained what happened and even told

her about Rose being a writer and looking her up. She watched her mother's face as she got to the part about meeting her. She noted tears in Sarah's eyes, and immediately regretted mentioning it to her.

She went over to her mother and took her in her arms. "*Mamm*, it's okay. Nothing has changed. She's like…a friend. Nothing more. You're my *mudder* and always will be. Please don't be upset."

"I shouldn't be. You have every right to correspond with your birth mother. She was *gut* to stay out of your life all those years. I know I'm being selfish. Always thinking of my own feelings. You're my baby—always will be. But sure, you want to know your roots. *Jah*, you have every right." She moved back and took a tissue from her apron pocket and blew her nose. "You say she's a writer now? My, my. *Gut* for her. Now is she married?"

"She was."

"But not to the Italian?"

"*Nee*. An older man. He passed away and she lives alone now."

"Does she want to come here to see you?"

"We've never discussed it, *Mamm*. She knows about your cancer."

"Ach. Maybe she hopes I'll die, so she'll be your only *mudder*."

Martha shook her head vehemently. "She's not like that. She really appreciates all you and *Daed* have done for me. She's not trying to take your place—not that she ever could. Please don't think so ill of her."

"So, you like her."

"As a friend. We don't write often."

"You ain't seen her yet, have you?"

"Just once. Please, *Mamm*, don't ask me anything else."

Sarah's heart nearly stopped, but she took a deep breath before responding. "Well read her letter. I'll try to act better about all this."

"I'll read it later. Let me help you now with supper."

"Ain't you curious?"

"Not particularly. It's not a big deal."

"So, you can add the mayonnaise to the potatoes. Your *daed* wanted potato salad tonight." She sniffed loudly as she continued to cut the meat, nearly cutting into her hand. "Oh my, I'd better pay attention to what I'm doing."

Martha patted her mother's shoulder on her way to the refrigerator to get out the mayo. In a way, she was relieved to have it out in the open. It had never felt right to do things in secret. Hopefully, her mother wouldn't dwell on it. Her mother sure didn't need to have more in her life to upset her. Poor dear woman. Maybe she shouldn't have told her, but she'd been raised not to lie. Sometimes, honesty didn't feel so good, but she knew it was best, in the end.

Chapter Twenty

It felt strange to be back home again. What a thrilling few days Rose had experienced. Was it a dream? She unpacked her suitcase and shoved it under her bed. Then she began a small wash and opened windows to let the fresh air in. It felt good to be back to the familiar, though she already missed Alex. Thankfully, September was just around the corner. They hadn't set a specific date for his visit, but he'd asked if she'd be ready for company sometime in September. Hopefully, he wouldn't wait till the end of the month. Maybe she should send him a text to say she'd made it home safely. No, she'd let him make the first move. Her Amish roots prevented her from being forward. It just wasn't done that way.

As Rose sat and booted up her computer, she wondered if Martha had received her letter. She hadn't mentioned her intention to look up Alexandro. There was no need to bring up that part of the past with her daughter. After all, it might not work out between her and Alex, and Martha might begin asking questions about her blood father. Rose wasn't ready for answers. She didn't have any yet.

She pulled up her latest manuscript and reread the last couple of chapters to refresh her memory. Just as she was prepared to continue, her phone rang. Glancing over, she noted it was Alex. A smile formed as she answered. "Hi."

"Hi," his wonderful voice came across the phone. "Are you home yet?"

"Just got in a few minutes ago."

"How was your trip?"

"Good. Uneventful, the way I like it. I just unpacked."

"Miss me yet?"

"And if I say yes?"

"It would make me happy."

"Okay. Yes. Very much."

"Ready for a visitor soon?"

"Anytime."

"How about September tenth?"

"Perfect! My signings will be over with, and I should have my manuscript ready to send off as well. How long can you stay?"

"Only two nights, I'm afraid. We have a gallery show coming up and there's a lot I need to accomplish first. I'm waiting to receive a shipment of new artwork from Italy in two or three days. Lots of paperwork and I'm the only one who does that part. Sometimes I reframe the ones I think need it."

"I understand, but it's better than nothing. I'm afraid I'll have to get you a hotel room."

"That's fine. Just make sure it's close by. I'm renting a car, but I haven't driven much in the last few years."

"While you're here, I'll take you around in my car. You can pretend I'm your chauffeur."

"Oops, my other line is going off. I have to take this call. I'll call you back tonight."

"Thanks for checking on me."

"Miss you."

He hung up and Rose held the phone close to her heart. She could picture him as if he were next to her—with his gorgeous smiling eyes and adorable cleft chin. He still had a full head of black wavy hair. He hadn't aged much in her eyes. Though more than twenty years had passed, it was almost like they had picked up from where they'd left off. Strange, but wonderful. She realized she'd never stopped loving him; she'd just refused to allow herself to think about him during their separation. Life is strange.

Time to face the day. She went back to work on her book.

Jeremiah and Hazel arrived at the rehab around noon, just as Martha's driver pulled into the lot. After greeting each other, they went into Paul's room together and found him sitting in his wheelchair, finishing up his lunch. After Jeremiah shook his hand in greeting, Hazel leaned over and kissed his cheek, embarrassing Paul and annoying Jeremiah and Martha. The girl was so forward. So un-Amish-like, Martha thought as she went over to greet Paul herself. She actually kissed him on his lips quickly, just to show everyone she was the girlfriend—in case anyone had forgotten!

Things got better as they sat and chatted. Hazel took hold of Jeremiah's hand and smiled constantly at him.

Then they discussed their wedding, which was to take place in late September.

"Your *Mamm* said you'd probably still be staying with them in October," Jeremiah mentioned.

Paul frowned. "Hopefully, I'll be much better by then and can stay with Martha's *aenti* and *onkel*. That seems like a long way off."

Hazel and Jeremiah exchanged glances. "Well, that would be *gut*," she said, "but a bit unlikely, according to your *mudder*."

"I'm improving every day," Paul said. "Of course, regardless of where I am at the time, Martha and I will still try to get to your wedding. For sure."

Martha squeezed his hand as she nodded. "I think you'll be near me by then."

"I can't wait to get married," Hazel said. "We've decided to live in the larger house—the one you guys were going to live in. You got a lot of it painted for us, Paul, without realizing you'd never live there yourself."

"What about the other place? What will you do with that one?" Paul asked.

"Ben's planning to live there. He's going to pay a small rent, plus cover the expenses. He's dating a new girl he met recently. It may end up being serious. They seem to get along real *gut*."

"I'm glad," Paul said.

"What about you guys?" Hazel asked. "When's the big day?"

"We may wait until spring," Martha said, attempting to smile.

"I want to be in better shape," Paul explained.

"Oh *jah*, I understand," Hazel said, as she cast her eyes to the floor.

"It doesn't matter to me," Martha said quickly. "As long as we're together soon."

Jeremiah cleared his throat. "You sure look better than the last time we were here, fella. Can you use your arm yet?"

Paul lifted it and bent it at the elbow slightly to show his friend. "That's about it."

"It's improving. That's all that matters," Jeremiah said.

"It may take a long time—if ever," Paul said with a scowl. "Maybe I can get my left arm working in its place."

"Maybe Martha can get a job in a store or somewhere. Even waitressing, like before," Hazel said.

"*Nee.* I'll be the breadwinner. I'll find some way." Paul's eyes flashed.

"Of course. I'm sorry if I said something wrong," Hazel added.

"I shouldn't have snapped, but I won't have my wife work. She'll have enough to do taking care of our *kinner.*"

"Of course."

Martha just sat and listened. Her heart was breaking. Would he ever be able to work again? And with his pride, would it end their relationship if he couldn't provide for her? It wouldn't bother her at all to waitress again. She rather enjoyed it, but Paul had his pride—something Amish are not supposed to have—but he took his future role as head of the family very seriously. There was no way around it. He'd have to heal, or there might never be a marriage between them.

After a couple of hours, Jeremiah and Hazel's driver appeared at the door and they left for home. Paul was exhausted, and though Martha knew he preferred to stay awake while she visited, he dozed briefly. Martha pondered her future. Everything seemed so uncertain. Oh, that her mother was cured and Paul had never had that terrible accident. If only...

One of the aides came in to check on Paul. He opened his eyes. "I'm okay," he said and then closed them again. The aide left a pitcher of fresh water by the bed and left.

Martha was surprised at how tired Paul seemed and wondered if it was his way of escaping temporarily from the realities he faced. She took hold of his hand again and he turned his head and stayed awake this time. "I'm sorry," he said.

"What for?"

"For sleeping while you're here."

"It's *gut* for you to rest. Was it hard to have company?"

"Maybe."

"Because it reminds you of—"

"*Jah*! The carpentry business. My situation! The whole mess we're in. You should go and forget me!"

Shocked at his sudden turn, she felt herself snap. "Stop it, Paul! We've been through this before. Don't talk like that. You're going to have to accept what's happened."

"I try," he said, turning from her. "You have no idea how hard I try."

"Really? I don't? Oh, so you're in this alone. I see." She took her hand away from his and folded her arms, scowling over at him.

"Don't be mad, Martha."

"Well, I am! This is tough on everyone, but if we just give up and feel sorry for ourselves, life will be even more miserable. We have to fight and not give up hope. It's not the end of the world. It wasn't very long ago that we didn't know if you'd even live, and look at you now. You can talk, get around in the wheelchair, eat, be grumpy," she added.

He laughed and shook his head. "Quite a lecture, but one I needed to hear. Why do I get like this? I know *Gott* will get us through. It's weird. My mind plays tricks on me. One minute, I can fight the world, and the next—I'm ready to give up and curl into a ball. Come give me a hug," he said, holding out his good arm.

Martha placed her head on his chest and they exchanged love language in the *Deitsch*. At that moment, Martha felt confident they'd get through it somehow, and come out stronger than ever.

Before she left, she told him about her mother knowing about Rose coming back into her life. Paul told her he was relieved she finally knew so there'd be no secrets between them. Martha nodded in agreement. "It was still hard to see how upset she got. She tried not to show it, but I could tell by her eyes. She can't seem to understand—I'll never think of Rose as my *mudder*. She's much more like a friend and always will be."

"It's possible to love both of them."

"Well, not at this point. I don't even know Rose that well."

"But if you see more of her and you do feel more attached, you shouldn't feel guilt over it. That's what I'm trying to say."

She nodded. "I guess only time will tell. Her letter was nice and she asked about you. I'd written her about the accident. I'll write back in a few days and tell her we've decided to wait until spring to marry."

"If I'll even be ready then."

"Paul?"

"*Jah*?"

"You *will* be ready by then. That's it! I'll stop to see Bishop Josiah some day this week and we'll set up time for him to council us weekly. Agreed?"

"*Jah*, boss. Goodness, are you really Amish, girl?"

She giggled and kissed him on his nose. "I'd better get ready to leave, Paul. It's almost supper time and Hank should be here with the car."

"You'll be back tomorrow same time?"

"*Gott* willing."

"I miss you already."

"It's not going to be forever. Someday, we'll be together all the time. You'll get sick just looking at me."

"Never, my beautiful *maed*."

Another parting. How many more? Martha sighed as she waited by the front door for her driver.

Chapter Twenty-One

One day ran into another. Martha's life became routine. Work all morning at home with her mother, take driver to see Paul, return and work all evening to catch up on what she was unable to accomplish earlier, collapse in bed and sleep seven solid hours and then start the same thing once again. There was a certain comfort in having a predictable life. She didn't have to think—about it, or anything much beyond her schedule. After more time passed, she got the news from Paul that he would be able to leave the rehab in the near future.

One morning, shortly after getting the news, she arrived at the rehab to find Paul's parents sitting in his room. They were with two staff members and the physician who handled Paul's treatment plan. When she walked in, everyone stopped talking to greet her. After a few remarks, the staff members left, along with the doctor, leaving the four of them alone.

Paul's mother told her plans were being made to have Paul leave the following day for Lewistown.

Paul was in his wheelchair and merely stared straight ahead, showing no emotion.

"Tomorrow? That's so quick," Martha said.

"*Jah*, but you knew it was coming, Martha," his mother reminded her. "You should be happy."

"I am. Of course. It's real progress." She looked over at Paul, who showed no change in his expression. "Paul, this is *gut* news, *jah*?"

He nodded slowly. "Can you come back with us?"

"Oh my. It's so sudden. I don't know. *Mamm* has an appointment with the oncologist in a couple days. I was going to go with her and *Daed*."

"I see."

"But if things are *gut* with *Mamm*, maybe I can come in a few days. Just give me time to work things out. If that's okay with everyone else," she added, looking over at his parents. They nodded.

"You'll have to stay with Paul's *schwester* though," his mother said. "It ain't right to be with us, you know. Not with Paul in the house."

"She lives right next door," his father, George, added.

"And she knows I'd be staying with them?" Martha asked.

"*Jah*, she even suggested it," his mother said. "Maybe you can help her with her *boppli* while you're there."

Martha smiled weakly. "Of course."

Paul spoke up. "She'll be with me most of the time. That's why she'd be there. Not to babysit for Susan."

"It's okay, Paul," Martha said quickly. "I can do both."

"It shouldn't be for long anyway," his father said. "You'll get well real quick, *sohn*. You're a strong one."

"I intend to," Paul said. "I exercise my arm three times a day. It is getting more flexible. See?" He held it up and slowly moved it.

"*Ach.* That's pretty *gut*," his father said, grinning. "*Jah, Mamm*?"

His mother nodded. "Still a ways to go, *sohn*."

"I used the walker last night and my therapist said my leg has healed well enough to put some weight on it now."

"Paul, that's wonderful-*gut*," Martha said as she moved closer to him and patted his shoulder. "You just keep it up."

He smiled over at her and added, "We may even be able to marry this winter. Maybe around Christmas, if I'm better."

"I doubt that," his mother said. "You're a long way from normal, Paul."

"Actually, he's not," Martha said. Everyone looked at her. "Well, look at how much he can do now! He's absolutely amazing!" She reached for his hand.

No one replied, but Martha felt a strain. She had spoken too quickly. It was not wise for an Amish girl to speak that way to the woman who would one day be her mother-in-law, and she regretted it. Though when she saw Paul's smiling face, she knew he needed to hear positive words. That was the goal. God works with people who put their faith and trust in Him. It was worth being a bit bold to see how Paul responded to her words.

It was decided his parents would go back home to set up the driver and get the house prepared. They left before Martha did, which gave the young couple time to discuss their future. Martha assured him she'd make the trip to Lewistown as soon as possible, but she also reminded him she'd only stay three days at a time, since her mother needed her the rest of the time.

She knew he wasn't looking forward to being home

that much. His mother was domineering, and as a good Amish son, he'd have to be compliant. Hopefully, it wouldn't be for long, now that he was using a walker. The main problem he'd face when he stayed with Martha's aunt and uncle, would be their only bathroom being on the second floor, whereas in his parents' home, they had a full bath on the first level. Stairs were still problematic. Once that was conquered, there'd be no reason for him to remain in Lewistown, and he and Martha would be close once more.

Rose talked with Alex nearly every evening after she returned from New York. They usually chatted for half an hour or more. It turned out, he was unable to visit in September, which was disappointing. His business was expanding, and his daughter was back in school, which put more demands on his own time. He had hired Todd full-time, but he was still in training.

Rose's book signings were well attended and she sold over fifty copies of her book at each event. Her writing flowed even better than it had previously, and she finished up the manuscript a week earlier than was expected. The edits would follow and then the cover design, which she had to approve before production began. It was exciting to see all the work finally culminating into a finished product.

Her church family knew nothing about Alex, but she had called two of her closest friends to tell them about their reunion after all those years. They were thrilled for her and encouraged her to see him every chance she had. Rose didn't mention how rich he'd become. It still was a shock to see how he lived. It was intimidating, to say the least. In fact, it was the one thing that both-ered her slightly. How would it affect their relationship? They lived in two different worlds. It might be easier if he still resided in Italy, she mused.

After supper, when Martha told her parents about Paul going home, her mother seemed pleased at first, but then became silent. Finally, she said, "I guess you'll be leaving us then."

"Well, I hope to split up my time between here and Lewistown. Paul needs me, too."

"If he's able to use a walker, why don't he go to Lizzy's place," her father suggested.

"It's the bathroom situation, *Daed*. He can't manage stairs yet with his leg."

"He could stay here."

"Now, Melvin," Sarah said, "that wouldn't look right. You know that. They aren't married yet."

"I guess that's true, but in his condition, you really think people would talk?"

"People always talk," Sarah said as she wiped down a counter. "Gab, gab, gab."

"The *gut* Lord don't like gossipers," her father reminded them.

"Tell that to Suzie Franklin! She'd have it all around town in minutes."

"Well, how many nights do you want to stay there when you go?" her father asked her.

"I'm thinking three at a time."

"It costs money to go back and forth," he reminded her.

"It's necessary, *Daed*. Paul will heal faster when I'm there. I know it."

"Oh, you have the gift of healing?" her father teased.

"It's just that his *mudder* always seems to look at the down side of things. He needs to have people with positive attitudes around him."

"*Jah*," her mother added. "We all do. You bring light into this family, sweetheart."

"*Danki*. That's so nice of you to say." Martha rose and went over to her mother and leaned over to give her a hug. "I hope you'll know more after you see the doctor."

"*Jah*, I'm a little nervous."

"They won't have all the results of your treatments yet, will they?" her father asked.

"*Nee*. Too soon. I'll need another scan for that. I'm just hopeful they won't need to give me any more chemo. They can tell some things by the bloodwork I had. We'll see what he says."

"So, you won't be leaving right away?" Melvin asked Martha.

"I'll wait till Friday. Then *Aenti* Lizzy can help *Mamm* more over the weekend."

"And I can do more," Melvin said. "Once the animals are taken care of, I can be with your *mudder* most of the time. I don't see a problem till harvest time."

"Goodness, I'm not a child. I can be alone, you know. I have plenty to do to keep me busy. *Mamm* and *Daed* like it when I go over and keep them company, if I run out of things to do here. So, stop worrying about me, you two."

Martha and her father exchanged looks. They knew when it was time to pull back. It was a good sign, for sure.

Chapter Twenty-Two

Melvin removed his socks and shoes as he prepared for bed that night. It had been a long day—longer than most. He'd tackled repairs on the barn by himself. It required using a fifteen-foot ladder and making multiple trips up and down with materials. The weather was unseasonably hot for September, and he felt drained from working in the direct sun. A cool shower would help. Before removing his bathrobe from a peg on their bedroom wall, he noticed Sarah had been unusually quiet—even at supper.

"Why so quiet?" he asked as he placed his soiled socks in the laundry basket.

"Am I?"

"*Jah*, why don't you tell me what's bothering you."

"Well, if you must know, Rose has gotten in touch with Martha."

"Well, I'll be. How did she find out where she lived?"

"It's a long story."

"So, after all these years, does it still matter?"

"To me it does."

"And to Martha?"

"She says things are the same."

"Then, believe her, and let it go."

"Melvin, they write to each other."

"That's it? They haven't met?"

Sarah began to weep. "Oh, they've met alright. They're even friends now." She sat on the edge of their bed.

"Well, that's okay, honey. That's all it will ever be. You know that."

"If I die, that woman will want to take over and be her *mudder*."

"Sarah, don't talk like that. That's not like you. First, you're going to live to be a real old lady, for sure. Next, we raised her from the very beginning of her life. In everyone's mind, you are Martha's *mudder*. Don't you forget that. Give Martha some credit. She's a deep-thinking girl. She ain't gonna be turned by a few letters and a couple of visits. Rose is like a stranger. If they become more like friends, that's okay."

"You really believe that? You don't think Martha will start going to her when she needs to talk? Like she does now with me? We're best friends, Melvin. Not just *mudder* and *dochder*."

"I know that, honey, and that's the way it will always be. Now wipe those tears away."

"You always make me feel better," she said as she dabbed at her eyes with a tissue. "You're a *gut* man, for certain."

"I try to be. Let me kiss those tears away." She leaned towards him and he caressed her back while he kissed her closed lids. "If I weren't so dog tired…"

Sarah opened her eyes and smiled up at him. "You go take your shower. We'll have other times. I'm pretty sad yet, but you have helped."

"*Gut.*" He rose and prepared for his shower.

Sarah hummed one of the songs they sang at their church service. *Jah*, she'd acted foolish. Nothing could change the bonds she had with her dear Martha. Nothing.

The next day, after cleaning up from their main meal, Martha waited outside for her ride. When she got to the rehab, Paul was using a walker, while his therapist stood by. Slowly, but confidently, he went from one wall to the opposite side of his bedroom, which was about fifteen feet in length. She stood and watched, grinning. "Paul, you're doing so *gut*. How does the arm feel?"

He stopped and held on with his good arm as he held up the other, turning it ever so slightly. "*Gut.* Doesn't hurt...too much," he added.

"You see? Someday you'll be making cabinets again. I just know it."

"I hope you're right. I sure miss it."

His therapist nodded. "Just takes time and perseverance."

He worked his way over to his wheelchair and waited for assistance. After settling down in the chair, the therapist said, "I'll be back to help you when your ride comes." He left temporarily to work with another patient, leaving Martha and Paul alone.

Martha went over and kissed Paul's forehead.

"I pray every day for you to get all better, Paul."

"I know you do. So do I. *Gott's* working in our lives."

"*Jah*, for certain. We just have to remain faithful."

"And patient."

"Oh, *jah*, and patient. That's a tough one," she said, smiling over.

There was a rap against the open door and Paul's driver, Skip, came in and greeted them. There hadn't been too much to pack up. Skip took the couple bags with Paul's belongings out to the car as his therapist returned to assist Paul. After he wheeled him to the car, a few of the other employees came out and gathered around Paul to say goodbye before he left. One of the aides had given him a list of phone numbers to call if he had problems or questions. They'd also arranged for physical and occupational therapy at the other end. Martha was confident he'd be well supervised even in Lewistown.

They'd had very little private time to talk, but she assured him she'd be heading to Lewistown in a few days' time. "And don't forget, we can talk on our phones. I charged mine up yesterday right here," she added.

"*Jah*, that helps. Once I can do the stairs, I'll be leaving for your *aenti*'s house," he said, smiling cheerfully. His attitude was so much better now that he could see progress.

She watched as he was helped into the car and then they waved to each other as the driver pulled away. Several of the aides remained beside her until his car was out of sight.

Then Martha called her own driver and sat on a bench to wait for him. He had remained nearby, so it was only a few minutes before she found herself heading back to her house. She had made plans to work on the garden. To keep busy was her answer to loneliness.

When Paul arrived at his parents' home, his sister, Susan, was in the yard pushing her baby in a carriage along the path. She called for her parents to come out when she saw the car pull up, and Paul received a warm welcome from his family. His father stood by with a wheelchair he'd borrowed from an Amish neighbor, who no longer needed it, and then Skip and Paul's father helped him make the transfer from the car to the wheelchair. It was getting easier to be mobile. Paul was confident he could have done it alone, though he didn't refuse their help.

After Paul paid the driver and he left, Paul asked to remain outside for a while. It was one of those crisp September days, the sky a deep blue with only a few random clouds puffing their way across the horizon. After being inside all this time, he savored the feel of the sun and fresh breeze on his face.

His mother and sister stood nearby, watching.

"So, let me see little Mary," he said to his sister.

"She's finally sleeping. You'll have to wait a few minutes. She was up half the night. Matthew walked with her for two hours so I'd get some sleep."

"Colic?"

"*Jah*, I guess so."

"Do you want anything to drink?" his mother asked. "What about medicines. Do you have to take any pills now? Are you tired?"

"Goodness. Everything is fine, *Mamm*. I just want to enjoy being outside."

"Well, you don't want to get sunburned."

"The sun's not that strong right now."

"You should go under the tree. I'll move you."

"It's okay. I can wheel this thing myself. Did *Daed* get the walker from the car?"

"I guess so. He just went inside with something. I'll

run in and see." She scurried away before Paul could say anything more.

Susan stood with her arms folded as she watched her mother hurry over to the house. "She's been a wreck, worrying about you."

"Goodness, I hope she calms down."

"Give her time. I'd better warn you. You'll be getting a lot of company today. All our sibs want to stop by and Jeremiah mentioned coming over with Hazel. Then of course Deb and Ebenezer will want to see you—with their tribe."

"I'd just as soon have the rest of the day to myself, but I guess I'll make it. I still need to rest a lot."

"*Jah*, I tried to tell people to wait a day or two, but it's like talking to that tree. No one listens."

"It's okay, I'll be fine."

"You know Jeremiah and Hazel's wedding is next week. Are you and Martha going to go to it?"

"I hope to. He's been such a *gut* friend."

"She finally got over you, I guess."

"If you mean Hazel? For sure, or she wouldn't be marrying Jeremiah."

"*Jah*, I suppose. She used to come over to my place and go on and on about you. Even when I mentioned you were in love with Martha, that *maed* just wouldn't give up."

"I sure hope she is a *gut* wife to Jeremiah. He's a great guy and deserves the best."

The baby let out a wail and Susan went over and picked her up. She calmed down immediately. Susan wrapped a receiving blanket around her and laid her on Paul's lap at his request.

"She's cute, Susan. Looks like you a little."

"You think so? *Mamm* says it too, but Matthew's *mudder* thinks she looks just like her *sohn* did at this age."

"Maybe she's a combination, and you're both right," he said as he let the baby grab his finger.

"Are you okay holding her? I know your arm isn't too *gut* yet."

"I have her in my *gut* arm. She's fine."

"Do you think you'll ever do carpentry again?"

He looked at her with a frown. "I sure plan to. It will take some time."

"*Jah*, probably be years before it's that *gut*."

"Susan, don't say things like that."

"I'm just being honest."

"Well, you're wrong. Even the therapist said maybe a couple of months—or more. Never mentioned years." His earlier mood of optimism was nearly shattered by her comment.

"I'd better go change her. Do you want me to get *Daed* to wheel you inside yet?"

"*Nee*. I want to stay here for a while longer. I can get myself to the door when I'm ready. I'll just need some assistance making it up the two steps to the house."

"*Daed* will help. If Matthew comes later, he can do stuff for you, too."

"*Danki*."

She took the baby and headed over to the house. "I'll be leaving soon. I just wanted to cheer you up before I left for home," she called back before entering the house.

You sure cheered me up, he thought sarcastically as he closed his eyes and allowed his senses to enjoy the scents and sounds of nature.

* * *

Martha and her mother spent a couple hours with her grandmother working on the quilt for her eventual wedding gift. They had completed almost three quarters of the top, but it was slow going, since her mother needed extra rest during the day now, and her *mammi's* eyesight was failing. Her Aunt Lizzy usually joined them, but today she had a dental appointment.

Martha's grandfather, Rubin, had taken up whittling and sat in the kitchen working on a pheasant, which he planned to present to Martha and Paul for their wedding. It was a bit primitive, but he had time to perfect it.

"And you think Paul will be coming here soon?" Martha's grandmother, Nancy, asked.

"He's doing everything in his power to make it happen," Martha said as she threaded her needle.

"Are his folks okay with his leaving them?" Sarah asked.

"I don't know how to answer that," Martha began. "I think it's been harder caring for him than his *mudder* thought it would be."

Sarah looked over. "Does he need that much nursing care?"

"*Nee*. Hardly any. Just help if he wants to climb stairs, and his therapist is working on that with him. His *Mamm's* just worrisome. Everything concerns her. Poor Paul is having a hard time with it, and I guess they're getting on each other's nerves."

"Oh dear, I hope it won't be too much for Lizzy," Nancy said as she pushed the needle through the fabric and out the other side. "I think you should let him stay with you, Sarah. That way he could see Martha. He could sleep on the sofa so he wouldn't have stairs."

"Now, *Mamm*, it would be unfitting. People would talk."

"Goodness me! Since when did you let gossip bother you? They sure wouldn't be doing anything wrong— not in his condition."

Marsha felt a blush run up her neck. She began stitching in the next patch, avoiding her grandmother's eyes.

"I don't know. I think it makes more sense to have him stay with Liz. She doesn't mind."

"Well, you know how she can get, if things rub her the wrong way."

"Paul could stay on our first floor, *Mamm*," Martha said. "We have a nice shower."

"I don't think your *daed* would allow it."

"He suggested it once, remember?"

"Well, I'm not in favor of it, but I'll have a talk with him. Now pass the thread over, please," she added. "I don't like the looks of this spool. Thread looks too thin."

"They're all the same, Sarah," her mother reminded her.

"Oh, I'm getting tired anyway. My eyes need a rest. Let's make *kaffi* and sit outside. It's wonderful cool today. Too nice to be indoors."

Dawdi called into the sitting room from the kitchen. "I agree. I need a pick-me-up and I can't stand looking at these sticky buns left from breakfast. They're begging to be ate up."

"Oh, what a sweet tooth," his wife said, shaking her head. "All right, we'll put this away till next time. I think we should wait for Lizzy, anyway. She's the best sewer in the family. She'll make us stick to it."

"*Mamm*, don't forget to ask *Daed* about Paul staying with us. If he says yes, he could come soon."

Sarah let out a long sigh. "You wear me down, *dochder*. I just hope people don't make nasty comments about us. Just keep your distance if he comes. I know it can be hard on young people. I was young once, you know."

Martha grinned. "You're the best."

"No flattery, young lady. It ain't happened yet." They folded the quilt carefully and headed for the kitchen.

The next morning, knowing she'd soon see Paul, her enthusiasm poured out in song, as she worked and used her lovely soprano voice to sing her praises with songs from the Amish songbook, the *Ausbund*. Sarah teased her about her exuberance, but added her voice as well, feeling encouraged herself.

As they fried up the sausage and set the table for breakfast, Martha stopped to give her mother a hug. "*Mamm*, I just know in my heart that you will get to see your *grosskinner* and live to be a real old lady!"

"Well, now wouldn't that be just wonderful-*gut*!"

Martha squeezed her so tightly, Sarah let out a gasp. "Unless my *dochder* squeezes the very life out of me first," she said cheerfully.

Chapter Twenty-Three

A couple days later, after clean-up from breakfast, Martha left for Paul's home. When she arrived, he was already waiting under one of the large shade trees in the front yard. He was not in his wheelchair, but sitting in a straight-back chair from their dining room. The walker resided next to him and when he saw the car arrive, he was able to rise to his feet and head towards her with the walker.

She jumped out and ran over to him. "Look at you! You're doing great!"

He beamed and waved to her driver, who came out to converse with them for a couple of minutes.

"Oh, I need to pay you," she said, fishing in her apron pocket for the bills she'd neatly folded earlier.

After he left, Paul, who was still standing, reached out his hand to her. She went over and received a tiny kiss on her lips. Out of the corner of her eyes, she saw the front door open and she moved away. His mother, Helen, came out and gave her a hug—more exuberant than previous hugs had been. Was that a look of relief on the woman's face?

After a few words of greeting, his mother retrieved a tube of sun block from her pocket and handed it over to Paul, without a word.

He nodded and stuck it in his pocket.

"He won't listen to his *mudder*," Helen said, looking over at Martha with furrowed brow. "Maybe you can get him to put that on his face before he gets skin cancer. He sits outside nearly all day. Think it's to get away from me," she added.

"Oh, I'm sure that's not the reason," Martha said, wondering if God would consider that a lie. Guilt feelings emerged, and she added, "But perhaps we'll never know." Now *that* was true. Hopefully, Paul wouldn't confirm or deny her statement. He just grinned instead.

"I'll ring the bell when dinner is ready," his mother said as she turned back to the house. Then Paul's father came out of the barn and headed over to say hello. He insisted on taking Martha's small suitcase into the house.

"Susan will be here after they eat their dinner. She has a room all set up for you. Clean as a whistle. She redded it up real special," he said as he walked toward the house.

Finally, it looked like they'd have a few minutes to themselves. Paul sat back down and pointed to a folding chair on the other side of the tree. "I'd get it for you, but…"

"*Nee*, of course not. Remember Amish *maedel* aren't used to being waited on. I'm no exception. You look so *gut*, Paul. Your color is better and you seem stronger."

He held up his damaged arm and moved it about to show his mobility. "See? I can use it more. I even played checkers last night with Susan's husband. Only dropped a piece once."

"That's so encouraging," she said as she set the chair next to him. "I've missed you tons."

They spent time catching up on their lives as they relaxed in the sun.

Later they went inside. His mother joined them and then she rose and disappeared temporarily. When she returned, she had some cleaning supplies in her hand, which she laid on the floor beside the sofa. She then pushed a feather duster around on every surface, sometimes more than once. It was obvious they weren't going to get much private time unless Martha could get Paul outside again for a walk in his wheelchair.

"Maybe I'll try using my walker outside for a few minutes," he said, looking for an escape.

"*Ach*, that could be dangerous," his mother warned, "with the lumpy grass and all. Besides, you spent a lot of time outside already."

"I could stay on the path," he said.

"Use the wheelchair, *sohn*. You could use the walker when you come back in."

"I think your *mudder's* right," Martha said. "We can't take a chance on you falling."

"All right. No point in trying to win this argument," he said, smiling his half smile.

"Now don't stay out too long in the sun," his mother reminded him. "I'll have some applesauce for you both when you get back. I'll add cinnamon, just the way you like it."

Finally, they were on the path leading to the barn, where they were out of sight of his mother.

"She's driving me crazy, Martha. I can't make a

move without her commenting. I can't wait to go to Paradise."

"I can't wait, either. It's hard not seeing you every day. Your *mamm* means well. She's concerned, is all."

"I'm not a little kid anymore. She seems to forget."

"I'll probably be the same with my *kinner*," she said in the woman's defense.

"You could stay straight through to the end of next week. That way you'd get to the wedding."

"I don't know."

"You could ask your folks if it would be okay."

"I don't have my best dress with me."

"You look great in anything."

"It would save me paying for another ride. But my parents don't have a cellphone."

"Can't you call your neighbor?"

"Let me think it over, Paul. I hadn't even considered it before."

"Don't forget, your mother has your *daed* and her *schwester*. It's not like she'd be alone."

"I know. Still…"

"Well, it was just an idea."

"A *gut* one, really. Would your *mudder* mind?"

"Of course not. I don't think so anyway. Why should she? You'll be sleeping next door."

"I eat my meals here though. I hope she'll let me help around the house."

"I'm sure she will. I heard her tell my *daed* she wants to paint the spare bedroom and she wondered if you'd help. I didn't say anything because I doubt she'll ever really buy the paint, but I'll make it clear, you're not here to paint a room we never use, but to help me."

"I wouldn't mind helping her. And be sure to let me help you. Did you attempt stairs yet?"

"Just getting into the house. You'll see, that's tricky, because I can't use crutches and we don't have a ramp. My leg doesn't like bending yet."

"How did you do it then?"

"I held onto my *daed* in case I needed his support. It worked okay, but I'm not quite ready for a whole flight. I'm hoping it will be soon though. I told my therapist and he said we'd start working on it. He's bringing some kind of a step or box with him tomorrow. You'll meet him. Nice guy. About my age."

"I liked the ones at the rehab."

"They were great. Everyone was."

"Paul, you're coming along so *gut*," she said, as she leaned over and kissed him soundly on his lips.

"Martha, I dream about you every night. I want so much for us to be married."

"Me, too," she said, returning for a second, longer kiss. She loved his minty breath.

They heard the farm bell ring. "It's not mealtime," Paul said, glancing at his watch. "We'd better see if anything's wrong."

Martha turned his chair around and pushed it swiftly to the back of the house where his mother stood with her arms crossed in front of her.

"Oh, there you are. I couldn't see you and got worried."

"We were over near the barn. No reason to be concerned," Paul said, his jaw tense.

"I was afraid you'd fallen over or something. Try to stay within my view, please."

"*Mamm*," Paul started.

Martha broke in. "We'll be more careful. I'm sorry. I guess it was my fault."

"For Pete's sake, stop treating me like a two-year-old," Paul said, angrily.

"Paul, your *mudder* is just concerned. Try to understand."

"*Jah*, try, *sohn*. At least Martha knows what I mean. Did you have enough water today?"

"That's it. I'm going to Paradise tomorrow."

"Paul!" both women said at the same time.

"The stairs!" Martha said.

"Your arm!" his mother said.

"My sanity!" he exclaimed and pushed the wheels of the chair with all his ability to get away from both of them. He made it as far as the horse stable and stopped, faced away from Martha and his mother.

"See what I put up with?" his mother said, shaking her head. "Sometimes, he's near impossible."

"I think we need to pull back and not tell him what to do, maybe," Martha said as cordially as she could manage. No wonder his nerves were shot.

"Hopefully, he can start getting up the stairs by himself and he can go stay with your family soon," his mother stated.

"*Jah*, I hope so," Martha said, in full agreement.

She would have preferred to go back home for a few days, just to get out of this tense situation, but she knew Paul needed her if he wanted to keep his calm at all. Plus, it would save her money to just stay on for the wedding. Perhaps, he'd even be well enough to go back with her and get out of everyone's hair when she was ready to return.

She took her phone from her pocket and dialed her

parents' neighbors. They took the message. She told them unless she heard to the contrary, she would remain with Paul till the day after the wedding—the following Friday.

Then she went out to the horse stable where Paul was watching their horses, still looking glum. When she informed Paul of her decision and the call she'd made, he broke into a huge smile and thanked her profusely. "You may have saved your future husband from total insanity," he said as he turned the wheelchair around and headed slowly back to the house. Not wanting to strain his sore arm any further, he allowed Martha to take over and push the chair the last hundred yards.

Alex and Todd stepped back and looked over the new arrangement of paintings on one of the large white walls of the gallery. "I think it looks pretty good," Alex said.

"Maybe the Rosso should be raised two or three inches though. What do you think?" Todd asked.

Alex placed his hands on his hips and pondered the idea. "I think you're right. Let's try it."

Now satisfied, Todd went to the front to check on a customer who had just come through the door, while Alex went over to his desk. He hadn't talked to Rose the night before since he'd been overwhelmed with paperwork, and had not realized how late it was when he finally found the time. Now seemed like a good chance to call.

She answered immediately.

"I know I don't usually call this early in the day, but since I missed yesterday—"

"I'm relieved. I waited for your call."

"I'm sorry. I got caught up in something and just

didn't realize how late it was getting. I didn't want to disturb you if you'd gone to bed."

"Never feel that way."

"I wanted to tell you, I think I can make it next weekend, if that works for you."

"Oh, Alex, I'm so glad. That would be perfect. Not a thing on the calendar. Still two nights?"

"Maybe three. I'll try my best. I can call the hotel myself to make reservations. I found a nice place online only three miles from you."

"Good. I'll surprise you with another Amish meal Friday night."

"That would be special. But I want to take you out to eat the other night or nights I'm there. Pick out your favorite places."

"You sure? I don't mind cooking."

"I want to try some of your local restaurants," Alex said.

"I'm afraid they can't compare to the great ones in New York."

"Either way. It doesn't really matter. I've just missed being with you. I could eat sandwiches, if I had to."

"I know. Me, too. It seems like it was a dream, doesn't it?"

"In a way. I still can't believe, after all these years…"

"I know."

"You're not still scared, are you?"

"Not as much," she said, smiling. "It will help to be together again. Make it more real."

"Yes. Soon. I'll let you go. I have more paperwork and three more paintings to hang before I leave for the day."

"Thanks for calling."

"I'll call you tomorrow night, even if it's only a five-minute call."

"Yes, please do that."

After they hung up, Alex joined Todd in the front to see if there were any unanswered questions that he could fill in. Todd was learning quickly, but Alex knew the history and biographies of each of his artists on display. It would be a while before he could rely on Todd to work on his own.

He'd been surprised when he asked Rosalind to work for him while he visited Rose and she'd been most agreeable. He had to wonder if it had anything to do with the fact that Todd was only five years older than she was and a pretty attractive guy—as well as single.

Chapter Twenty-Four

Rose spent the next three days scrubbing walls, polishing furniture and vacuuming every corner and heat vent in the house. She may not be rich, but she liked being clean and orderly. When she put her cleaning paraphernalia away Friday morning, she stood back and admired her efforts. The house gleamed. She'd even purchased new accent pillows for her sofas and added scented candles and a couple of new house plants for the living room.

Satisfied, she went to the grocery store and purchased top quality coffee beans and a quart of half-and-half. She planned to make Amish Pot Pie with apple dumplings for dessert. The noodles were already made and the dumplings were ready to pop in the oven later in the day. Hopefully, she hadn't forgotten anything. She wanted everything to be just perfect for Alexandro Gionnardo!

After getting her nails done, she stopped at her favorite beautician's where she'd made an appointment and had her hair streaked and trimmed. Alex wasn't expected to arrive until around five, so she still had time to stop at the florist for a small arrangement for the table.

Once she arrived home, she showered and changed into a white blouse and aqua skirt, both made of silk. She checked herself out in the long mirror in her bedroom. Satisfied, she slipped into comfortable heels and went downstairs to set up the table and work on the meal.

At four, her phone went off and it was Alex. "I got in town early. I'm already checked in—and bored. Can I show up early?"

"Of course!" It was earlier than she was prepared for, but what could she say? After giving him directions, she lit the candles and made sure everything was in order. It was. Everything.

It took only fifteen minutes for him to arrive. Oh, he was even handsomer than she'd pictured. Those eyes! The gorgeous hair! No wonder their daughter was such a beauty. She certainly didn't take after her.

"This is nice," he said standing inside the doorway, a bouquet of pink roses in his hand. "Here, these are for you, sweet Rosie."

"Thank you," she said, standing back to allow him entry. "Come on in to my humble abode," she said, smiling. He handed her the flowers and removed his jacket, flinging it over a chair. "It's hot out there."

She just stood there and stared. It seemed surreal. She felt eighteen again—nervous and overwhelmed. Then he took a step towards her, took the bouquet from her hands and set it on his jacket. He drew her to him. Their kiss lasted several minutes. She could barely breathe.

He moved back a few inches and ran his hand

through her hair. "You are *bella*. Very beautiful. But I'm going to slow down before I upset you. I know we must be careful. Thank you for allowing me to come here to your lovely home, Rose. It reflects your personality. Now show me everything. First your art. What do you have hanging?"

She finally caught her breath and walked him around her small, but attractive home. Most of her furnishings were contemporary and light in color and texture, but a few unique antiques added an eclectic touch. Most of her art was not original, but the prints were in good taste and many were of the French Impressionists. He seemed pleased with her choices.

"Everything is so you. In such good taste."

"Thank you." Her cheeks were flushed. "Are you hungry yet?"

"Anytime you say. It smells fantastic in here."

"Nearly everything is done, but I haven't made the salad yet."

"Let me help you. Just put everything on the counter you want in it, and I'll figure out what to do with it."

"You don't sound too familiar with food prep," she teased.

"I have to admit, my idea of cooking is throwing a steak on the grill or frying up bacon for breakfast. But I'm very good at eating."

Rose found herself relaxing, as she worked alongside him in the kitchen. He pretended to know nothing about putting a tossed salad together. She went along with his fabricated ignorance and gave demonstrations on cutting each article of food, which he followed meticulously.

Rose played some Chopin nocturnes while they

worked, and then when it was actually time to eat, she lit more candles and turned down the music. The table was already set with her finest linens and crystal glassware she'd picked up for a song at a local auction. He went out to the car for a bottle of wine he'd purchased earlier, but when she told him she didn't drink, he set it by the door. "Then I'll skip it myself. Water will be fine."

He raved about the Amish meal and when she brought out the dessert, he whistled a drawn-out note. "Do you know the last time I had apple dumplings was at your home? It's like going back in time." He stopped speaking and reached across the narrow table for her hand. "Thank you for inviting me here. We're going to have a great time—just like the early days."

And they did. After dinner, they danced to a few old songs and even sang together with the music, as they had when they were younger. Then they sat and talked about the years when they were separated. Nothing was said about the child they'd had together, now grown and a beauty in her own right.

The next day, there was an art festival a few miles from her home. They drove over and spent most of the day there. He bought three hot dogs and devoured his two within five minutes. "Do you know how much I've craved hotdogs? Sometimes I buy one from a vendor near one of the parks in Manhattan, but these are so much better."

They were too exhausted by evening to do much, so she pulled up an old movie on Netflix and made a huge bowl of buttered popcorn. They sat and watched together, as they managed to devour the popcorn. He put his arm around her at one point, but didn't attempt to kiss her again, which gave her mixed feelings. She might have refused, but it would have been nice to be asked.

Around eleven, he rose and she walked him to the door. Before leaving, he asked if he could kiss her goodnight and she nodded. He pulled her close and slowly lifted her chin and placed his lips on hers. It was so tempting to ask him to stay, but she prayed for strength and soon suggested they part for the night. He smiled gently and left, turning once to wave. After he was gone, she cleaned up from their movie party and made her way to bed. There was no doubt in her mind. She was in love—head over heels in love.

Chapter Twenty-Five

Martha's parents agreed to have Paul stay with them until he could do the stairs. Then he'd have to move over with Lizzy. He was more than pleased.

"I can't wait. I didn't tell you, but a couple days ago, my *mudder* heated up a glass of milk and insisted I take a nap like I did as a little *bu*. Can you believe it?"

"Did you do it?"

"*Jah*, it was that or hear about it all day."

Martha giggled. "Did you sleep?"

"*Nee*. Now don't make fun of your future husband. One *mudder* is enough."

"She's a *gut* lady, Paul. Just a little overprotective."

"A little? I feel like I'm ten years old."

"Well, pretty soon, you can leave. How are you doing with the steps?"

"Better, but I still need some support. I can't believe how weak I am since the accident."

"They warned you it would take time. You forget how bad it was."

"I guess you're right. It seems like a long nightmare."

"*Jah*, I know what you mean. For me, too."

"I can't even imagine if it was reversed and I thought you might not make it. I forget how hard it was on you, Martha. Forgive me."

"Nothing to forgive. I'm just thankful you're doing so *gut*."

"It's hard to be separated. I want to go back with you. I feel ready now and we can get moving on the baptism preparation if I'm there. I'm determined to marry you—soon."

"I'm excited! Should we leave the day after Jeremiah and Hazel's wedding?"

"I don't see why not. I'm not particularly looking forward to their big event, but Jeremiah has been such a *gut* friend."

"And Hazel, now that she's backed off and accepted the fact we're to marry."

"*Jah*, she's still a little forward, but I can sure handle it. We don't ever see each other alone anymore."

"Would you still feel temptation, if she tried to do more?"

"Not at all. No, Martha, I'm yours—only. Always will be, even when we're too old to work and we become part of the rocking chair group."

"I hope I'll always look young in your eyes."

"I'm sure you will."

"My *dawdi* still thinks *Mammi* is just about perfect."

"That's true love, *jah*? Through thick and thin, couples must stick together."

"*Jah*, *Mammi* told me once that love is more than a feeling. It's a commitment as well, and a decision. I think I'm beginning to understand."

"I hope we never argue."

"That's not too realistic, but I hope it never gets hurtful where we say things we don't mean."

"We have to pray together always, and keep *Gott* in the center, *jah*?"

"*Jah*. You are a Godly man, Paul."

"And you, a *gut*, Godly *maed*."

Martha moved her chair closer to his and they sat holding hands in the pleasant stillness of the early autumn day. A colorful male goldfinch perched nearby and his cheerful chirping song continued for several minutes, till he flew off. The ringing of the farm bell came to them and they reluctantly left their haven and walked slowly towards the house—Paul, supported by his walker, with Martha next to him. Maybe they'd never have to be parted again, at least not in this lifetime, on such a beautiful planet.

Chapter Twenty-Six

Alex took Rose out for breakfast at a small family restaurant she recommended. Rose ordered pancakes with blueberries while Alex settled on bacon and sunny-up eggs. They lingered over their second cups of coffee after their waitress removed the empty plates, and discussed their ideas for the rest of the day. They decided to visit the famous Hawthorn Hill House, which was built by the Wright Brothers. Then she'd show him around the town and they could browse in some of the shops.

After a few more minutes just relaxing, they left and headed over in Rose's car to the famous house. It was a stately home and they were given the tour by an elderly gentleman, who had been an avid airplane pilot in his own right. Then Rose parked in town and they walked through shops she frequented. They went through a mall, more for the exercise than purchasing anything, and spent a full day enjoying each other's company.

Around five, they returned to her home and she took off her shoes and relaxed on the sofa while Alex made several business calls. When he got off his phone, he sat next to her and took her hand.

"It's official, I'm heading off to Italy the end of October for a couple of weeks—maybe a full month."

"Business?"

"Most of it. I'll take some time off to visit my parents and some other members of my family before I head back. Want to go with me?"

"Oh, I'd love to, but—"

"I know, it wouldn't be appropriate, unless we were married."

Her heart jumped at the word, and she wondered if he was about to propose to her. She merely smiled over and nodded.

An awkward silence prevailed for several moments. Finally, Rose asked what his itinerary would be and he told her the major cities he'd visit. "I'm scouting out a couple of new artists I've read about and checking on some of my current ones, to see their new works."

"It's a pretty nice job, which takes you overseas and you can write it off."

"It's very enjoyable. I can't imagine doing anything else. I have to ask you, Rose," he said, hesitantly, "Would you consider moving to New York?"

"You mean now?"

"In the future."

"It would depend. I can't say I'd mind. It's a pretty exciting place to live, though I am used to my quiet life here."

"You know, I think we'd do well to get married. We should have done it years ago. We'd probably have had children and—"

Children.

"Alex, I need to talk to you about something. Something important." She cleared her throat and sat forward on the sofa, turning to face him.

"Sounds serious. You're not ill are you? Because if you are, it wouldn't—"

"No, I'm fine. It's just that there's something you need to know before we go any further."

"I'm listening." He continued to hold her hand as he waited.

"I was pregnant when you left America twenty years ago."

He stared at her, his mouth dropped open, but he didn't say a word.

"I had a baby girl eight months after you left. You have another daughter."

"You're not serious." He moved his hand away from hers.

"I'm very serious."

"Why wouldn't you have gotten ahold of me somehow? And we've seen so much of each other lately, and you never said a word?"

"I'm not sure why."

"I'm not either." His voice took on a tone she'd not heard—a mix of incredulity and anger. "I'm in shock. I don't know what to say. I've been denied knowing my own child all these years?"

"I didn't raise her, Alex. She was adopted by an Amish family."

"You gave *our* baby *away*?"

"You don't understand, I had no choice."

"No choice? You just handed her over to others to raise—*just like that*?" He raised his hand as he snapped his fingers, inches from her face.

Her voice began to tremble. "My parents. You know how strict they were."

"Don't, Rose. I don't want to hear any more. I need to process this." He stood up and headed towards the door.

"Alex! Don't leave. We need to discuss this."

"Not now, Rose. You can't believe what a shock this is. Maybe I'll call you later—or tomorrow—or never."

She sat and watched as he headed for her front door. Before turning the handle, but without looking back at her, he asked in a voice shaking from emotion, "What's her name?"

"Martha."

And he was gone. Rose sat in shock, staring at the empty spot where he'd been sitting only moments before, speaking about marriage. Her dream had died as quickly as it had arrived. For a second time, the man she loved with all her heart, was leaving her. This time, if he left without calling, she knew she'd never see him again. It was more devastating than before. She didn't even weep. Her pain was beyond tears. It tore into her very soul. *Alex, Alex, I need you.*

Alex nearly crashed into a car coming out from a side street. They each squealed their tires as they braked to avoid hitting each other. He hadn't even seen the four-way stop. The other driver screamed through the closed window, though Alex just kept driving.

A daughter. She'd be twenty years old. All those years he'd never known there was a child living somewhere with his blood in her veins. A living child, taking first steps, cutting her first baby tooth, first day at school—first—first—first…everything! And he never saw her as she grew from infant to young woman. And neither did the woman who gave birth to her. No, she'd given the child away. Like an old pair of shoes or an out-of-date jacket. The girl—or now woman—he'd loved, even after all these years. He hadn't really known her. No girl he loved and loved him back could have done such a thing. Surely. Thank God, she hadn't chosen abortion! At least she gave the girl life. *Rose. Rose. How could you have? I would have returned on the next plane and married you.*

Would he? He was so young. Had such plans for his life. What would he know about raising a child? Then again, why would she give up her own child? Surely, her parents would have raised it for her. Or would they? The Amish were not tolerant of immorality. They weren't even supposed to kiss before marriage. He had made fun of Rose when she hesitated on their third date to even allow him to kiss her. She'd finally told him he could kiss her cheek. Once. She was a proper young Amish girl. That was part of the fatal attraction. He was fascinated with the Plain people and especially this lovely young woman with her beautiful blonde hair so carefully tucked under her prayer *kapp*, with such fair skin and gentle ways. She attracted him far more than the girls back home, many of whom sought his attention without restraint.

Had he been unfair from the beginning? Had it been seduction on his part? She'd been so innocent—so reluctant to become intimate—until that night.

He pulled his suitcase from the closet and laid it open on the bed. Too bad he'd unpacked it when he arrived. He could be gone by now.

He opened the bureau drawers and reached for his undershirts, but closed the drawer instead and sat on the edge of the bed.

Why didn't he stay to hear her story? She had a right

to explain it to him. He wasn't being fair. Maybe she felt she had no choice. Her parents destroyed all his letters. Rose had no idea how to get in touch with him. Would she have, if she'd known his address?

He stood up and paced the floor. What did she look like? Martha. Pretty name. Does she see Rose? Did they stay in touch during those growing up years? Did Rose ever try—in any way—to find him?

Oh, Rose, my Rose, what have you done?

Soon he'd be leaving for Italy. He could stay there longer. It might take a lifetime to forget her. Would that be long enough, since he never had? It had been so much more than a 'fling.' He'd never experienced that kind of feeling for any other girl. He'd wanted to return the following year to see her and find out why she never wrote back, but with his father suffering a major stroke shortly after he returned from the States, he didn't feel free to travel overseas. Not only did they need extra income from his part-time job waitering, but he was expected to help care for his father, who had paralysis of his left side. And she never wrote back. He'd never heard one word from the lovely fair-haired Amish girl.

If he was ever to meet his daughter, he couldn't just leave and pretend it never happened. Even though it was over between him and Rose, maybe he could establish some kind of relationship with Martha. He suddenly realized, Rosalind had a half-sister. If for no other reason, he should try to get as much information as he could before he walked away. Away from his dreams… away from the woman—the only woman he'd ever truly loved. He put his head in his hands and wept for all that was missed. All the crushed dreams—and for a little girl who never met her father.

Chapter Twenty-Seven

Martha spent as much time with Paul as she could. He walked inside the house, sometimes without the walker, but usually took no chances outside, due to the unevenness of the grassy areas. She noticed he used his damaged arm sometimes without realizing it, and when she mentioned it, he'd grin and nod. "*Jah*, it's feeling more like an arm all the time."

It was fun to be part of Susan's family in the morning. Usually, they were already in bed when she went over in the evening; so she'd head for bed herself. She rose early, usually when she heard the baby crying, and helped by starting the breakfast while Susan nursed her child. Susan's husband, Matthew, was fun to be around. He had a cute sense of humor, and made her feel at home almost immediately.

Right after cleaning up from breakfast, Martha would head next door to see Paul, and usually end up having coffee with his family. The therapist took about an hour to run through the exercises with Paul, at which time Martha would give his mother a hand with the cleaning. She noticed the woman had calmed down since she'd arrived, and had stopped overseeing every move her son made. All-in-all, it was a pleasant stay.

Sunday was church day and Martha enjoyed meeting some of the people she'd heard Paul mention to her. The main sermon held her interest and was not as long as some she'd listened to at her home church. Afterwards, she helped with some of the other women as they set up the meal. Hazel and Deborah cut up the cakes and other desserts while Martha filled the water glasses and pitchers with ice water.

Martha kept an eye open for Paul, in case he needed something, but he seemed pleased to be in the company of so many friends and family members. He would be giving up a lot to move to Lancaster County after their marriage. She appreciated his sacrifice even more than ever, after seeing the closeness of his church group. The children in the congregation played outside together, with the older children watching the younger ones and keeping them out of trouble. Martha loved the Amish get-togethers and felt fortunate to be raised in an Amish home with loving parents.

The day of the wedding, Martha went early to help Hazel's family with some of the food preparations. Women came in carrying casseroles and extra desserts. It was an exciting time. Hazel was in a flurry, checking on every detail. When she saw Martha arrive, she ran over and hugged her. "I'm so glad you could make it. I'm so happy, Martha."

"Of course you are. And you look real pretty."

"I wish we were allowed to let our hair loose, but at least the pimple on my chin went away yesterday."

Martha giggled. Then she looked around. "Is Deborah here yet?"

"Oh, I told her to wait till the ceremony. I don't need her tribe of little ones tearing things apart. Their new *boppli* doesn't sleep all night yet, you know. Poor Deb looks so awful tired."

"*Jah*. I don't know how she manages with triplets and twins as well."

"Ebenezer helps her a lot, and I go over nearly every day to help. Of course, I won't be able to once I have my own *boppli*."

"You've been a great *schwester* to Deb. I don't know how she'd manage without you."

"And you were so *gut* to come stay with her when the twins were coming."

"I was glad to be able to help, and of course, I met Paul here."

"I guess you'll have to postpone your own wedding," Hazel said, frowning.

"Actually, Paul's doing so *gut*, we may be able to marry this winter—or at least in the spring."

"You know, I'm sorry I had such a hard time giving Paul up. I'm embarrassed when I think about my behavior."

She almost looked about to cry. Martha leaned over and squeezed her. "It's okay. I'm just glad you and Jeremiah will be together. He's a real *gut* man."

"*Jah*, I know it. I really do love him, Martha, with all my heart."

"I'm so glad," Martha said, with unexpected relief at her words. She had wondered if the girl would ever give up her pursuit of Paul. Finally, things would be right, and they could be good friends again.

"I'd better help *Mamm*," Hazel said. "She's not the greatest organizer. She looks lost at the moment."

Martha looked over at Wanda, Deborah's elder sister, who was scurrying about as their mother stood with her hands on her hips, looking utterly confused. Once Hazel made it over to her, she seemed to calm down, so Martha went outside to work with some of the older women as they set up plastic tablecloths on the long tables, which had been placed in the yard for the reception.

She pictured herself as the bride, surrounded by family and friends. It hadn't been that long since she'd wondered if it would ever happen. Paul had come a long way from the first horrible days of his accident. *Danki, Gott*, she said aloud softly, as she went over to the stack of tablecloths and took the top one off to place on the next table.

About a half hour before the ceremony was to begin, Paul and his parents arrived in one buggy as his three married brothers and two sisters arrived in their buggies right behind them. Martha went over and greeted everyone as two of his brothers went over to help Paul out of the buggy. He looked somewhat embarrassed by all the attention, but it was not easy to exit from a buggy, even with aid. Once on the ground, his father came around with the walker and placed it in front of his son. "I'm going to try to do without it for now," he said. "You can leave it in the buggy."

His mother overheard them and clucked her tongue. "Foolishness. Don't take chances."

"Paul, your *mudder's* right. If you fall—"

"*Jah, jah.* Okay, I'll take it along for the rough spots."

Several of his friends came right over and shook his good hand or patted him on the back. He grinned at the attention and assured everyone he was getting better every day.

"You'll soon get back to work, I guess," one of the young men said.

"Not for a while, I'm afraid. Still don't have my strength back or the full use of my arm." He held it up to show the limitations of motion.

"Mmm. May take some time to get back into carpentry," one of the other men said, shaking his head. "It ain't easy work."

Martha sidled up next to him. "He'll get there. He works real hard doing the exercises."

Martha knew most of his friends, but she had never met one of the young men. "Is this the famous Martha?" he asked, grinning.

"*Jah*, my Martha," Paul said, nodding.

"I thought you lived in Paradise," the man continued.

"I do, but I came to help out."

"Oh, nice to have a nursemaid, *jah*?" he said, winking at Paul.

"She's been *wunderbaar*."

"So where are you staying?" he asked Martha.

"With Paul's *schwester*, Susan."

"Ah, I see. Very nice. You used to come help Deb and Ebenezer, didn't you?"

"*Jah*. We're related."

"Oh, I see. That was kind of you."

"She really needed help badly," Martha said, glancing over as she saw Deb and her family arriving. "Excuse me, I think I should go help them out."

Paul made his way to a group of chairs and sat down. One of the young men came and sat next to him. Paul's eyes followed Martha as she made her way over to Deb. What a sweet wonderful woman he was going to marry.

His heart was filled with love for her and appreciation for life itself. How close he had come to meeting his Maker. He never feared death, but it sure was nice to be alive, even if he never touched another cabinet again. God would open a door for him. He felt a wave of peace flow through him as he realized he'd finally resigned himself to a future, yet undetermined. As long as it included Martha, he'd be just fine.

The wedding went smoothly. Jeremiah and Hazel spent time alone with the bishop and then the sermon followed. It was a long service, but at last their vows were said and the reception took place. Martha judged there were well over four hundred people in attendance. Fortunately, the weather couldn't have been better. The sky was clear, with very little breeze, and the temperature hovered around seventy. Martha had been surprised the bishop had agreed to a September wedding. Usually, it was after harvest time, but Jeremiah had pushed hard to have an earlier wedding date. It was only a couple months later when she realized the date had been pushed up for a reason. It was then she noticed Hazel's clothes were tight across the abdomen. Goodness, she certainly wasn't your typical Amish maid. Paul was fortunate not to have fallen for her!

The next day around ten in the morning, Skip Davis, the family's driver, arrived to take Martha and Paul to Paradise. Paul's parents had given no objection to his leaving them to recover in Martha's home. In fact, his mother appeared relieved. She had lost at least three pounds in the short time he'd been staying with them. Martha had grown to care more deeply for his family, especially for dear little Mary, Susan's baby, who was her alarm clock each morning. What a sweetheart she was. It made Martha excited to think about her own future family.

Martha and Paul were ecstatic about not being separated anymore and talked about their future with optimism. When they got to her home, they spent an hour with the family enjoying their main meal together. Sarah insisted on giving them the rest of the day together and wouldn't allow help cleaning up from the meal.

The young couple sat outside, delighting in the cool afternoon breezes. After a while her parents and grandparents joined them and her *dawdi* kept them entertained with stories of his youth and the tricks he'd play on the little girls in his one-room schoolhouse—including the woman he married. They'd known each other their entire lives, and his wife still laughed at his jokes, though Martha was sure she could have recited them herself from hearing them so often.

"That's the kind of marriage I want for us," she told Paul before she went upstairs for the night. He nodded. "*Jah*, it will be, Martha. We have something very special." He kissed the tip of her nose.

Before turning in for the night, Sarah made up the sofa for Paul and added a quilt in case it got chilly during the night. She stuck around until Martha said good night and even followed her up the stairs. Martha realized that was the way it would be and knew someday she'd be the same way with her own daughters. When they got to the top of the stairs, she hugged her mother and thanked her for allowing Paul to stay at the house while he recuperated.

"*Jah*, he'll do okay here till he can do the stairs. Nice young man. We approve of your choice, Martha."

"*Danki*. That means a lot to me, *Mamm*. I want us to always be a close family."

They parted for the night and Martha slept soundly, dreaming about her wedding. Life was good.

Chapter Twenty-Eight

Alex wasn't able to sleep. He tried reading, but the book he'd brought along no longer held his interest. He watched the late news and tried to find a movie, though he couldn't concentrate on the plot and soon turned off the television. He decided to take a walk around the hotel. After several trips around the parking lot, he returned to his room and just sat in the armchair. Prayer was difficult. He attempted several times to pray, but he simply couldn't come up with words.

He pictured Rose laughing and smiling at him. He tried to rid himself of her image, but to no avail. All these years... And now Martha. His own child. He still had trouble believing he had another daughter. What did she look like? Did her adoptive parents treat her kindly? Were they overly strict with her, punishing her for everything she did that they didn't approve of? Some of the Amish were like that.

Maybe she was married by now. A mother, perhaps. He might never know. Why did he walk out without hearing more? And what about Rose? Hadn't she suffered enough?

He'd been too abrupt, not allowing her to explain her actions. She was a kind person. She used to talk about having a large family. Certainly she would have wanted to raise her own child. Why didn't she?

He stood up and went over to the large picture window and looked down the three flights to the ground where he saw his car parked next to the building. Maybe Rose would still be awake. He knew he'd hurt her terribly. She'd probably never want anything to do with him again. She'd not had it easy. A marriage without love. It may have helped with her loneliness at the time, but he knew how painful it was to try to create a meaningful marriage out of a poor relationship. Worse than remaining single.

He could drive by and just see if there were any lights on. He wouldn't wake her if she was asleep. He wasn't sure what he wanted to say, but the words would come. He just couldn't leave things the way they were.

He reached for his keys and headed down the elevator, and then drove over to her neighborhood. He drove past her home, slowly. The house was completely dark. Disappointed, he made a U-turn at the next corner and actually stopped in front of her house, pausing to consider his next step. Then he drove away and returned to the hotel. Since he couldn't sleep, he'd pack up and head for New York. What made him think Rose would even talk to him after he acted that way?

Rose watched from her bedroom window where she had just walked over to draw her shade. Only ten minutes before, she had closed up downstairs and come up to try to sleep. When she saw the car, she prayed it was Alex. She recognized his rental car, but he slowly drove away. Her hope died once more, and for the first time since he'd left, she allowed her tears to flow, and flow they did. She laid on her bed and didn't even attempt to stop the sobbing. Finally, when there was nothing left, she wiped her eyes with tissues and prayed for strength. She also prayed for Alex's safety as she knew in her heart he'd be heading home.

If she'd remained downstairs, would he have come in? Would he have allowed her to explain everything? She might never know the answers. She just had to accept what had happened and go on. Before he re-entered her life, she had found happiness. Well, contentment, anyway. It was better that way. You couldn't be hurt, if you no longer felt. Now that she'd known him again and allowed her emotions to emerge, she was vulnerable once more to the pain of his absence. Oh, if only she had never visited his gallery.

It was a good thing she would have church to attend. Hopefully, she'd catch a couple hours' sleep first. Totally exhausted, she found herself drifting off and thankfully, she didn't dream about Alexandro.

It was mid-October already. Martha was amazed how quickly the time passed now that Paul was living with her family. He was making remarkable progress and one day, as they were having an afternoon coffee break in the backyard, one of the men who worked at the carpentry shop where he intended to work eventually, stopped by to check on him.

"We sure are busy, with the holidays coming. Think you can give us a hand, Paul? You wouldn't have to use any of the power tools. Maybe just use your good arm to help with waxing or staining some of the furniture. Maybe even take care of customers."

"I think I could do that," he said.

Martha sat with them, listening to every word. She handed a plate with fresh macaroons over to the man, whose name was Ken. He took one and nodded over.

Paul looked over at Martha. "What do you think, Martha? *Gut* idea?"

"If you think you can handle it. You still get tired kinda easy."

Ken quickly added, "Part-time would be fine, except you'd have to hang around to get your ride home."

"I could start out part-time, and then if you need me and I'm able, I could put more hours in for you, a little at a time."

"Sure, that would work. We really would appreciate it, Paul." They talked a few minutes more and actually made arrangements for Paul to start work the following Monday. It was decided, Ken would pick him up at eight in the morning and return around five.

Now that the therapist only came once a week and had talked about discontinuing his visits anyway, Paul had time on his hands—too much time. He was getting restless and Martha was relieved that he would be able to work and feel he had a purpose once again. It was a major step forward.

The day after he began his job, Sarah went for her CT scan. The chemo treatment was over with and this scan would determine whether her cancer had been eliminated. Many prayers were sent asking for her total recovery. No one mentioned it in the family, but everyone knew this was a marker, which was extremely important. The doctors were running out of further options.

The next day Lizzy planned to join them when they went to the oncologist. Hopefully, the oncologist would have the results of the test, and Sarah would be clear of cancer. Martha was nervous just thinking about it, but she didn't discuss it with her mother.

Martha had written to Rose to tell her of all the changes in her life, but she hadn't heard back from her and considered calling, especially if the results were good. Rose had told her she was praying for her mother's condition. She had also mentioned wanting to see Martha before winter set in, but nothing further had been discussed. Martha realized she hadn't heard a word since early September, which was unusual. Hopefully, Rose was okay and just too busy to write.

Alex sat with Todd and went over paperwork with him and showed him the books. There was so much to know. His daughter, Rosalind, was going to help out on Saturdays while he was in Italy, since that was their busiest day.

Todd closed his notes when they were finished and stretched back in his chair. "You've been pretty preoccupied lately, Alex. Anything I can do to help?"

"No. Not really. I'm going to take a run to Ohio though on Sunday. I'll drive back Monday, but I need you to handle things without me that day."

"No problem. That's a long way to go for one night. Whatever happened on your last trip? You seemed so anxious to spend time with a certain someone there."

"It just didn't work out. I don't want to go any further."

"I'm sorry, it's none of my business, but you're a good friend. I hate to see you unhappy."

"Am I?" Alex folded his arms and firmed his mouth, unconsciously. "Yeah, I guess I am. I have to go back and get a few answers before I write off that whole deal."

Todd sat silently, waiting for more.

"I thought I was in love," Alex finally added.

"But you weren't?"

"I was, and still am."

"Then, maybe I'm missing something, but why are you writing it off? Is she married?"

"Heavens no. I wouldn't have gone out with a married woman."

"I didn't think so. Kids? She has problem kids?"

"I may as well tell you. She had my child twenty years ago."

"No way! Wow! That's a biggie."

Alex nodded. "I never knew about it. She gave the child up for adoption."

"What a shame. Or was it? She was pretty young, wasn't she?"

"She was. And Amish. Amish women didn't have children out of wedlock. It just wasn't done."

"Why didn't she tell you?"

"She didn't know how to get in touch with me. Her parents destroyed all my correspondence."

"That's pretty bad. So I guess she didn't have much choice, but to give the child up. They were probably too ashamed to have an illegitimate child in the house."

"That's about it."

"I don't understand though, Alex. What does all that

have to do with your feelings about the woman now—twenty years later?"

"She gave our child away!"

"Wasn't it better for the child? I mean, she gave the kid a chance to have a family without the stigma attached."

"True."

"Doesn't she love you?"

"I doubt she does now. I walked out and didn't give her a chance to explain everything. I was just in such a state of shock. You can't believe it."

"I guess I understand. Somewhat. So you're going back to find out what?"

"Where my daughter lives, mainly."

"Not to see if this woman still cares about you?"

"How can she? It was a month ago and she hasn't called."

"Hey, Alex. It's not up to her to call. You're the one who walked out. Right?"

"Yeah, I guess."

"Guess?"

"Okay, I did. I shouldn't have. I realize that now since I've had time to think it through, but I'm embarrassed, I guess."

"To admit you were wrong? I think they call that pride."

Alex stared over at his friend. "I've really messed up. I'd be lucky if she ever speaks to me again."

"Right."

"I have to go see her. I can't go on like this. It's more than Martha. I do still love that woman. Her name is Rose. I've loved her for most of my life. I don't know why I've been so blind."

"Well, hopefully, it's not too late. Love like that doesn't come along too often. I wish you well, my friend. And if you want to spend a couple more days there, just call. I'll cover the gallery."

"Thanks. I appreciate it. Now, let's wrap up that Pinelli painting and get it ready for shipment."

Chapter Twenty-Nine

Martha sat with her parents and her aunt as they waited to be called into the doctor's office. It seemed to take forever. Finally, his nurse, Milly, directed them into the small room where Dr. Harriman sat at his desk, Sarah's chart before him. He looked up as they entered and stood to shake Melvin's hand. He nodded to the rest of them and then motioned for them to take seats.

"Well, I have here the results of the latest scan," he started. Everyone remained silent. Melvin reached for Sarah's hand and Aunt Liz held on to Martha's.

"I have very good news. There are no signs of cancer at this point."

"Oh, praise *Gott*," Sarah said, fighting back tears.

"*Jah*, that's amazing news, doctor." Melvin was grinning from ear-to-ear. "So she's done with the chemo."

"Yes, for now. We'll be checking frequently, but I have to confess, I didn't have much hope in the beginning for success like this."

"*Jah*, but we were all praying our hardest," Martha said, smiling widely.

"Whatever you did, it seems to have worked," the doctor said, smiling over.

"My sister is a tough lady," Liz said. "She's a fighter."

"Well now, I almost gave up," Sarah admitted. "I couldn't let you all down though without trying my hardest."

The doctor nodded. "You've been strong through this, Mrs. Troyer. You all have and I'm sure your faith helped you get through some of the roughest moments."

"Oh *jah*, the *gut* Lord is always there right along with us when we need Him."

"Even when we don't think we do," Melvin said, still grinning.

"We'll set up an appointment with you before you leave," the doctor said, "and I'd like you to follow the instructions the nurse gave you about diet and exercise. We have to keep you in good health now so you never have to deal with cancer again."

"I'll be *gut*. I'll try not to eat too much cake and sugary things."

He laughed. "If you have any to get rid of, you can bring it here to the office. I'm sure there'd be a few people willing to help you out."

After they got back in the buggy, Melvin suggested they celebrate by eating at a local diner they liked.

"But I put a pot roast on before we left," Sarah said. "I was going to add vegetables when we got back. *Mamm* and *Daed* are coming over."

"Well, we'll go for a buggy ride later, then," Melvin said. "Maybe just you and me. Want to do something special after such *gut* news."

"It is wonderful-*gut*," Martha said. "Paul will be so happy when he hears."

"There's another reason to celebrate," her aunt said. "Your Paul is able to work again. Goodness, so many blessings at once!"

The women began singing one of their favorite songs and even Melvin, who couldn't hold a tune, joined in. Yes, it was a memorable day for this faithful Amish family. One they'd never forget.

That night, after Sarah and Melvin were lying next to each other in bed, Melvin drew her close to him and she rested her head on his chest. "Can you believe it, Mel? No more cancer."

"At first, I was afraid to believe it, afraid there'd be a 'but'…but it's true. I'm so grateful to *Gott* and the doctors." He kissed the side of her head. "I don't know what I would have done if something had happened to you."

"Oh, you would have managed. You're strong. Someone would have stepped into my place in time."

"*Nee*. Impossible. There is no one as sweet and wonderful-*gut* as you, Sarah-love. I would have survived, I guess, but I would have just worked night and day till I was too exhausted to think at night. But, let's not talk like this. You're well, and when you get your strength back—"

"And my hair!"

He laughed. "You look kinda cute with your little bald head."

"Oh, stop. I hate it. That's vanity, *jah*?"

"Well, don't be hard on yourself. No woman wants to lose her hair, even Amish women who don't show it much. It'll grow back. It did before."

"I know and that's the least of it. I'm kinda kidding around."

"Martha and your *schwester* looked like they were gonna cry when they heard."

"They've been so faithful, helping me through. Everyone has. My *Mamm* and *Daed*—I even saw tears in their eyes when we told them. My *daed* never shows his emotions."

"But he feels them, just the same. We Amish try so hard to be stoical."

"Wow. That's a big word I've never heard you use."

"*Jah.* I like it. Sounds like I went to college," he said with a grin.

"Ever sorry you couldn't go on in school?"

"Never. I was taught everything I needed to know— and more some. I love my life, Sarah. Especially now that I know you're okay and we'll face the future together."

"I've been thinking, Melvin. Maybe we should meet with Rose. If she came back to get to know her *dochder*, she'd probably want to hear about the *maed's* early years."

"Could you manage that? Really?"

"I think so. Nothing has changed between me and my Martha. Our love is just as strong. Maybe even stronger. I'd rather they didn't sneak around. It ain't right."

"If you think it wouldn't be too hard on you, talk to Martha about it. She may not want you to meet Rose again."

"I don't see why not. I had nothing against the poor young thing. I saw how broken-hearted she was. I can't even imagine what she went through."

"It's *gut* of you to consider it. Now let your poor husband get some sleep. I have a lot to do tomorrow."

"You want to sleep already?" she asked, pouting.

"Well, I'll be. My sweetheart has plans."

"Now, I didn't say—"

"Shhh." She felt his lips press against hers and she thrilled to his touch. *Jah*, there was much to celebrate, and their bonds of marriage were indeed one of their many blessings.

Chapter Thirty

Rose went out for lunch with three of her friends Sunday after church. She tried to concentrate on their conversation and contribute to it, but she was attracted to two couples about her age dining across the room. She watched their actions, trying to read into them. Maybe it was the writer in her, but she loved imagining people's lives. The one couple preferred checking their phones to talking, and they pretty much ignored each other, while the other couple carried on a non-stop conversation, animatedly gesturing at some points and laughing together at other times. That's the way it had been with Alex. They'd been so close. Past tense. She hadn't heard a word from him and frankly, never expected to again. In fact, she wanted no part of him after his departure that brutal evening when he wouldn't even listen to her explanation. Apparently, he had no interest in his daughter, either.

"Rose, did you hear Mary Beth? She wanted to know how your new book is going."

"Oh, I'm sorry." Rose turned her attention back to her friends and they discussed her latest book project.

It forced her back to reality and she temporarily became part of the discussion and the real world around her.

Once she got home, she sat and read the Sunday paper and then turned on the television. This was her life—again. Put the time in doing mundane things, work on her writing project and then get enough sleep to start all over again the next day. She lived vicariously in the characters she wrote about. Their lives certainly were more interesting than her own.

It was now the middle of the afternoon. In a few hours, she could get ready for bed and her routine would begin all over again. At least she no longer cried.

A car pulled into her drive. Probably making a turn. It didn't turn though. She heard the engine shut off, followed by a car door closing.

Her heart started beating quickly. No one just popped in like this. They'd call first. Perhaps it was a burglar—or worse! A killer!

Goodness, what an imagination! She read too many ghastly stories on the internet.

Her doorbell rang as she tiptoed towards the front window. She certainly wasn't about to open her door to a stranger. It was a man. Tall. Good-looking. Alexander!

She quickly opened the door. Then she unlocked the screen door, but didn't make an attempt to open it.

"Rose."

"Alex."

"May I come in?"

"I…don't know…"

"Please." They stared at each other for several seconds, and then she nodded and turned towards the sofa. She heard his footsteps behind her. As she sat down, she pointed to a chair across from her. He took it and leaned forward resting his arms on his knees.

"Rose, I came to apologize."

"So…apologize."

"I know I've hurt you and it grieves me. Oh Rose, I'm so sorry I behaved the way I did. It was totally unfair to you. It's tortured me to realize how I acted."

"It's taken you long enough to realize."

"I deserve your anger. I know that. Believe me, I was just in a state of shock."

She nodded. "Why are you here?"

He left the chair and tried to hold her hands, but she drew back. "Don't."

He returned to the armchair and sat back down. "I'd like another chance, Rosie. I know I was horrible, but I love you so much."

"It didn't feel like love," she muttered softly.

"No, I'm sure it didn't. I don't know what got into me."

"You truly thought I didn't want your baby. That's what got into you. You figured I was a cold, uncaring person who wouldn't want to have your child. I just gave it away to the first person who came along. Admit it! That's what you thought."

"No, no. I didn't think that far about anything. I just felt so cheated at that moment. Denied the joy of raising my own child. It was irrational. I know that now. You were a sweet Amish girl, and I'm sure your parents were instrumental in having you give up your child."

She nodded. "Very. They told me I'd have to leave if I wanted to keep the baby. I had nowhere to go. I asked friends and an aunt, but no one offered to help me. I was desperate."

"I'm so sorry."

"Are you?" She looked at him closely and detected his eyes filling. Maybe he truly was.

He closed his eyes and shook his head. "If only I could live that night over."

"Yes."

"Please give me another chance, Rosie. I can't give you up. You're the only woman I've ever truly loved."

"You make things very difficult, Alex. I was finally getting used to being without you again."

"And you were happy?"

"Are you serious?" She turned to stare into his eyes. "I was devastated after you left. I couldn't believe you'd taken off like that. Surely, you'd come back the next day."

"I drove over that very night. I didn't sleep at all. Your lights were out. I figured you were in bed."

"Why didn't you ring the doorbell? I saw you from upstairs."

"You did? So, you weren't asleep. But how could I know that? I went back and packed up and left for New York that night."

"Why didn't you call me then?"

"I don't know. I ask myself the same thing. I guess I felt too ashamed."

"Pride."

"Yes. You can call it that. Stupid pride. But I'm here now, Rosie."

"I'm scared, Alex. I want to say everything is fine and we can pick up again where we left off, but…"

"We can. Look, every couple has their moments, but love can get you through. You don't just give up when you have a misunderstanding."

"Is that what it was? A misunderstanding?" She

stared into his eyes. Beautiful searching eyes. "Perhaps that's all it was to you. Do you think we can forgive and move on?"

"Yes, we can do that, Rosie, because we love each other. I know you still care."

"I can't deny that. I don't want to, but my feelings run deep—deeper than I'd even realized; otherwise it wouldn't have hurt so much when you walked out."

"Then talk to me. Begin with my leaving you years ago. I want you to tell me everything about your life. Please."

"I guess I owe you that." She sat back and closed her eyes. "First, I didn't know I was pregnant until you'd been gone about two weeks. I was late, but I often was, so I didn't think anything of it. Besides, we had only been together that one time. As guilty as I felt, I didn't think I could have a baby that easily. One time?"

"It happens, I guess."

She nodded. "Anyway, when the second month came around and I still hadn't, you know, then I started to question it."

"Did you tell your parents then?"

"Oh, no. I just suffered in silence. I wanted to get in touch with you. I couldn't understand why you hadn't written. I had no idea my parents sent my sister out to meet the mailman every morning. I was usually too busy milking the cows or weeding the garden to even notice. I learned only recently that every letter from you was immediately destroyed. They didn't even suspect we had been that close, but they found out from my sister that we'd been pretty serious, and I guess it scared them to think I might leave the Amish for you.

"Around the sixth month, I couldn't hide it anymore.

Even with loosening my apron, I was bulging. It was my older sister who actually figured it out first. She came right out and asked me one day, and I confessed to her. She was horrified and instead of guiding me or comforting me, she ran directly over to my mother, who was hanging clothes, and told her. From then on it was a nightmare. No one told my father when they first heard, but it was getting obvious, so he actually brought it up with my mother—in front of me. I thought he'd beat me, Alex. I never saw him so angry. I actually ran to my room and pushed the bed over to the door. That's how frightened I was."

"What did he do?"

"He came up the stairs and pounded on the door, calling me all kinds of names. He said they'd put the baby in an orphanage and send me away somewhere. It was horrible. I actually wished I'd die. After a while, he left me alone. I remember lying on the floor. Why I didn't lie on the bed, I'll never know, but I laid there on my back and placed my hands over my abdomen. I could feel my baby kicking and stirring about. I vowed I'd do the right thing for this innocent life and find loving parents for my—*our* child. Even if it meant giving the baby up. I couldn't try to raise it alone—no money— no home. I prayed out loud, it seemed for hours, though who knows? I didn't leave my room for two days. My younger sister brought me a sandwich and some milk. No one else even cared to check on me. You'd think after this experience I wouldn't want my child raised in an Amish home, but unlike our home, where there was so much tension and unspoken anger, I saw how many of my friends lived. Most had wonderful lives, surrounded by love and generations of family. I knew that was what I wanted for my child. A week or so later, I told my mother I would be willing to give my child up for adoption, but it had to be to an Amish family, and I wanted to meet them."

"So, you didn't actually know the people who ended up raising Martha?"

"I knew of them. They couldn't have children of their own and were anxious to adopt. The woman had had cancer and had a hysterectomy. It seemed like a perfect solution."

"How did you feel when you actually met them?"

"Oh, Alex. That was the hardest day of my life. Just remembering it makes me choke up. When we went into their home, it smelled of pumpkin pie. The house was humble, but well-cared for. The woman, Sarah, smiled so tenderly at me. Then when she held little Martha, I could see love pour out from her. Martha responded to her immediately. At first, I felt horribly jealous. She was my baby, after all, but then I realized God had had His hand in this whole thing. Even Melvin was emotional as he asked to hold the baby for a few minutes. I knew, as hard as it was on me, it was the right solution."

"And then you had to leave."

"Yes. I couldn't talk. My throat felt closed up. I was sure my heart had physically broken. My baby." Rose put her head in her hands and wept as she relived that terrible moment of separation.

She felt Alex's arms surround her and his tears mingled with hers as he rested his cheek against hers. His pain was real, but she knew at that very moment, he understood—and forgave. They remained intertwined for several minutes. Then they just sat holding hands, pondering life as it had been twenty years before for a young Amish teenager who became a woman overnight.

"We can talk more later, Rose. I'm sorry you had to relive it."

"No, I'd rather tell you everything and then maybe I can go on with my life." She proceeded to tell him of her need to leave a year later. "My father never forgave me, though Amish are known for their forgiveness. He'd ridicule me sometimes and humiliate me in front of the others. My mother did not defend me. I think she was afraid of him. I left the Amish religion as well and lived in a mansion outside of Dayton, where I served as a maid. I actually saved enough money to attend a community college after receiving my GED. The family I worked for helped me so much. They allowed me to live with them in exchange for watching their two children as well as clean. And then they helped pay my tuition to take writing courses at Indiana Wesleyan College, and along with grants, I was able to eventually get my degree."

"Why did you marry someone you didn't love then?"

"The family I stayed with moved to California. They asked me to come with them, but I didn't want to be that far from Martha. I still had hopes of one day having a relationship with her, even though I had agreed not to get in touch with her for at least eighteen years.

"Monty had a pharmacy where I worked part-time while I attended school. He was very kind to me and he was a lot older. He was more of a father figure to me, but he offered me a safe life. I hoped it would help with the loneliness. I didn't trust men my own age. I guess after you left. Don't forget, I didn't know you'd written to me until much later."

"Did your husband know about Martha?"

"I didn't tell him."

"Did he want children?"

"We never talked about it, but it didn't happen. It was only five years later that he died suddenly from a heart attack. It occurred one morning at his pharmacy. I wasn't even beside him. I felt guilty about that, but of course, it couldn't be helped."

"Did you see your family again?"

"Just my one sister. She's the one who told me about your letters. Then she wrote when my father died. I may one day see my mother again, but it would be like seeing a stranger."

"It's been so difficult for you, Rosie. And I went and made it even harder. Please let me make it up to you."

She looked up at him and finally smiled. "I still love you, Alex. I don't want to, but I'm stuck, I guess."

He kissed her passionately on her lips. She returned his fervor and then he separated slightly and looked down at her. "I want to marry you, Rose. Soon."

"I… I don't know."

"Why should we wait any longer? We've already lost too much time. I'm leaving for Italy in two weeks. Come with me. We'll honeymoon in Florence."

"Oh, my. This is unreal."

"Let's make it real then. Please, say you'll be my wife. We can marry right here, if we can get the paperwork done."

"What about Rosalind?"

"I'll fly her in if she wants to be here for it. If not, we'll go to a justice of the peace if we don't have time for your minister to perform the ceremony. I just don't want to be separated from you ever again. Say yes."

She nodded, grinning. "Yes, I can't think of anything I'd rather do. I've been dreaming of being your wife, it seems forever. I'm never spontaneous about anything. I'm so overly cautious. This would be totally uncharacteristic of me."

"Then it's decided. We'll go to your courthouse tomorrow and see how to go about this."

"And I'll call my pastor."

"I'll call Rosalind."

"I wonder if I should call Martha. Oh, Alex, what if she came to the wedding? Would you like that?"

He laughed. "Like it? I'd be overwhelmed! It doesn't hurt to ask her. I'll pay for any expenses, of course."

"We have a lot to do! What about a plane ticket for me?"

"Uh oh. You'll need a passport."

"I have one! I needed it last year to go to the Bahamas. I can't believe this is happening!"

He crushed her again with his embrace and kisses. Then she pulled back. "You'd better control yourself. It's not official yet."

"I'll wait! I've waited my lifetime for you, Rosie. I can sure wait a few more days till you're my wife."

Chapter Thirty-One

Martha folded up the towels as she removed them from the clothesline. Her mother worked in the vegetable garden, weeding between the rows of ripe tomatoes. They planned to do canning when Lizzy arrived. Martha's grandparents sat nearby, her *dawdi* nodding off in the cool October air while her *mammi* mended his socks.

Paul's ride had picked him up for work several hours before. She kept her phone in her pocket now that he was away from home. This way, they could talk when he took his lunch break, even if just for a few minutes. She lifted the large wicker basket of clean laundry and took it into the house. The phone began to vibrate. After setting the basket down on the kitchen floor, she retrieved her phone and noted it was from Rose.

Surprised to hear from her during the day, she answered with a cheerful greeting.

"Oh, Martha, I'm sorry I haven't been in touch. So much has been happening. I can't wait to tell you!"

Martha grinned into the phone. She'd never heard so much excitement in Rose's voice.

"Tell me! What's happened?"

"I don't know where to begin. I guess I'll just get right to the point. What are you and Paul doing weekend after next?"

"What? Goodness, I have no idea. I guess not much. He's working part-time though. I wrote to you about it, but you may not have received that letter yet."

"Oh, that's wonderful he's able to work again. You must be thrilled."

"We are, but he could take off. Are you coming this way?"

"No, I want you to fly to Ohio! Martha, I'm getting married, and I'm marrying your father—Alexandro!"

Martha actually dropped the phone. Fortunately, it landed on top of the towels. She quickly picked it up. "Slow down and say it again, Rose. I think I heard something crazy."

"It's true! Alex and I have been seeing each other and we still love each other and he wants to marry me right away and we're going to fly to Italy and have our honeymoon there!"

Martha could barely take it all in. "How? When? Oh, goodness, this is so amazing!"

Finally, Rose slowed down enough to fill Martha in on the events leading up to this moment. Martha plopped down on a kitchen chair and tried to catch her breath. "And you want us at your wedding? I'll meet my birth father? Is this really happening?"

"And we'll take care of all the expenses. Can you get a ride to the Philadelphia Airport?"

"Probably. Mercy! Let me absorb all this. It's too much to grasp at one time."

"Of course it is! And just one other thing. You have

a half-sister named Rosalind, who is a couple years younger than you, and we hope she'll be at the wedding as well."

"Oh my! A half-sister? I'm going to cry! I can't believe it!"

"Wait, hold on. Alex is tapping my shoulder."

Martha tried to hear what was being said, but their voices were muffled. Then Rose got back on with her. "Alex has a new idea. He thinks we should marry in New York City. It would be closer for everyone. That's where he lives."

"I've never been to the city," Martha said. "I wouldn't know how to find you."

"We'd explain everything first, Martha. It can be done. Just say 'yes,' and we'll work out all the details."

"I need to talk to Paul first. This is all happening so fast... I'll call him and get back to you. Is that okay?"

"Of course. I know it's all very confusing at the moment, but we'll work on things at this end. I have to pack up for Italy first and then we have to figure out about my house and...oh my, there is a lot to think about!"

After a few more comments, they hung up. Martha sat stunned. A father. A half-sister. A wedding between her birth parents. Goodness, it was more than she could process! What a book this would make! And what would Sarah and Melvin, her real parents—in her mind—think about all this. She certainly didn't want to hurt them. What should she do?

Paul will help me decide. She went up to her room and called her fiancé. They didn't make any plans without discussing it first. Her head was spinning. Too much information at one time!

Paul was not nearly as excited as Martha. He sug-

gested caution when mentioning it to her father, Melvin.
After discussing the whole thing, he agreed to attend the
wedding, though he was hesitant to stay with someone
he'd never even met, even if he was related. He'd been
to New York City only once himself, but remembering
how expensive everything was, he accepted the invitation to stay with her father. Martha made plans to call
Rose for further details once Paul said he'd arrange to
take a couple days off for their trip.

After they hung up, Martha went downstairs where
her mother was setting up the canning kettles and cutting boards. Martha asked her to sit a minute first. Once
they were seated at the table, Martha blurted out the
news. Sarah's jaw dropped open as the information
poured out.

"Isn't it exciting?" Martha asked her, barely able to
remain seated.

"Oh, *jah*, for sure. So you'll meet the man who is
your blood father." Sarah looked down at her lap and
twisted her apron strings around her fingers. "Your
other *daed*, Melvin, may be upset to hear it."

"Oh, *Mamm*, he shouldn't be. He'll always, always
come first in my heart."

"You'd better be sure he hears that. We don't want
him hurt. He loves you so much, you know."

"I know. He's a wonderful-*gut* father. I'll reassure
him. I'm curious, is all. You can understand, *jah*?"

Sarah nodded. "You have a right to know your birth
parents. I'm not afraid like I was before. I'm glad I know
what's going on. I don't like being in the dark."

"Maybe you can go to the wedding," Martha said
patting her mother on the knee.

"Oh, mercy no. I never want to set foot in a city the

size of New York. It ain't my thing. I'd probably collapse from all those mobs."

"I can't wait. I've read all about New York. They say the skyscrapers are enormous—they can touch the tips of the low clouds."

"Well now, I kinda doubt that."

"Paul said it probably wasn't true."

"Would you be gone long?"

"I don't think so. A couple days, maybe."

"Where will you stay?"

"Probably with Rose. She's staying with my father. I honestly don't know any more than I've told you. Rose said she'd give me more details next time I talk to her. She sounded so excited. It's real romantic, don't you think?"

"Like out of a storybook. He must be a rich man to live in New York. I heard it was very expensive there. I heard it costs over five hundred dollars a month to live in a nice apartment."

"Wow! But it must be a beautiful one."

"This is real sudden, Martha. I need time to think it all through. I am worried about Melvin though. I've kind of gotten used to the idea of you meeting Rose, but now the father? My. *Jah*, your *daed* may be upset."

"I'll make sure he understands my feelings will never change towards him. In my mind, he'll always be my real *fodder*."

Sarah nodded. "It will take time for everything to sink in." She let out a sigh and tilted her head slightly, a smile forming on her lips. "Are you too excited to help your *mudder* can tomatoes?"

Martha grinned back. "Probably, but let's try." They went outside together as Lizzy pulled in. Martha would have to give her aunt the exciting news; but right now, the three women gathered the ripest tomatoes they could find. It had been a wonderful summer for tomatoes and these were the late blooming ones. When they were put up, they'd be through for the year. Next would be putting up corn. Their work never ceased, but how enjoyable to eat your own produce in the dead of winter.

Chapter Thirty-Two

Many calls were made between Martha and Rose over the next few days. Finally plans were finalized. The wedding would be held on the last Saturday of the month in New York City in a small chapel, which Alex had attended several times. He really didn't know the minister, who would be presiding over the service, but he and Rose liked him right away, and the man was more than willing to perform the wedding. Then the next day, they'd fly to Italy.

Martha and Paul made arrangements with their driver to take them into the city and they were given Alex's address as the destination. Rose wanted them to arrive two days before the wedding so Martha could spend private time with Alex before the big day. She suggested that Paul and she would go out for lunch together, while the get-together took place.

Probably Rosalind would join them for dinner one night.

The actual event would be very small. Only a few close friends of Alex's would be added to their small family.

* * *

Rose and Alex discussed selling Rose's house in Ohio, but ended up deciding to rent it out instead, at least for a year while they adjusted to city living together. A few of Rose's furnishings would be moved to his apartment, but they hadn't attempted to figure out all the incidentals at this point. There'd be plenty of time after they returned from Italy.

Rose packed up clothing for their honeymoon and also took cartons that would fit in the trunk of her car, which she filled with other clothes. She decided to sort out what was left at a later time. Most of what was left would go to a thrift shop as a donation. Everything was happening so fast, she had trouble sleeping, and had to keep a notepad by her bedside to add notes as they popped into her head.

Alex made many of the arrangements by phone. It was his responsibility to set up the wedding itself. Dinner would be held in the Plaza Hotel for the attendees of the wedding in lieu of a real reception. Not only was there no time to set up anything elaborate, but they both preferred having something simple and more intimate anyway.

When Martha told Melvin she'd be meeting her blood father and about the upcoming wedding, he merely nodded. He didn't speak at first. She watched his countenance for signs of his true feelings, but he wore a blank expression. Finally he commented. "That's nice for Rose. You'll see where you got your coloring from, Martha. You sure look Italian sometimes."

"And you're not upset that we're going to the wedding?" she asked.

"*Nee.* I understand. It sure don't matter to me. You'll always be my baby girl," he said. She went over and embraced him. She felt his arms tremble ever so slightly. What a kind man. How grateful she was for his love and his support all these years. Nothing would change.

At first, when Paul started working again, he came home fatigued, but he grew stronger as time went on. He learned to do some of the detail work on an ornate desk using his left hand. It pleased him to know he'd one day work full-time at his craft and be able to support his future family, even if he didn't regain full use of one arm. Now that he was productive again, Martha was able to get more done around the house and help her mother.

Sarah convinced the young couple that it would be wiser for Paul to sleep in the *dawdi haus* now that he could get around better. Her mother had suggested it after hearing from friends that there was talk about Paul staying with Martha and her family. At least he and Martha were able to spend most of their time together. It turned out that *Mammi's* sofa was a little longer and he was more comfortable sleeping there.

The bishop stopped by twice a week in the evening to continue their baptismal classes. They planned a December wedding, though it wasn't in stone as of yet. Just knowing it was a strong possibility gave the young couple hope. Her Aunt Liz and Uncle Leroy offered to hold the wedding in their barn, which was a good deal larger than the Troyer barn; and Lizzy's sons offered to get it cleaned up for the event.

When the family sat down to make out lists for invitations, they were coming up with between three and four hundred guests. That included Paul's family and friends, many of whom would most likely rent a bus for transportation, since it was too far for buggies. There was no such thing as a small, intimate wedding in their community!

If they'd decided to live in Lewistown, they would have had a home already, but they planned to stay with Martha's parents until they could afford their own place. Paul had the money invested earlier in the business with Jeremiah, which was reimbursed when he left. Now that he felt more like himself, he planned to check with the realtor and see if the land he'd looked at earlier was still available. If so, he knew he should make an offer immediately. It was two acres of prime land and close by.

It seemed there was so much to do. The accident had set their plans back by months, but at last they could see the bright future that lay ahead of them. They thanked God every day for His blessings on themselves and their families.

Rose and Alex took turns driving her car back to New York. He was fortunate to have a parking garage below his apartment and had already made plans to park her car there—at least until they decided whether to sell or keep it. He was used to driving now, and found it relaxing. They left early one morning, the car filled to capacity with miscellaneous articles Rose wanted to keep, including some small kitchen appliances.

When they arrived at his home, she and Alex made several trips on the elevator with all her articles. "Good thing my daughter moved out. We have her room to stash all this until we have time to find permanent homes for everything."

"I hope you don't mind me bringing some of these things. It's just hard to part with some of them."

"Honey, if you want to move everything here and get rid of what I have, I'd be fine with it. I just want you to feel at home."

"Your place is lovely! It's amazing, really. I can't believe you're such a good decorator."

He laughed and shook his head. "I let a professional decorator do anything she wanted. I have no idea about fixing up a house. The only thing I did on my own was choose the paintings to be hung."

"Well, you did an outstanding job of selecting them," she said, trying to make him feel pleased that he'd at least done that much.

Once everything was in the vacated bedroom, they relaxed over coffee. He pulled out some sweet buns from the freezer and they defrosted them in the microwave and consumed them rapidly. "We'll go out for dinner tonight," he said. "I don't have anything in the house except some frozen burgers."

"I can make them if you want."

"Rosie, thanks, but I'd rather take you out. I guess you may have realized, I'm pretty well set financially. You don't have to worry about anything. You don't even have to ask if you want to purchase something. Whatever I have will be yours."

"That's really sweet of you, but I live simply. You know, it wouldn't have mattered one iota if you made only a small income. That's not why I want to marry you."

He took hold of her hands. "I know that, Rosie. Money has never been an issue for either of us. When we get home from our honeymoon, we can sit down and make a list of things we may wish to purchase for our apartment, if you want. For now, I just want to concentrate on you and our wedding."

"I know. There's just so much to think about. A week ago, this would have seemed impossible. In fact, I didn't really like you very much," she added, grinning over.

"But you still loved me, right?"

"Mmm. I'm afraid so. I didn't want to, but…"

He leaned over and kissed her. "We were meant to be together."

"To use one of my Amish clichés, 'that's for sure and for certain.'"

Alex had one phone call he'd put off. That was to his daughter. She would not be happy to learn of his plans. But call, he must. He decided to put it off one more day. Life was too good right now, to listen to a lecture from Rosalind.

Chapter Thirty-Three

After Sarah learned of the upcoming wedding between Martha's blood parents, she planned to sew up a fresh dress for Martha to wear. She decided on a soft green colored fabric. It would complement her dark hair and maybe Martha would even want to wear it to her own wedding. She couldn't keep it a secret, since Martha spent most of her time helping her around the house. Martha was delighted with the color and thanked her mother profusely for thinking of presenting her with a new frock for the occasion.

Though Martha had many friends, she no longer attended the sewing bees and work frolics. While her mother had been cancer-ridden, she wanted to spend as much time with her family as possible. Now, however, she occasionally dropped over to visit with a couple of her friends from church. Most of the girls she'd known from school were already married, some with children.

As was the custom, couples usually kept their budding relationships secret until it was time to publish their wedding plans, though when couples were seen together more than two or three times, it was assumed there was a romance forming.

The fact that Paul was seen staying at the farm, and Martha had made many disappearances after the accident, had tongues wagging.

When her friend, Elizabeth, told her people were talking about her, she told her Paul was now staying with her grandparents—not with them. Then she confessed they planned to marry soon. Elizabeth, who was still single, was sworn to secrecy about the wedding plans, but Martha told her she wanted her to be included in the ceremony as one of her *novahuchers*. Elizabeth seemed honored to be asked and the young man she was seeing would also be included, as well as another single couple, whom had not been chosen yet. Two couples were usually selected to act as attendants.

Martha was dying to tell her friend about meeting her blood parents, but not too many of her friends knew she had been adopted. It was too much to get into, so she kept it to herself.

On the Thursday before Rose's wedding, she and Paul had their ride set up for nine in the morning. When Martha said goodbye to her parents, she detected reluctance from her mother, though the words spoken were cheerful and encouraging. She and Melvin waved to the young couple as the car pulled out of the drive and made its way to New York.

Martha had decided to present Rose and Alex with a crocheted tablecloth she had made for her own trousseau the year before. It was small, card-table size, but had taken many hours to make. Hopefully, they'd find a use for it. She'd wrapped it carefully in white satin-finished paper and added a large white bow, along with a poem she'd written specifically for them.

When they finally made it to the address, Paul paid the driver and then they stood on the sidewalk with their two small suitcases and present in hand. Paul looked up and let out a long, slow whistle. Martha, too, was overwhelmed.

"What do we do now?" she finally asked.

"Go in, I guess," Paul answered.

They hesitated at the large glass entry door. A uniformed doorman smiled and then opened the heavy door with a large brass handle and nodded for them to enter. He didn't seem to notice their plainness, though they suspected he was just being courteous. Had he ever seen Amish people before?

They walked in, Paul carrying both suitcases and Martha clutching her beautifully wrapped gift, and made their way over to the concierge's desk where Martha handed him a slip of paper with Alex's name and apartment number. A call was made and within five minutes, Rose appeared and went over to the young couple. "So this is Paul. It's so nice to finally meet you," she said, smiling affectionately at the overwhelmed young man standing before her.

"Likewise," he stated, forcing a smile back.

"Alex had to run over to the gallery for a few minutes. Come, I'll take you up to his apartment. You must be thirsty after your drive."

Martha nodded. "I'm so nervous," she said on the trip up in the elevator.

"I'm sure," Rose said, putting her arm around Martha. "I think Alex is, too. Paul and I will stick around before leaving for the restaurant till you and Alex seem more comfortable."

"*Jah, gut* idea," Martha said, reaching for Paul's hand. She noted it was rather clammy.

Once inside, Martha and Paul just stood motionless as they gazed about at the luxurious living room. They'd never seen anything so extravagantly furnished.

"Yes, it's a bit overwhelming at first," Rose said, as she looked at their faces.

"He must be as rich as the president," Martha said.

"Probably more so," Paul added.

"He's very humble about it," Rose said. "Try not to let it intimidate you."

"I could never live here," Martha added. "I'm afraid to sit down."

Rose laughed. "Oh, it's made to live in. Honest. Come on, try to relax. You two sit over on the loveseat while I find something for you to drink."

Martha made her way over to the small sofa, Paul lagging behind, and they sat together, continuing to look around at the sculptures and paintings. It resembled a museum in Martha's mind. Everything so perfect and not a shred of dust. Goodness.

Rose called out from the kitchen area. "We have lemonade or iced tea."

"I think I just want water," Martha called back, fearful she might spill something on the immaculate white carpet.

"*Jah*, me too," Paul said. At that moment he was wishing he was back at the carpentry shop where he felt so comfortable and productive.

There was the sound of a key at the front door, and

in walked the handsomest man Martha had ever seen—next to her Paul, of course.

Alex strode over to greet them, removing his suit jacket at the same time. He smiled broadly, his cleft chin deepening as his midnight dark eyes twinkled.

"Come, stand my pretty girl," he said softly to Martha. He was mesmerized by this plain, but beautiful young woman sitting so awkwardly on his designer sofa. So incongruous.

Martha rose slowly and looked into his eyes, seeing herself reflected. She took hold of his outstretched hands and he brought her close and surrounded her with his strong arms. Father and daughter.

Rose stood off to the side, swallowing with difficulty. If things had only been different. She glanced over at Paul, who was emotional as well at this moment. Not a word was spoken for several minutes. Then Alex led Martha over to the matching sofa across from Paul and they sat together silently. Rose handed them each a tissue and took the seat next to Paul.

Finally, Alex addressed Paul and thanked them both for coming. "I hope you had a pleasant trip."

"*Jah*, very nice," Paul said.

"No problem finding the place?"

"*Nee*. Our driver uses a GPS."

"Ah, yes. Wonderful gadget. Have you been to New York before?" he continued to speak directly to Paul. Martha was visibly emotional.

"Only once, a few years back."

"Well, it's a bit overwhelming sometimes," Alex stated. "Rose is just getting used to it, aren't you, honey?"

"Yes. I've never been partial to crowds, but I stay inside during rush hours."

Paul nodded. "I think my Martha may find it a little scary."

At this, Martha spoke for the first time since Alex arrived. "Oh, *jah*. I never saw so many people and cars at one time. I don't know how you can stand it."

Alex laughed. "You get used to it. I lived in Rome for a while. That was even worse in some ways. Romans have no idea how to drive."

Rose jumped in. "I'm not too impressed with New Yorkers and their driving skills, either," she said.

The conversation continued in a light vein and soon the tension first noted evaporated, and everyone shared in the discussion.

After about an hour, Rose and Paul left for the restaurant. Before leaving, Rose told Martha and Alex she had made a chef's salad for them and mentioned finding butter almond ice cream in the freezer.

"Huh. I didn't know I had any," Alex said as he rolled up his shirt sleeves. "We'll be fine. Enjoy your meal," he added before the door closed.

"Are you hungry yet?" he asked Martha.

"A little, but I'll wait until you are," she said.

"I'm always hungry. Come on, you can help me set the table." She followed him into his immaculate and efficient kitchen. A small table was already set up for them, even with linen napkins and a plate filled with bakery-purchased cookies.

After adding the salads from the refrigerator and heating up some rolls Rose had set aside, they sat across from each other to eat. They bowed their heads and silently prayed a blessing on their food.

Martha took longer to eat than usual, chewing each mouthful carefully before swallowing, since she wasn't sure her swallowing mechanism still functioned. When they were finished, they continued to remain at the table.

"I want to hear all about your life, Martha. What you liked, what you hated, what you ate…everything."

"Oh, goodness. I don't know where to begin. I was just like every other Amish girl I knew. I ate whatever was put in front of me and I didn't hate anything— or anyone. I guess my favorite food was *Mamm's* chicken pot pie."

"Rose made that for me!" he blurted out. "It's great! I had eaten it when I was in Pennsylvania at her parents' home."

"That was when you met Rose," Martha stated.

"Yes. Lovely Rose. The joy of my life. I've loved her from the first day I met her."

Martha nodded.

"Martha, if I'd known…known about you… I would have come back to Rose."

"*Jah*, I believe that."

"The poor girl had no choice."

"I know that, too."

"And you have forgiven her," he said softly.

"I was never angry. She did what she had to. I had wonderful-*gut* parents. Still do."

"I'm so thankful. We owe them a debt of gratitude."

"They wanted me from the beginning."

"Yes, that's what I understand. Good people."

"And Amish. Rose made sure they were Amish."

"Yes, she felt that was very important. And you're glad you're still Amish?"

"Oh, I could never be anything else. Paul, too. He loves being plain. We love each other very much and plan to marry in December."

"That's wonderful. I know you'll be very happy."

"We will."

"Do you have any reluctance about Rose and me marrying?"

She looked over, confused at the question. "I have nothing to say, except I'm glad you met again. She's a wonderful person and deserves the very best."

He smiled. "You look just like me, Martha. Do you realize that?"

"*Jah*." She felt herself blush. "We both have dark eyes and hair."

"You'll meet my other daughter tonight. She too, is dark, but resembles her mother as well, whereas, you…"

"I'm glad you had another child."

"Yes, I felt betrayed when I first heard about you. I missed out on so much, but it was wrong to blame Rose. I hurt her, I'm afraid, and I'll regret it forever. There was no blame to be had. It was such a difficult time for the poor girl and she made the best decision under the circumstances."

"*Jah*."

"I know you love the people who raised you—"

"Very much. They are like my real parents."

His mouth drew down. "I understand exactly how you feel, but I truly hope you can allow Rose and me to be part of your life as well. It would mean the world to Rose."

"And you?" She questioned with her eyes as well.

"Yes, and to me."

"And I have a half-sister," she added, smiling.

"Yes, Rosalind. I have to warn you, she may not be ready for a relationship quite yet."

Martha's brows rose, but she didn't say anything.

"She wasn't thrilled to know I was going to remarry. Especially since it was Rose."

"Why?"

"I guess it was loyalty to her mother. I'm not sure. But be patient, because it would be good for her to know she has a sister and I think you'd be good for her."

"I'll try to be nice."

He laughed. "I doubt you have to try too hard. You seem like one of the nicest young women I've ever met."

"Oh, no. I can be really fussy."

"No, I don't believe it."

"Oh, just ask my *fodder*. I can be grumpy like you can't believe."

"Well, I'm sure it's not often."

She nodded. "Not too often, but I'll warn you, if I feel it coming on."

"Thank you, Martha." He held back a chuckle. What a dear young woman. He loved her already. *Oh, Lord, thank You for bringing her into my life.*

Chapter Thirty-Four

Paul ordered the cheapest item on the menu, a portabella mushroom burger, which still cost more than he'd ever spent in his life for a meal out. Rose ordered Manhattan clam chowder and a piece of crab quiche. They had a few minutes to wait for their order. Rose asked about his arm and listened while he told her about the progress he'd made, and he even went into some detail about the piece of furniture he was working on. She was attentive to his story and nodded with approval as he gave an enthusiastic appraisal of his progress.

As he talked, she pictured his life with Martha someday, being head of a large family, living in a picturesque country home. Her heart swelled as she realized, even without her raising her own child, Martha was exactly where she would have wanted her—ready to marry a fine Amishman and begin her journey as an Amish woman and mother. It's what she had one day hoped for herself, until circumstances turned her world upside down.

The waitress set down their meals and refilled their water glasses before heading to another table.

"This is sure a pretty place," Paul said. "Busy, too."

"It's always like this, according to Alex. We were here yesterday."

"Do you like the idea of living in the city?" he asked.

"Well, I wouldn't have chosen it, but as long as I'm going to be married to Alex, I don't have much choice. He's worked hard to make his business so profitable. I like the travel part. I've never been to Italy. We'll spend a few days in Florence and then go to Milan. Then we'll fly back home out of Rome."

"How long will you stay?"

"Nearly a month. Part business and part pleasure. I'll be meeting his parents."

"Sounds exciting."

"Do you think you'll ever get to travel?"

"Probably not. At least not overseas. We may go to the islands someday. I'd like to stay where I can look out at the sea. I've seen pictures."

"Yes, it's beautiful down in the Caribbean. I like the sunny skies, even in winter."

"New York can get pretty cold, I guess."

"I'm afraid so, but not as cold as Ohio."

"I'd like to ask you something."

"Sure. Anything."

Paul cleared his throat. "Would you like to see the Troyers to learn more about Martha's childhood and stuff?"

"Oh yes, but I don't know if they'd want to see us."

"Martha thinks they would. She thinks they'd like to thank you."

"If that's true, you can mention to them that it would be wonderful to get together, at least once."

"I think it would be *gut* for Martha, too. It took her a

long time to tell them she'd met you. She was so afraid to hurt their feelings, but they took it *gut*, if you ask me. They are really nice people. You couldn't have picked better people to raise your *doch*—daughter."

"I know. God was in the mix."

"For sure. He always is."

"How do you like the burger?" she asked.

"Oh, it's real *gut*. Not like any I've ever had before. *Mamm* makes venison burgers usually."

"I'm sure these are quite different," she said smiling.

When they were done, they ordered dessert. Rose had gelato while Paul settled on New York cheesecake. He wanted to see if it was different from his mother's. It wasn't.

When they got back to the apartment, Alex and Martha had made themselves chocolate sundaes and they were laughing together over some of Alex's stories about his childhood. If there had been fears of their not bonding, those fears were gone now. It was a pleasurable day.

And then they heard the buzzer. Rosalind was on the way up the elevator.

Alex opened the door and waited as the elevator came to a stop at his floor. Rosalind emerged, scowling. She wore a designer dress, down to her ankles, with a slit up her leg and a low neckline with an enormous pendant drawing the eye.

"Am I late?"

"No, in fact you're on the early side. Come on in."

She removed her spike heels and set them next to the door. Martha wondered if she should have removed her shoes upon entering. She just noticed Rose was bare-foot, as well.

Rosalind kissed her father on the cheek and then nod-ded over to Rose, who greeted her with a pleasant smile.

"And I guess this is your Amish daughter," she said to her father as she went over and extended her hand to Martha, who reciprocated and shook her hand loosely.

"*Jah*, I'm Martha."

"I'm Rosalind, but I guess you figured that out." Turning to her father, she asked for a glass of lemonade.

"You want ice?"

"Sure," she said as she took a seat.

Paul had stood when she walked in, but now he sat down awkwardly, having been ignored by the new guest.

"This is my fiancé, Paul," Martha said, squeezing his hand as he took his seat next to her once again.

"Hi, Paul. So, when's the big day? I'm surprised you're not planning a double wedding," she added, look-ing over at her father, who was headed over with a glass of lemonade. He made no response.

"We hope to marry in December," Martha replied.

"Whoa, that's not far off."

"We couldn't plan ahead because of Paul's accident. Did you hear about that?" Martha asked her.

"I think Dad said something about a buggy or some-thing."

"*Jah*, that was it. It went into a ditch because of a crazy driver."

"You look okay now," she said, turning her atten-tion towards Paul.

"*Jah*, I'm pretty *gut*, considering."

"Are you a farmer?"

"*Nee*, although I know how, and I help when I'm needed. I'm a carpenter."

"Oh, you build houses?"

"Mostly furniture, kitchen cabinets, inside things."

"I see. And what do you do, Martha?"

"I'm not working now—just working at home."

Rose stepped in. "She's been helping her mother mainly. She's recovering from cancer."

"I thought you were her mother."

There was silence.

"I explained the whole situation, Rosalind." Her father stood behind Rose's chair and held her shoulders. Rose patted his one hand.

"Are you hungry yet?" she asked Rosalind.

"I had a late lunch, but I can eat whenever. I have to leave when I'm done. I made plans with friends."

"I see," Rose said. "I just have a meatloaf in the oven. Your father wanted to take us out, but I thought it would be nice to have an evening at home together—to get to know each other better."

"Mmm." Rosalind took a long sip of her lemonade. Paul pulled on his suspenders, and Martha twisted her *kapp* ribbons.

Then Rose went to check on dinner and Martha followed her into the kitchen. "Let me help. Can I make salads?"

"Thank you, dear, but I made extra salad early in the day. You can fill the water pitcher, if you'd like. It's on the counter. I'm sorry Rosalind…"

"Oh, she's fine. She's very nice, I'm sure. Maybe she's a little shy."

"I don't think that's her problem."

"Well, it takes time to build friendships. We'll have

to spend more time together. I'm sorry she's going out later. Maybe after the wedding we'll have more time to chat."

"Maybe. What do you think of your father?" she asked softly.

"He's really, really nice, Rose. I can see why you never forgot him. We enjoyed our time together."

Rose hugged her briefly. "I'm so glad, Martha. I know it meant a lot to Alex. Here, I forgot to put the cheese and crackers out. Do you mind? The meatloaf isn't quite done yet."

"That looks yummy!" Martha went back out to the living room and placed the dish on the glass coffee table right in front of Rosalind. The girl looked up and actually smiled.

"Thanks."

"You're welcome."

"You speak English at home?" she asked her.

"Sometimes. Usually the *Deitsch* though, unless we have guests."

Paul was listening. "We learn the high German in school, too."

"Really?" Rosalind actually looked impressed. "I thought you didn't go to school much."

"Till eighth grade," Paul said. "Not much need to go further. We learn all we need to know to function in our community."

"It must be strange to have to use outhouses and not have electricity."

"Oh, we have nice bathrooms," Martha said. "Some Amish still use outhouses, but we're more advanced. And we use gas generators for electricity or windmills, so we have some lighting. Even a refrigerator."

"Huh. I didn't know that. But not cars, right?"

"No, not cars. I love to ride in our buggy. If you ever have a chance, I hope you'll visit us in Lancaster County, and we'll show you how we live and take you to some beautiful sights."

"Watch out, I may take you up on it," she said with a grin. Rose and Alex exchanged glances.

"Do you want to see some of our photo albums?" Rosalind asked both Martha and Paul.

"I'd love to," Martha said quickly.

"*Jah*, sure," Paul chimed in.

"Come with me into the office. They're in there." The three of them got up, excused themselves, and went down a wide hallway into the room at the end.

Alex raised his brows. "What do you think?"

"I think it's going way better than we predicted."

"Same here. And we get five minutes to ourselves. Sit next to your future husband and give him a kiss."

She moved next to him and he leaned over and kissed her lightly on the lips. "Wouldn't it be great if they became friends?"

"Absolutely." She closed her eyes and waited for a follow-up kiss, which he provided with relish.

"Maybe I'll turn off the meatloaf and give them more time," Rose said.

"And us," he said, winking at her.

Chapter Thirty-Five

A<small>S</small> Rosalind flipped through the photo album, she identified some of the family on her mother's side and then came to some photos taken in Italy of her father as a young boy. He always had a grin on his face and Martha mentioned it.

"Dad's a good guy. He deserves the best."

"I believe he's getting the best with Rose. She's wonderful-*gut*," Martha said.

Paul stopped them at one page and pointed to a photo of Rosalind as a toddler. "I bet you looked like that," he said, turning to Martha. "You two would easily be taken as sisters, you know."

"Aren't you lucky," the girls both said at once. They looked at each other and burst out laughing as Paul joined in and shook his head. "Yipes, that sure sounds like *hochmut,* to me," he said, still grinning.

"*Hochmut*? What a funny word," Rosalind said. "What does it mean?"

"Oh, you don't want to know," Martha said, patting her hand. "Pride."

"That's a riot. I have to remember that word. Teach me some others."

They taught her a few rather derogatory words and then spoke a few phrases like 'outen the lights,' 'redding up the house' and 'stribbled hair,' which meant messy.

"You guys are awesome. Why don't you come with me and my friends tonight? We're going to a club for dancing."

Paul and Martha looked at each other, each thinking the same thing. What would their bishop think?

"I don't think we'd better," Paul finally said.

"Oh, I guess it would be strange for you. I'll try to get you to meet them another time then. Do you think you'd ever want to live in New York?"

They shook their heads vehemently at the same time and it set off a new round of laughter.

"I wonder what's going on in there," Alex said, enjoying the happy noises.

"I don't know, but I'm not going to go check. We can always eat cold meatloaf," Rose added.

At the back of the album, there was an envelope with loose photos, which Rosalind was ready to dismiss when a couple fell out. One included a young teen-aged girl with blonde hair. She was wearing a plain dress and her hair was drawn tightly into a bun. In her hand was a crinoline hat. "Oh, my goodness, she looks Amish," Martha said, picking it up to inspect.

"Huh. I never noticed it." Rosalind peered over.

"I think it's Rose," Martha said, passing it over to Paul, who nodded. "It does look like her. Turn it over."

Martha did and sure enough, it was marked 'Rosie' in pencil.

"I wonder if Dad even knows it's in here," Rosalind said, taking it back. "Let's go show them."

They went together and handed it over to the adults without a word.

Alex smiled. "Rosie, it's you. Just before I went back to Italy. Remember that day? We went wading in the brook?"

"I do remember. And you splashed me."

"Yeah, and you splashed me back—tenfold."

"Goodness, that was a long time ago," Rose said.

"Is that why you have your *kapp* off?" Martha asked.

"Yes, it was sopping wet. I think your father wanted to see my hair down."

"Did you take it down for him?"

"I… I don't remember."

"I do," Alex said. "You did, and I thought you were the most beautiful girl in the whole world."

"Oh wow! You two are so nauseating!" Rosalind said, giggling. "Yipes, I'm glad I moved out!"

Martha and Paul joined in the laughter and before they knew it, the whole family was laughing. It was a moment to remember. The years and distances were non-existent in that moment of time. They were as one.

After Rosalind left to meet her friends, Rose rinsed the dishes and placed them in the dishwasher. Alex insisted on doing the pots. While they worked in the kitchen, Martha and Paul played a game of checkers in the office where they had spent time going through the photo albums. One wall had lovely cherry shelving filled with books arranged by category. It had been designed to match a desk which housed Alex's computer.

Once their game was completed, Paul went over and ran his hands along the smooth surface of the desk. "This is beautiful wood. I'm sure he had to have it crafted specifically for this room. Did you notice, Martha? The trim matches the top cornice piece above the shelves." He pointed towards the wall of books.

"Oh, goodness, it is nice. I hadn't noticed."

"I guess because I'm a woodworker… I'm afraid I could never do this kind of perfect work…not now, anyway."

"You will eventually, Paul. I'm sure of it. It may take longer than it would have before, but you're a perfectionist. You wouldn't be happy until it was just the way you wanted it."

Alex appeared at the doorway as they were discussing it. "You like it?" he asked, pointing towards the wall. "I just had it done last year."

"It's very fine work," Paul said, placing his hands on his hips as his eyes took in the beauty of the carving.

"I hired a craftsman who studied the design of antique Italian furniture and he used some of their ideas for the carvings."

"I'd love to work under someone like him."

"If you moved to…"

Martha wagged her finger at Alex. "Don't even tempt him. We'd never survive in the city."

"I'm teasing. No, it would be nearly impossible to leave the countryside of Pennsylvania for the hustle and bustle of a metropolitan city like New York. I love it, but then I've spent most of my life living in cities."

Rose came in and Alex put his arm around her. "I just hope my wife will be happy here."

"I'll be happy—wherever you are."

Martha smiled a wide smile. "This is so much fun, being here with you. *Danki*, I mean thank you for inviting us."

"The pleasure is all ours. You're making it even more special," Alex said.

"I put some music on, Alex. I wanted to see if you'd like it played while we have our dinner at the reception. I'm glad we'll have a separate room."

"We'll all go listen then. The more opinions the better," he added as they left the room and returned to the living room. They listened to several selections and decided on Vivaldi—part of the Four Seasons. Then around eleven, Rose and Alex turned the sofa in the library-office room into a bed for Paul, and Martha was shown the bedroom they used as a guest room. There was too much furniture and too many cartons stuffed into Rosalind's old bedroom to use it for sleeping.

"Once you're married, you can stay in the guest room together," Rose said as she tucked in the bottom sheet on Paul's bed.

"Maybe you and Alex can come to our wedding," Martha suggested timidly.

"Oh, Martha, that would be so marvelous! We'd love to come, but you need to talk it over with your parents first. I wouldn't want to do anything to upset them. Paul mentioned that maybe we could come visit them though sometime. We'd love to hear about your childhood from their perspective and also to thank them for doing such a wonderful job raising you. I'm so proud of the woman you've become."

"*Jah*? Do I seem more Italian or Amish?" she asked, courting a crooked grin.

"Oh, that sounds like a trick question! You're just a perfect combination. There, how's that for diplomacy?"

"You got out of that one pretty *gut*, I'd say," she said, laughing.

"I'll put an extra blanket at the foot of the bed in case it gets chilly during the night."

"Would you like to open our wedding present tonight? You'll be real busy tomorrow, I'm certain of that."

"Yes, let's join the men and do just that. Then we should turn in. Alex sleeps on the sofa in the living room. He's given me his room for now."

They went in and joined Paul and Alex, and Martha handed Rose the present she'd brought.

When she opened it and Martha explained she had made it herself, Rose was ecstatic. "You didn't! It's amazing! It must have taken you years."

"About a year, actually. I started out wanting to make it to fit a long table, but I gave up. It does fit a card table though."

"Perfect! Then it will fit the kitchen table, where we'll probably have most of our dinners together."

"It's too nice for a kitchen," Alex said, studying the lovely handiwork.

"Well, with candles and a solid colored cloth underneath, it will add a touch of glamour to our meal."

"You're the expert, Rose. Just as long as there's food on the table, I'll be happy."

When they prepared to separate for the night, Martha went over, first to Rose and then to Alex, and gave them each a hug and a good-night kiss. Alex held on a moment longer. "It's wonderful to have you here. I still can't believe you're my daughter. Thank you for coming."

She nodded. "At last I can see where I got my dark hair. I never could understand how two blonde people could produce someone who looked like me." They laughed and retired for the night.

Chapter Thirty-Six

The wedding between Rose Esh and Alexandro Gion-nardo was especially meaningful to Martha.

She allowed her tears to surface as the vows were spoken. What if it had transpired twenty years before? What if one letter had gotten through to Rose and she'd told Alex of her condition? Would he have returned to marry her? Where would they have lived? Would she be speaking Italian now instead of English and *Deitsch*?

She sat with Paul on one side and the beautiful Ro-salind on her other, her long black hair flowing loosely over her shoulders. Her eye make-up made her look even more glamorous, with eyelashes curved to expose her deep mahogany eyes. The contrast to herself was even greater with their dress. Martha's simple green frock, tucked closed with straight pins and her starched *kapp* hiding all but a few inches of her own dark hair compared to Rosalind's turquoise silk dress, raised above the knees in the front and flowing to mid-calf on the sides and back, seemed a century apart. If things had been different, Martha would most likely be dressed in similar fashion.

As she contemplated her 'other' life, she glanced at Paul. His profile was strong, openly honest and handsome. She wouldn't have known him. Of course, there were wonderful English men, she knew, but she couldn't even imagine life without her Paul. She reached over and touched his knee and he placed his hand over hers. What was going through his mind? Was he too, wondering how life would have played out if the adoption had not taken place?

Her attention was drawn back to Rose and Alex as the minister pronounced them man and wife. Alex gave a tender kiss to his bride and then they turned towards the few people watching the ceremony and those in attendance applauded enthusiastically.

The group was taken in limousines to the Plaza and shown into a small private dining room. It was so elegant. At first, Paul and Martha felt awkward as they stood out in their plain clothing; but once everyone was seated at the large round table, they adjusted and began to join into the gaiety of the occasion. Rosalind kept up a light conversation with Martha who was amazed at how quickly they were bonding. So different, yet in ways, so similar. It was mainly their sense of humor. The same things struck them as amusing and a couple times, Rosalind rolled her eyes at something that was said, causing Martha to giggle aloud.

Rose and Alex sat together holding hands. Every few minutes, Alex would lean over for a kiss, which Rose was delighted to provide. Alex's friends were fun to be around as well, and even Paul, who had been quiet most of the meal, began to discuss carpentry with one of the other men, who had a hobby of carving decoys.

After the meal came to a close, the family returned

to the apartment where they changed into casual clothing and sat around to chat.

"When can I come visit you?" Rosalind asked Martha as she curled up on the long sofa next to Martha and Paul.

"Anytime," Martha said. "And stay as long as you'd like."

"Will you teach me to milk a cow?"

Alex, who sat on the opposite sofa next to Rose raised his brows. "Do I hear you right? You want to milk a *cow*?"

"Or a goat, I guess," she responded.

"You'll get your hands dirty," he reminded her.

"I think it would be fun. I could even help make bread," she added.

"*Ach*, you don't know what you're asking for," Paul said, grinning. "Our Amish women work themselves to their bones."

"I'm strong. I can run five miles."

"Running isn't the same as scrubbing floors on your knees," he added.

"I think Rosalind would be *gut* as an Amish *maed*," Martha said, patting her sister on her knee.

"Really?" she grinned over. "So you'll teach me?"

"Oh *jah*. And you can get the fresh eggs and feed the chickens and—"

"I'll skip the chickens. They scare me."

"Have you ever held one?" Martha asked.

"No, only a baby chick once in a pet store. I wanted one for Easter, but then it pecked me and so I stopped pestering for one."

Alex laughed. "I remember. That was a close call."

"Are you allowed pets here?" Rose asked him.

"Small—very small—dogs are allowed and I guess cats, but I'm sure chickens would be frowned upon."

"So I had to leave my boa constrictor home," Rose joked.

Since the newly married couple was leaving for Italy the next day, Paul had arranged for their driver to pick them up around five. No one was hungry after the elaborate dinner provided at the reception, so around four thirty, they began to say their goodbyes. Rosalind left first, but before she did, she gave her father and Rose hugs and then turned to hug Paul, who put his hand out for a shake before she got too close. As an Amishman, he kept his intimate moments only for those close to him.

She seemed to understand and backed off before shaking his hand. Then she turned to Martha with outstretched arms. Martha hugged her tightly. "Well, sis, expect a call from me soon. I want to play Amish before the winter sets in. I like my warm snuggly apartment too much to leave it in the cold weather."

"I can't wait. It's so exciting to know I have a *schwester*!"

"*Schwester*. Okay—new word. You'll have to teach me your language as well. This is going to be so cool! My friends will all be so jealous!"

After she left, Martha went over to her father first, who embraced her tightly. "It's been wonderful, Martha. Absolutely wonderful. I'm so proud of you."

"I never thought I'd get to meet you," she said, feeling herself become teary.

"Nor I."

He reluctantly released his grip and turned to shake

Paul's hand. "Thanks for coming with Martha. I know you two will be very happy together."

"*Jah*, for sure. And I know the same for you and Rose."

Rose stood watching and then took Martha in her arms. "Thank you for sharing this special time with us, Martha. You can't believe how much it's meant to Alex and me."

"I'll talk to my folks about our wedding plans. If it's okay, I hope you can come to our wedding as well."

"Yes. Please let us know. We can find a hotel nearby, I'm sure."

"Maybe we'll see you sooner. It might be easier on everyone if you meet each other first."

Rose nodded. "Just call or write when you know."

"Maybe you should call when you get back from your trip."

"Yes, that's what we'll do. I can call from Italy, too, if you want to just talk."

Martha smiled and nodded. "If you have a chance, that would be *gut*, but you'll be real busy."

"I called my parents to tell them about the wedding," Alex said. "And they're going to meet us in Rome when we're there. I don't have time to go to Positano this time. It's too far south, down on the Amalfi coast. We'll spend a few days with them in Rome."

"Alex, you didn't tell me I'd get to spend that much time with them. How wonderful!"

"They weren't sure when I talked with them earlier, but I got a message on my phone today. I just forgot to mention it."

"This is all so exciting," Rose said.

"Oh, my," Martha said. "They'd be my grandparents, *jah*?"

"That's right," Alex answered. "I hadn't thought of that. Wait till they hear about you," he added. "And I sneaked in some pictures when you and Paul weren't looking."

"Naughty you," Rose said, grinning. "I got a few, too, with my phone."

Paul and Martha laughed. "We're like celebrities," Martha said.

"And we're the paparazzi," Alex quipped.

Martha's brows rose. "That sounds Italian."

He nodded.

Then the four of them went down to the lobby to wait for the ride. The driver was right on time, and Martha and Paul began their journey back to Lancaster County—their real world.

Chapter Thirty-Seven

Martha sat with her parents and grandparents at the kitchen table the next morning after Paul left for his job and the farm chores were completed. They sat with a fresh pot of coffee Sarah had made along with Martha's sticky buns, fresh from the oven. Lizzy and Leroy knocked on the back door and then let themselves in. "Have enough *kaffi* for us?" Lizzy asked her sister, Sarah, as she pulled out a chair. Leroy joined his niece on the long bench and took off his straw hat, laying it beside him.

After pouring their mugs full of fresh-brewed coffee, Leroy reached for a bun and placed it on a paper napkin in front of him. "You make the best, Sarah."

"Martha made these," Sarah said, nodding over at her daughter. "Got up early today to bake them."

Lizzy grinned. "It's my recipe."

"*Nee*, it's mine," Sarah stated.

"Well, ladies, I hate to tell you," their mother said, somewhat proudly, "but that recipe came down through the family, beginning I don't know where. My *oma* made them, too."

"They're the best," Melvin said. "I don't care who wrote the recipe."

"So, tell us all about the wedding," Lizzy said, reaching for sugar for her coffee.

Martha proceeded to give them the details—first, of the beautiful apartment Alex lived in, and then the wedding itself. When she got to the part about the Plaza, Lizzy and Sarah leaned forward for details.

"My, he must be very rich," Lizzy said.

"He is, but he doesn't act all snooty. He's humble about it."

Melvin listened to every word, but made no comment.

"And Rosalind wants to visit us and learn how to milk a cow," Martha said, looking around to watch their varied reactions.

Melvin let out a low whistle. "My goodness, what a thought. Some fancy girl, all made up with lacy clothes, wants to get her hands dirty."

"She'll be sorry," Sarah said, clucking. "It sure ain't easy being like us."

"She's so much fun to be with. After a while, I forgot how rich and fancy she was."

"How did Paul feel about being there?" Lizzy asked.

"He was pretty quiet most of the time. I think he was glad to get back here."

"And you?" Sarah asked.

They all stopped and looked over at Martha. She hesitated before answering. "I'm glad to be back home. I felt a little like a flapping trout on a dry river bank, but it was interesting to see how other people live."

"You might have ended up there, if things had worked out different," Melvin said, somberly.

"I'm so thankful to *Gott* that they worked out just the way they did. I love you all and I love being Amish. You can keep the city life."

Sarah looked relieved as well as the rest of the family, and she picked up the plate of buns and passed them around again. "We have plenty more where these came from. Eat up."

"Sure want to help you out," Leroy said, adding a second bun to his plate.

Soon the topic went to the weather and the fruitful harvest. The past few days seemed more like a dream than a reality. Martha didn't mention wanting Rose, Alex, and her half-sister to attend her own wedding. It wasn't quite the right time. So far, things had gone smoothly. She wanted to keep it that way. She had over a month to worry about adding to her wedding list.

Later, when Paul came home, he pulled Martha aside and gave her a huge kiss. "It's *gut* to be back," he said.

She nodded. "*Jah*, and that's the first *gut* kiss I've had since we left."

"I guess I never felt comfortable enough to be myself."

"I'm sorry if it was awkward for you."

"Well, it wasn't that bad, but I'm sure glad to be working again. I started a rocker today, Martha, and I was able to use both hands."

"Oh, Paul, that's amazing. See? You're healing real quick now. *Gott* is *gut*."

He nodded. "He got tired of hearing all your prayers, I guess."

"I'm not letting up, so expect to be getting even better."

"Now, did you leave me any sticky buns?" he asked as he glanced over at the counters for a goodie. When he spotted the plate with the few remaining buns, he walked over and took the largest one he could find. After taking a huge bite, he chewed it slowly, closing his eyes in ecstasy. "You could become a millionaire selling these in the city," he finally said.

"*Jah*, probably, but I'd rather just make them for you and the family," Martha said. "Your smile is worth more than a whole bunch of money."

The flight over to Italy was uneventful, though fatiguing. When they arrived in Rome, Alex rented a car and they settled into their hotel room before touring part of the city by foot. Rose wanted to see the Colosseum and some of the famous fountains, which were in walking distance from the hotel. Alex was amused at her enthusiasm for everything he'd taken so for granted.

They devoted the first five days to their honeymoon, checking out the sites and spending many hours enjoying the marvelous food in some of Rome's finest restaurants and smaller family-run trattorias.

Then Alex attended to his business, checking the new work of some of his best-selling artists. Not wanting to be alone, Rose tagged along. He and the artists spoke in English so as not to be rude to Rose. Occasionally, when they found themselves alone in the studios, Alex would ask her opinion about the paintings he was considering for his gallery. Pleased he listened to her and seemed to respect her views, she took the questions seriously and evaluated each one carefully before responding. There was one lovely painting of a child wading in the Mediterranean, that she hoped they might purchase for their apartment. It could easily have been Martha—the likeness was amazingly strong. Later that evening, when she mentioned it, he picked up the phone and told the artist to include it with his selections for the gallery. She was thrilled at his thoughtfulness.

The visit with his parents was planned for the end of their stay when they returned to Rome for their flight home. Rose was disappointed not to be going to Positano so she could see where Alex spent his childhood, but he promised their next visit would include the southern part of Italy as well.

Every day was exciting for Rose and the two of them were inseparable. She was learning a lot about the art world, and Alex shared much of the business end with her. With his daughter preparing for her studies, it would be fun to work together in the gallery. Rose was enthusiastic about the prospect of partnering in his thriving business.

Back home, Rosalind told all her friends about her Amish sister and showed pictures she had sneaked of the lovely young woman, so similar in looks to herself. When she mentioned wanting to visit Martha's farm, one of her friends, Ashley, showed an interest in joining her. "My grandparents lived on a farm," she told her. "I don't remember it much. I was too little. They had to leave the farm when they got old, but that's all they talked about when we were together. If you want company, I'd go with you," she added.

"Yeah! I'd like the company. Of course, I'd have to ask first."

"Just let me know if it's okay. Would it be overnight?"

"Sure. I might have to get up early to get the eggs."

"Ooh wow! What fun," Ashley said, all bubbly.

That night, Rosalind called Martha and they planned their visit for the following weekend. Rosalind would hire a driver for Saturday morning and then they'd return to New York Sunday afternoon. Rosalind even asked about church, but it was the alternate week, which meant they'd go visiting instead. "In a buggy? A real buggy?" she asked.

Martha giggled. "That's the only way we get around unless we pay someone to drive us somewhere. I'll take you out a couple times, if you'd like."

"That's just way too cool. Ashley will flip out."

Later Martha told the family about Rosalind's reaction to taking a buggy ride. Sarah was amused. "It will be fun to have her here and her friend. We'll have to plan to have some special food for them. How about shoofly pie?"

"*Jah*, and whoopee pies! They probably never had them."

"I hope they don't mind going to bed early."

"They'll need to, if they want to do chores with us."

"Oh, we shouldn't make them work while they're here."

"*Mamm*, they want to. Honest."

Sarah shook her head in disbelief. "I guess it will be fun for them, since they will only be here a short time. Our house is going to look pretty plain to them, I'm afraid."

"Well, it sure doesn't look like a fancy New York apartment, but it's clean and it's comfortable. Please, not to worry, *Mamm*. She's not snobby. I thought she would be, but she's just like any other young *maed*."

Melvin wasn't quite as excited as the women about having two young girls hanging around. He made a

comment that he was going to feel like a zoo animal—
an odd one at that, but Sarah scolded him. "You'll enjoy
it, Melvin. They'll probably think you're very mascu-
line and like a movie hero, what with your strong muscles and all."

Martha giggled. "You can roll your sleeves up and
lift the couch to show them how strong you are."

"All right. You ladies have made your point. I'll try
to keep them from swooning over me. Now let me go
groom my horses." He chuckled on his way out to the
stable.

It was warm for November when Rosalind and her
friend arrived. After a huge hug for Martha, they were
introduced to the rest of the family. Even Martha's
grandparents were there when they arrived. Martha
noticed the family had worn their Sunday clothes and
she was proud of the way they looked. Plain and clean.
Her *Mammi's kapp* was crisp and white as always, but
special care had been given to her hair. Not a single
loose hair made its way out of the *kapp*.

Martha took her friends through the whole house and
then they sat for their main meal. Her mother had made
a roast chicken with typical Amish bread filling. They
had cornbread and mashed potatoes, along with corn
casserole. Everything was made with their own produce
from the summer. Paul seemed unusually quiet. Martha suspected he was as uncomfortable as he had been
when in New York. Poor man didn't like any changes
to his routine. He'd be looking for that in his marriage,
she was certain of that. Routine and peace. And very
little variance. Of course, when the children would start
coming, there'd be a little less peace, though they were

taught at an early age to be respectful of their elders and to be seen, rather than heard.

After the young women insisted on helping with the dishes, they went for their much-anticipated buggy ride. Martha and Paul took them to Lizzy and Leroy's house where they were given the tour of their farm. A couple of their daughters-in-law came by to meet the fancy New Yorkers. It didn't take long for people to relax in spite of their many differences. Lots of questions were asked, mostly by Rosalind, but Lizzy seemed to enjoy being the 'expert' on Amish ways, and Martha heard some stories that were new—even to her. She sensed her aunt might be exaggerating somewhat.

The only negative comment was when they all entered the barn. Rosalind pinched her nose and let out an 'ewww' which amused the others. "*Jah*?" Leroy said, grinning. "Worse than all those exhaust fumes you get in your big city?"

"Sorry, I guess you get used to the smell."

Martha leaned over and whispered. "You never do, completely. I still prefer nice kitchen smells."

On the way back, Rosalind asked if she could sit up front and 'drive' the horse. Paul's brows rose as he looked with hesitation over at Martha. She shrugged, so he okayed the idea, but suggested he'd remain up front, in case she had any questions.

Rosalind had ridden horses at summer camp three years in a row, so she had some knowledge of horse behavior and it went well. Ashley complimented her friend at her aptitude for her equine skills. When they arrived back at the Troyer farm, Paul excused himself and went out to give his future father-in-law some help, leaving the three young women time to themselves.

They went up to Martha's room and Martha sat on her rocker as the two girls sprawled out on her bed. "Paul is a hunk," Ashley stated, pushing her long auburn bangs away from her eyes. "I bet he's pretty romantic in—"

Rosalind looked horrified. "It's not like that, Ash. They don't do anything till they marry. Right, Martha?"

"Right. At least we try not to. Of course, there are exceptions."

"Yeah, like my father and Rose," Rosalind said.

"Oh, I forgot about them," Ashley said, casting her eyes downward. "I didn't mean to offend you, Martha. Anyway, Paul seems like a real cool guy and he sure adores you."

"How do you know that?" Martha asked.

"I don't know. You can just tell. He grins at all your jokes—even dumb ones—and watches your every move. Stuff like that."

"I've never really loved anyone else. I thought I did for a while, but it was puppy love or infatuation. Not the real thing. What about you, Ashley? Do you have anyone special yet?"

"Don't I wish! No, I've had tons of crushes, but nothing serious."

"But she has been kissed," Rosalind added, winking over at her friend.

"Oh, a few times," she responded.

"And you, Rosalind? Serious about anyone yet?"

"No, I don't want to be. I want to get through school first and have a career for a while. Eventually, I'll probably settle down and have kids and all, but I'm way too young."

"I think it would be hard to wait too long," Martha said. "It's hard for us to stay apart, especially when we were living in the same house. It takes a lot of discipline."

"More than I'd have," Ashley said. She sat up and stretched her arms over her head. "I think I'd like to live like this. There's so much stress in our home. My folks are so worried I won't become a cardiologist like my father. I don't like pre-med. There's too much to memorize. Every stinking nerve and bone... I'd rather be a dancer."

"Oh, she's good, too," Rosalind added. "You should see her sometime."

"I'm not that good."

"You know you are. She's been on TV and everything. You should just take off for Hollywood when you have a chance."

"I'd be scared to go out there by myself."

"So, find a guy and convince him to go with you."

Martha looked from one to the other. "Oh, that sounds scary. I think you should stay put and try to convince your folks you want to concentrate on your dancing."

"They think it's a waste of time. What would you have wanted to be, Martha, if you'd had a chance."

"I don't know. Maybe a nurse. I like helping people and taking care of them. I'm used to it since I had to help my *mudder* when she had her cancer and would be sick, and then Paul after his accident."

"Why don't you then?"

"Oh, not now. At this point, I can't wait to marry. I want to have at least six or seven children."

"Whoa! That's a lot. It sounds like a nightmare," Ashley added.

"Oh, I know someone who just had number twelve."

"Ugh," Ashley said. "I may never have kids."

"I'd be so sad if I couldn't have *boppli*—babies," Martha said, rocking slowly in her chair.

"Maybe because it's been drummed into you by your family," Ashley said.

Martha shook her head. "*Nee*. I don't think that's it. I've taken care of lots of little ones, and some have been bratty at times, but they just need more love when they get rambunctious. My *mamm* says, the worse a child acts, the more love he needs."

"Wow, that's profound," Rosalind said. "I'll have to remember that. Amish people are smart."

"Well, we are practical, I think."

"You are," Ashley said, nodding.

"This has been so much fun. I can't wait until tomorrow to milk the cows," Rosalind said.

"You don't have to wait," Martha said with a grin. "In half an hour, they get milked again."

"Twice a day?" Rosalind asked with a grimace.

"Oh, *jah*, for sure. The ladies can't wait longer than that. They get pretty grouchy if you keep them waiting."

"Yipes, that's a lot of work," Rosalind said.

"We do work hard," Martha said. "But I could never be anything but Amish. When someone needs help, there's always someone willing to come to their aid. We pray for each other and care about each other, like you can't believe. And I love having my grandparents close. Paul had a chance to be a partner in a *gut* business, but it would have meant my moving away. He cared enough to leave everything for me. We will try to live close to my family. In fact, he made an offer on a piece of land just, which would be real close by. We're just waiting to hear if it will be accepted."

"Then will you build your own house?" Ashley asked.

"In time, with the help of our friends. They can build a barn in a day or two, so a house wouldn't take that long, once we can pay for all the materials."

"Amazing!" Rosalind sat up and folded her arms. "If life ever gets too crazy, maybe I'll come and live near you, Martha."

"Oh, what fun! We'd be like real hundred per cent sisters then," Martha said.

Ashley pushed her long tresses back off her face. "You two are lucky. All I have is a brother and he's a real pain."

"I missed out on having a large family since my *mamm* couldn't have children," Martha said quietly.

"And you know about my situation. Mom was killed and Dad never wanted to remarry."

"Maybe he and Rose will have a baby," Martha said.

"Oh, they're too ancient. Rose is nearly forty," Rosalind said.

"*Jah*, but it could happen," Martha said.

"I wouldn't count on it. So, let's go for a walk to the barn. Maybe we'll watch them milk this time and then I can help in the morning—if I wake up in time," Rosalind said.

Martha smiled to herself as they went down the staircase together. She had a feeling the morning milking would take place without her sister.

Chapter Thirty-Eight

The warm days of early November were a thing of the past. Single digit days quickly made records as the late autumn took on the characteristics of mid-winter. It snowed a week before Thanksgiving and the six inches remained frozen on the ground for two weeks before thawing in the slightly warmer days that followed.

Paul missed two days of work due to the dangerous road conditions, which Martha thoroughly enjoyed. He kept her company while she baked off batches of cookies for the Thanksgiving holiday and then they sat and played Canasta while her parents read the bible together in the kitchen. Her grandparents stayed put in their cozy *dawdi haus*, though Martha and Paul took dinner over to them each day so they wouldn't have to take a chance on falling while making their way to the main house. As fast as her father chopped up and cleared the thick patches of ice, the sun would melt some of the snow covering, and then that would freeze as temperatures dropped in the late afternoon. It was a frustrating battle.

Rose called a couple times to see how things were back in the States and report on their trip. They were in Florence. Martha had finally brought up the idea of inviting Rose and Alex to come to Paradise to meet with them all soon after their return from Italy. Martha's desire to invite them to her wedding was not yet mentioned. One thing at a time. Though her parents did not seem overly enthusiastic about the idea of a re-union, they agreed to it. It helped when Martha mentioned they'd be staying overnight at a hotel and would only come by for a couple of hours on one of the days.

When Martha told Rose about the get-together, she seemed pleased. "That's kind of them. Tell your mother we won't be able to stay for any meals. I really don't want to be a problem in any way."

"Oh, she won't—"

"No, please. It would be better this way. At least for the first time we all get together."

"*Jah*, maybe so. Okay. It seems strange, but you are probably right. A little at a time."

"And I don't want you to worry about inviting us to your wedding. I don't want any strain on your special day. So please, don't even give it another thought. Wait, your… Alex wants to say hello before we hang up."

Alex got on the phone and asked her a few questions about her health and the weather and then he told her to say hello to Paul for him. After a few more impersonal remarks, they signed off. Conversation felt strained on the phone. Much better to see each other in person. She and Paul had discussed the whole thing and he agreed they'd try to get together once or twice a year after their marriage.

He wasn't excited about the prospects, especially if it involved going to New York again, but he also knew how much it meant to Martha to keep some kind of relationship going, so he didn't raise any objections.

Martha and Rosalind talked every week for at least an hour. They had developed a real friendship over the past weeks. Sarah had seemed surprised when Martha told her about their frequent calls, but she was pleased for her daughter. It had always been painful for Sarah to know she'd never bear her own child and Martha would not know the joys of being raised with siblings.

The bishop announced one evening just before Thanksgiving that he'd completed the pre-baptismal instruction and suggested the young couple take their kneeling vows as soon as possible if they planned to marry in December. It was cutting it close, but because of Paul's unexpected accident, the kind bishop did all he could to speed up the process. Paul and Martha were grateful for his willingness to work with them. A date was set for the baptism. It would take place the Sunday following Thanksgiving.

The morning after the bishop's visit, Paul received a call while he was working. It was from the realtor. He had wonderful news—the owner of the land they wanted to purchase had accepted their offer. Paul was ecstatic, but waited until he got back to the house before telling Martha.

He broke the news to her parents at the same time as they finished up their supper. Sarah wiped her eyes. "Such wonderful-*gut* news. It's close enough for the *grosskinner* to walk over when they're old enough."

"Now, that's certainly looking ahead," Melvin said, grinning over. He turned to Paul. "It's real nice that you decided on settling nearby. You've made your future in-laws real happy."

"And your future wife," Martha added, grinning over.

Time began to move quickly as so many events were lining up. Thanksgiving included most of Lizzy's family as well as Martha, Paul and her parents. Lizzy held the meal at her home, but everyone contributed to the occasion. Martha and Sarah brought the baked candied sweets and three pumpkin pies, as well as homemade fudge. Martha hid the fudge from the men so there'd be enough for the whole crowd.

It was a great occasion. A child's table was set up in the kitchen and their dining room table was extended to the fullest length for the many adults. Their home had been planned ahead for large get-togethers and especially when it was their turn to hold church service, so the partitions were pulled back allowing full view of the young ones from the dining room and living room area.

The following Saturday, Paul and Martha went to a special session before their baptism. It would be their final chance to change their minds about being baptized. There was no hesitation. They were well prepared to take this important step in their faith.

Paul waited till he and Martha were alone with the bishop to thank him for all he'd done to aid them through the instruction. Though the nine sessions were normally done before regular church services, the bishop had made it a point to do it through visits to their home, due to the fact of Paul's serious accident. He'd also made the exception to hold the baptismal service in November, after most of the baptisms were already performed.

The next morning, Paul's parents came for the service, but left later the same day so their driver could hang around and not make two trips.

Dawdi dressed in a new suit since, as a deacon, he'd participate in the service. Martha and Paul prayed together before leaving in the buggy for the event. Martha's hands were clammy, but Paul seemed more elated than nervous. The whole family attended as well as the rest of the congregation. After two of the sermons were given, Martha went up first and answered the bishop's questions about her commitment to follow the faith and renounce the devil, as well as the world. While she knelt, her *Dawdi* came over with a small pitcher and poured some water through the bishop's hands onto her head. She felt a chill run through her at the sacred moment. Her tears flowed as she accepted her new position with Christ and her people. Then she rose and the bishop's wife embraced her and gave her a holy kiss.

She took a seat as Paul went forward and the same ceremony was performed for him. It was a moment neither of them would ever forget. Paul realized he was also committing to serve in their ministry if he was called to do so. A powerful moment.

Once the service was concluded, the women of the congregation set up their food for the meal. Martha had difficulty concentrating on helping. Sarah took note and told her to go off with Paul to reflect on their meaningful commitment and the others would get the food prepared.

She motioned to Paul, who was in the process of setting the benches at the tables with the other men, and he followed her out to the screened-in porch of the Zook family's home, where the service was being held. They held hands and Paul prayed for them. He was already the spiritual leader of their relationship and soon he'd be her husband. So many emotions, she barely ate from the bowls of salads and the homemade cold cuts. Life was good and God would see them through to the end of their lives, but there was more than life on this planet. Through the Savior, and her total faith in Him, she knew there was much more. She smiled as Paul put a close to his prayer.

There wasn't much time left before the wedding. Rose and Alex had arrived back in the states, coming home several days earlier than originally planned, and Rose had called that same day to settle on a date for their trip to Lancaster County.

It would take place the following Saturday. Martha had already okayed the date with her parents. Sarah immediately took her pad and pen and made a short list of chores that would have to be done before their arrival. Then she and Martha made a list to include cookies and brownies to be baked off midweek. "Is Rosalind coming too?" she asked as she tacked her list onto their bulletin board in the kitchen.

"No. She had other plans made already."

"She's a nice *maed*," Sarah added, nodding her head.

"*Jah*, we have fun talking."

"You know I'm glad, Martha. I'm not upset, you know that, *jah*?"

Martha went over and put her arm around her mother's waist. "I know. And you have no reason to be. I feel like I've just added some friends in my life. They'll probably never feel like real family."

"Well, maybe in time."

"*Mamm*, I wanted to ask you something."

"Before you ask, I want to mention that if all goes

well when we meet Rose and her new husband, maybe you'd like to have them come to your wedding."

Martha's mouth fell open. "Oh, my goodness! That was what I was going to ask."

"I'll leave that decision up to you. It's your big day. Just know it's okay with your *daed* and me."

"You're the best," Martha said and kissed her cheek. "Now let's see if we need more chocolate for the brownies," she added, heading for the cupboard.

Chapter Thirty-Nine

Alex and Rose packed a small suitcase before driving to Pennsylvania. Rose made sure she had the boxes of Italian stationery purchased in a gift shop in Florence with them. One box, with prints of some of the religious paintings on the covers, was designated for Martha and Paul, and the other one had floral prints of early Italian paintings on their covers. It had been difficult to find anything for her plain daughter and her parents.

As much as Rose had prayed about this reunion, she was still nervous about the outcome. Hopefully, any feelings of jealousy on the part of Sarah and Melvin would be a thing of the past. Rose had made it a point not to invade too much in Martha's life, though at times it had been difficult not to pick up the phone and call, just to chat.

They stopped on the way at a pizza parlor where they shared a small pizza with pepperoni. Alex was impressed and made a point to thank the young man in the front of the store who spent his time flipping and twirling the blobs of dough into works of art. He left a ten-dollar tip.

Using his GPS, he managed to find their farm without

any difficulties and when they turned down the drive, Rose's heart did a quick jump. Before they got to the front of the drive, Rose saw Martha open the front door and wave. The sight of the lovely young woman standing at the open door of the white clapboard farmhouse would be imbedded in her memory forever. Her daughter. The child she carried for the first nine months of her life, her body nourishing the newly formed human, conceived of love, though not the way it was intended to be, now standing before her as an adult, ready to launch into her own marriage. Would she have preferred to raise her herself? No question, but she was the product of a loving Amishman and woman, whose life was enriched by the blessing of a child, not of their own flesh, but a child in need of a home where friction and strife were absent. They had indeed been sent by God.

When they entered the small tidy vestibule, hugs were exchanged. Melvin and Sarah had stood back in the kitchen to allow their daughter a degree of privacy before they walked out and introduced themselves.

"It's been a long time, Rose," Sarah said, taking hold of her hands and then embracing her.

"Yes, it seems like a lifetime," Rose responded.

"*Jah*, my lifetime," Martha said with a grin.

The couples smiled and then Paul came in from the back door, his jacket covered with fresh snowflakes. He'd removed his boots before coming to the front. He shook Alex's hand and then shook Rose's. She then leaned forward and pecked his cheek.

"Come, let me take your coats," Sarah said. "Help me, Martha. We'll put them right here in the hallway on hooks."

Martha took Rose's dark green woolen coat while Sarah reached for Alex's Italian leather jacket. Melvin stood with his thumbs behind his suspenders and then nodded towards their sitting room. "Come on in. It's not fancy, but it's warm by the fireplace."

Alex took Rose's elbow and steered her in where they sat together on the plump couch set next to the snapping wood fire. "This is real pleasant," Alex said as they settled in.

Martha and Paul waited for Sarah and Melvin to take seats across from the others. Her parents had their own favorite armchairs and awkwardly took possession of them. Then Paul pulled over a side chair for Martha and one for himself. There was a moment of unease as silence predominated. Finally, Martha asked about Italy, and the dam was broken. Rose passed her phone around with some of the photos she'd taken. Melvin was particularly interested in the pictures of the country-side around Rome and commented on the farmhouses. "I see everyone has their own grapevines. Guess they like grapes a lot," he said, tongue in cheek.

Rose named each building or fountain as the phone got passed back and forth.

"It's real pretty there," Sarah said.

"Oh, yes, it's beautiful. Amazing artwork," Alex said, smiling.

"Did you find much to bring back?" Martha asked him.

"About thirty canvases. They'll be shipped. They have to be crated first. It takes a while to get them into my gallery, but it's worth the wait."

"Do you paint yourself?" Melvin asked him.

"No, I leave that to others. I've always admired people who have that talent."

"Martha sings real nice. Have you heard her?" Sarah asked.

"No, I don't think so," Alex answered.

Rose joined in. "Alex has a beautiful tenor voice," she said.

"Oh, that's nice," Melvin said, pulling on his beard. "Guess she got it from him then. I can't sing worth a dime."

"Oh, but she has your humor," Sarah said, quickly.

"Ain't much of a talent."

Martha squirmed. One thing her father Melvin didn't have was much of a sense of humor.

"We have fresh *kaffi*, I mean coffee made," Sarah said. "Anyone want a cup?"

"Oh, and homemade goodies," Martha said, rising to bring them out.

"We can sit in the kitchen," Rose said. "It would be easier, wouldn't it?"

"You're our guests," Sarah said. "We want you to be comfortable."

"Maybe they'd be more comfortable in the kitchen, *Mamm*," Martha said. "Kitchens are for cozy talk. You always told me that."

Rose stood, followed by her husband. "Please, I prefer kitchens to any other room," she said, looking over at Sarah, who relaxed her jaw and nodded.

"Come along then. Melvin, bring in the side chairs, please."

"I'll bring one," Paul said as Melvin reached for the other.

Things seemed to be less tense now as Martha poured coffee into the mugs already set upon the table, and Sarah busied herself passing the plates of cookies and brownies over to her guests.

Alex raved about everything and it certainly sounded sincere to Martha's young ears. After an hour of chatting, while a fresh pot was brewing on the stove, Rose cleared her throat. "I just want to tell you…you have both done a wonderful job raising Martha. She's such a lovely young woman."

"Oh, she'd be lovely no matter who raised her," Sarah said.

Rose and Alex both shook their heads. "No, we were too young and I was too self-centered to be a good father," Alex said, his lips drawn. "I realize that now. I believe God had it all planned out."

Melvin grinned. "I don't know about one part of it being His plan," he said.

"Well, maybe not the way it all started," Alex agreed, a slight blush forming on his neck.

"Now, Melvin. That wasn't necessary," Sarah said. "*Danki.* Thank you, for telling us that. It means a lot to us, don't it, Melvin?"

"*Jah*, sure does. We love this girl with our whole hearts."

"Please," Martha said, lowering her face in her hands. "I can't hear any more. You are all so wonderful-*gut*. I've been blessed beyond words. And I even have a *schwester*—sister, too."

Paul reached over and patted her knee. "I don't know who to thank, but I'm getting the sweetest girl in the world to be my wife, so whoever is responsible, I'll be forever grateful."

"Now, you folks may be too busy to make it," Sarah started to say, "but it would be real nice if you could come to Martha and Paul's wedding."

Rose and Alex smiled over at each other. "That would be wonderful-*gut*," Alex replied, lending a little *Deitsch* to the conversation. It brought a wave of laughter.

"*Jah*, you have to teach Alex the *Deitsch*," Melvin said, grinning over.

"I have to learn Italian first," Rose said.

In spite of their original plans, Rose and Alex stayed for supper. Alex was taken out to the barn when the women cleaned up after their meal. By the time they left, they had bonded. Martha was sorry Rosalind hadn't been there as well, but the three of them would be attending the wedding, and Martha hadn't even had to discuss it with her parents. So often the things she worried about the most never even happened. Another lesson learned.

Less than two weeks to go. The marriage was to take place at her aunt and uncle's farm. The excitement was almost too much to bear. There were so many things to prepare and the guest list continued to grow as forgotten names were added. It seemed there was nothing else going on in the county of Lancaster as more names appeared on the 'yes' list.

At last the big day arrived. Lizzy gave Martha a front bedroom for her to use and then came in to help her with her dress. "You look real pretty, Martha. Not that you don't always, but there's a glow about you. Only brides get that special look." She leaned over and kissed her on the cheek. "You'll always be special to your *onkel* and me," she added. "You can't believe how thrilled we are to have you live nearby."

"I don't know how I could have stood being far away. I think Paul knew that more than I did."

"He's a *gut* man, Martha."

"*Jah*, the best."

After Lizzy went downstairs, Martha stayed up in her room till it was time. The weather was cooperating. There was no snow predicted and the temperatures had risen to the forties. As buggies arrived, she peered from behind the window shade to see who was coming. About a half hour before the ceremony was to begin, she saw Alex drive in with Rose and Rosalind. She smiled tenderly as she watched them, dressed in simple clothing with very little jewelry, get out and shake hands with some of the others and then head towards the large clean barn set up for over three hundred guests. It would be crowded and many might end up standing, but that's the way it was in Amish homes.

She glanced at the small wind-up clock on the dresser. Goodness, it was to start in only fifteen minutes. Martha said a quick prayer as she heard her mother knocking at the door.

"It's time, Martha," she said through the simple wooden door.

Martha opened the door. "I'm ready, *Mamm*."

Sarah nodded and took her daughter's hand. They walked slowly towards the staircase. Her baby girl was a woman now, ready to take on the responsibilities of a good Amish wife and mother. It was time to let go, though the bonds of mother and daughter were bonds that could never be broken. Not by time or man. The cycle was beginning again.

* * * * *

Please feel free to write to me at www.junebelfie.com. I hope you have enjoyed this series as much as I've enjoyed writing it.